The Bridge
and the Butterflies

Part 1 of The Filey Chronicles

The Bridge
and the Butterflies

Janet Blackwell

First Published 2018 by Fantastic Books Publishing

Cover design by Gabi

Cover art is an original work by Jolanta Dziok

ISBN (eBook): 978-1-912053-90-2
ISBN (paperback): 978-1-912053-89-6

DEDICATION

For Paul, Amy and Emily. My Superheroes.

Chapter 1

She came to us at midnight in the back of a police van.

I was in my room in the attic when she arrived, angry that I'd been made to stay in all night to wait for her. I had missed Will's party. There was no way I was going downstairs to play happy families.

The policewoman threw open the back doors of the van and the next minute this girl was out on the street. If I hadn't been sulking, I might have felt sorry for her. It was obvious that the police were happy to get rid.

Mum had said that she was about fourteen, the same age as me, but she looked a lot younger dressed like that. She was very small and she had a long blonde plait right down to her waist. It was tied with a ribbon.

I saw Mum rush out. I opened my window a little to try to hear what they were saying, hoping that there had been a mistake and that the girl would be taken away again. It didn't seem likely.

Suddenly a firework exploded like a gunshot and one of the policewomen strode off in the direction of the beach. The girl just stood there, shivering under the street light, in a pair of pyjamas that were way too big for her. She was

1

gripping a black bin bag as though she thought Mum was going to take it from her. I noticed that she had no shoes on her feet.

Just for a moment she glanced up. I thought that she had seen me but then I realised she was looking up at the sky and the fireworks being set off, probably from kids messing about on the sands. They'd be out celebrating the start of the summer holidays. Not like me. I couldn't stop thinking about the party at Will's. It all seemed so unfair.

Mum had taken her cardigan off and put it around the girl's shoulders. They walked towards the house.

I slammed my window shut.

The girl wasn't my problem.

Well not then, anyhow.

Chapter 2

The sand was cold and much darker than usual. I knew I was on Filey beach although it seemed different somehow.

I had no idea how I had got here.

I looked down at my feet and realised I'd forgotten to put my shoes on. The tide was out and the empty beach stretched for miles in both directions.

Suddenly there was a loud explosion from somewhere behind me. I shot round but there was nothing there. I remembered something about fireworks but it was daytime now.

Everyone had gone.

A breeze fluttered about my face for a moment and then turned into a gust of wind. Before I had time to do anything, a storm blew up out of nowhere. The wind blasted into my face. Spiteful yellow and orange clouds churned around me and spat needle sharp sand at any skin I had left unprotected.

'Enough!' I shouted. 'Pack it in!'

I'm not sure who I thought I was talking to but it seemed to work. The clouds dissolved and the wind died.

Everything went quiet.

Then I saw that the girl who had arrived last night was standing a few feet in front of me in those huge pyjamas, her long yellow plait shimmering in the early morning light. I was going to call out to her but then I realised I didn't know her name. Tears were streaming down her face.

'I want to go home,' she said.

I tried to speak but no sound would come out of my mouth. The girl glared and there was a kind of fire in her eyes now. It all felt wrong. I didn't even know what I was doing down here. I took a small step backwards but my feet started to sink into the ground.

Someone, something grabbed hold of my ankles. I was being pulled, down and down. I floundered about, trying to stop myself from being dragged under but the sand was too soft and it sifted through my fingers. I tried to scream but I knew it was no use. Sand flew into my mouth instantly, coarse and gritty and choking.

'You have to help me!' the girl screamed.

She was directly above me. I was sinking fast and I reached out my hand, desperately trying to get her to grab me, to stop me from suffocating but she just kept shouting, getting louder and louder until she was almost perforating my eardrums. I made a last frantic attempt to heave myself out of the ground but something smacked me hard on the side of the face.

I woke up on the floor, my phone buzzing in my ear.

Missed call.

Will.

I looked around as though I hadn't seen my bedroom before. I rubbed the side of my face where I had slammed it against my bedside cabinet. Probably an attractive bruise brewing already. Sighing, I clambered back into bed, dragging my duvet into place.

My phone sounded again.

A text.

Hey Meg . U ok? Last night a train wreck. Meet later? ☺

I hadn't considered that the party last night might have been rubbish. Will had been really excited about it and loads of people were going. Perhaps I hadn't missed anything after all.

I thought about the girl that had arrived last night and I felt a bit bad about staying up here sulking now. A picture of her standing on the beach in my nightmare came into my head and I shuddered. I hate it when dreams are so real that you can't shake them off.

There was a loud knock which made me jump.

Mum stuck her head around the door.

'Rise and shine!' she said. 'You alright? What was that crash?'

I didn't answer. I was hoping that if I kept quiet then she would go, but she didn't. She came right in, flung back the curtains and started picking things up off the floor.

'Sorry you didn't make it to Will's last night,' she said. 'I didn't think ... never mind. You've got six weeks off now. Are you ready to come downstairs?'

'I'm having a lie-in,' I mumbled.

'Right. No rush. The girl they brought to us is still fast asleep. It was gone midnight when she arrived. I shouted for you to come and join us but you must have dropped off.'

Yeah. Right.

5

My face was stinging from where I had bashed it and I didn't want to listen to her any more. I slumped down into the bed and pulled the duvet over my head.

It didn't make any difference.

I could still hear her.

'Her name's Mirabel,' she went on. 'They found her wandering about on Filey beach near Happy Valley. She's got quite a few cuts and bruises but she won't say what happened to her. The only thing I got from her was that she lives with her aunt but to be honest, the rest of what she said made no sense. Perhaps she'll feel better this morning and want to talk properly.' She paused. 'I wish you would keep this room more tidy. Now it's the summer break I think you could at least try.'

'I'm tired,' I moaned from under the covers. 'And stressed.'

'Dad will go mad if he sees the state this room is in. He'll be working away this week and I'm going to need you to help out more.'

'Fine. I'll do it later.'

'You always say that. No wonder you're always losing stuff.'

'No, I'm not.'

That was a lie. Things were always going missing. She was going to have a fit when she knew I'd lost yet another house key. She'd even taken to putting a spare cellar key on top of the door frame. Perhaps I should have a tidy up.

'Please Meg. I need you to get dressed. Have a chat to Mirabel.'

I didn't respond.

'She told the police that she lives in one of the big houses on the cliffs. But that's all nonsense apparently. You're the same age and … well she might say more to you.'

I heard coat hangers clanging together.

She wasn't giving up.

I emerged from the covers.

'Leave it, Mum. I'll do it.'

'I gave her one of your old nighties for last night but she could do with something to put on now really. Is there anything in here that would fit her? She's quite small.'

'Mum, will you please get off my stuff!'

'I'm not asking you to give her anything special. I don't remember you wearing these for a while.'

She pulled out a pair of blue jeans that I didn't even remember owning and threw them on to the bed.

'I don't see why I always have to be involved,' I grumbled, pulling myself upright.

'Because you are part of this family and this family helps children who haven't got the advantages in life that you take for granted,' she said.

She paused and turned towards me. 'Look, I know I said … oh my goodness. What … what did you do?'

'Nothing. Bashed my face on the bedside cabinet. It's fine.'

'There's blood!'

'What?'

I swung round.

There were bright red stains all over my pillowcase.

'No. No. That's just my hair,' I said.

'For goodness sake! I thought you were bleeding to death for a minute. I don't know why you put that streak in. You've got nice hair. You don't need to play around with it

7

and look at the mess you've made of your bedding. I bet that won't come off.'

'Sorry,' I said. 'I'll wash it myself.'

'You'll probably make it worse.' She sighed. 'Never mind. We'll discuss it when you come downstairs and I'll have a proper look at your face.'

She headed for the door. 'Don't be long,' she said. 'There's bacon and eggs.'

'No thanks. I'm a vegetarian.'

'Since when?'

'I just need you to …'

My door banged shut.

'… respect my views … or something.'

I sighed and lay back down but I was wide awake now. I was pretty sure that this was not the way I had imagined the start of the summer holidays.

I gave in and got up.

Walking over to the window, I could see that it was still raining and in the distance the sea looked grey and un-inviting. You'd think that living at the seaside would be cool but it's really not.

Nothing ever happens.

I walked over to my dressing table mirror to assess my bruise in the daylight.

'Bloody hell,' I exclaimed. 'You have got to be kidding.'

It wasn't the swelling on my cheek that caught my atten-tion. A few days ago I'd put a small red streak in the floppy fringe of my black hair as a kind of statement. For some reason, overnight, it had faded to a weird sort of orange.

'I don't believe this,' I said to the Meg in the mirror. 'You are such an idiot.'

I brushed it quickly to try and flatten it down but some of the hair seemed to break off.

Perfect. I was going to have a bald patch.

I sighed.

I'd liked my short hair with the long fringe when I'd first had it done. All the girls at school had long Disney princess type hair and I had wanted to separate myself from them. I'd done that alright. Now with my ghostly pale skin, green eyes and ginger streak I looked like a demented cat.

A cat that had been in some sort of fight.

It was no use.

I couldn't realistically stay in my room forever. And it was the holidays so at least I'd escape any more 'witty' comments from my super intelligent classmates.

I got up and walked over to the bed.

The jeans Mum had picked out would never fit me. I had grown way too tall. But they wouldn't be the right size for the girl downstairs either.

As I chucked them on to the floor, a thought struck me. If I did lend Mirabel, or whatever she was called, some clothes, there was a chance Mum might be in a better mood and let me go over to Will's. It would also mean that the girl would be ready to leave straight away if someone came to collect her.

Good plan.

I rummaged around and found several pairs of black leggings I didn't wear any more. There were a few t-shirts that I had got sick of and I added them to the pile. I needed some new stuff really but there was no way I could afford any.

My text signal sounded.

Hey Meg . U ok? Last night a train wreck. Meet later? ☺

Same message again? What was Will playing at? He really needed to learn how to use a phone.

I tried to send a reply but nothing on my screen seemed to be working. There was a crack in the glass at the top which was spreading and some of my apps wouldn't even load up. If I did help Mum she might be willing to get me a new one. It was a long shot but worth a try.

Downstairs, Mum was busying about in the kitchen and talking loudly down her phone to someone.

'Yes … well what I'm saying is that it isn't really good enough … Yes but I need you to let me know … Yes … Yes … I understand that but what if you can't …?'

I was carrying the clothes I had found for the girl and she waved at me.

'Take them upstairs to her and then tell her to come down and have some breakfast … Sorry, no, not you. My daughter. Where was I?'

Mum was really pushing her luck but I thought about my dodgy phone and smiled at her.

The foster kids always slept in the room next to Mum and Dad's. I knocked sharply and the door swung open. I was half expecting her to be standing there in her pyjamas, screaming at me to help her, like in my dream.

She wasn't of course.

'Er … Hi … Mirabel?'

You'd think because we'd had so many kids over the years that I'd be good at this sort of stuff but I'm not. I'm actually a bit shy around the foster kids for the first few days. I don't always find it easy to get on with anyone to be honest.

There was no answer.

I went further into the room and decided to just dump the clothes on the bed and leave her to it. 'Mum said I had to bring you these,' I muttered.

No response.

The curtains on the window blew suddenly and there was a gust of cold air.

'It's freezing in here,' I said, louder this time.

The window must be open.

I went over to close it and as I drew back the curtains, light flooded into the room.

I could see at once that the bed was empty and Mirabel had gone.

Chapter 3

'Well I think it's cool,' said Will. 'Makes you stand out.'

'Will, it's bright orange. It's a disaster.'

'What happened to your face?'

I prodded the bruise on my cheek speculatively. It still felt a bit sore. 'Nothing,' I said. 'It doesn't matter. Just tell me about the party.'

'You didn't miss anything. It was totally crap if I'm honest. The worst party I have ever been to and it was mine. What does that tell you?'

'I can't believe Mum made me stay in.'

'Meg. It doesn't matter. You probably had a better time than I did.'

'It must have been bad.'

'Like I said. Train wreck.'

We had reached Will's favourite café on the seafront. It was cold and still drizzling a little but he wanted us to sit outside.

'It's raining,' I pointed out.

'Of course it is. It's summer.'

He wiped the plastic chair with the sleeve of his hoodie. 'Now, Mademoiselle. Would you care to sit down while I procure us some refreshments?'

I smiled. It's hard to feel bad when Will's around.

'What did you order?' I asked as he came back from the counter.

'I got us both a caramel macchiato.'

'What's a maccy whatsit?'

'No idea. Sounds very Italian. I bloody love coffee.'

'Only because you drink it with ten sugars.'

He laughed.

'I keep telling Dad we ought to have a proper coffee bar on our caravan park,' he said. 'I'd run it. Make it really cool. Only to be honest I don't think he's talking to me after last night.'

'Why? What happened?'

Will leant forward and banged his head down on the table. 'I can't bear to tell you.'

'It can't have been that bad.'

'I may have to move to another school,' he groaned. 'Maybe another country. Join the army or something.'

'No offence but I don't see you doing that. You'd have to shave your head for a start.'

Will sat back up and ran his hands through his thick blond hair. 'You're right. And I don't agree with war of any kind so that might be a drawback.'

'Yeah. It could be. Now tell me what happened last night!'

He sighed. 'Well, loads of people dropped out …'

'I told you I …'

'No. I don't mean you … I mean you had a proper reason. The others just got a better offer. Laura decided to have a gathering at hers so most people buggered off there.'

'So who came?'

'Just Marcus and Tom and his mates ... and Abbie and Kathryn of course. Plus some kids I didn't even know off the caravan park.'

I flinched at the sound of Abbie's name. I knew she would be there. We used to be friends but she changed when we were in year nine. She started hanging out with Kathryn who is barmy and scary and I could tell Abbie thought I was too uncool for her now. She liked Will though and she was always turning up when he was around. That was really annoying.

'If it was so lame, why is your dad freaking out?' I said.

'It wasn't too bad at first, then Abbie's big bro Simon turned up with some of his loser mates. Brought some cider he'd got cheap from someone. No kidding, it was actually in a bucket.'

'Classy.'

'Yeah. It smelled like ... well not like cider. There were bits of straw and stuff floating in it.'

'Tell me you didn't drink it.'

'No way. Abbie did though. Drank some of it straight from the bucket for a dare. Threw up all over my dad's new van. Never seen him so mad. Made everyone go home and it was only about eleven. Shaming.'

I laughed. 'Did he make you clean it up?'

'No ... I did offer but he said I'd only make a mess of it. I was glad he turned me down though. It was rank. Dunno what she'd been eating but ...'

Thankfully he didn't complete his description as the waitress arrived with the drinks. Will bent his head down and sniffed his coffee. 'Bloody hell!' he said. 'That smells nearly as bad as the cider.'

'Why didn't you order something we'd actually like?'

He started sipping his drink and grimaced. 'Revolting,' he said. 'Needs sugar. At least they always give you a free biscuit here. It might take the taste away.'

'Anyway,' I went on. 'I'm sorry you didn't have a good night. I …'

'I wasn't having a go at you. I think it's great what your mum and dad do, taking in kids and that. It's brilliant, actually. She must be in a state, that girl, running off like that. Where do you think she went?'

'She said she lives in Filey. She wanted Mum to take her last night so I think the police have gone over there to try and find her.'

'Poor kid.'

I didn't answer. Of course I felt sorry for Mirabel but Mum didn't have to have a go at me about it all. She'd only agreed to me going out to meet Will because she wanted us to look for Mirabel on the promenade. I wasn't going to get Will involved and anyway there was no point. It was raining and there was hardly anyone around. It was obvious that the girl had tried to get back to Filey. She wouldn't be anywhere near here.

I took a sip of whatever it was Will had bought me. He was right. It was disgusting.

'Perhaps it's an acquired taste,' he said, as he shoved the biscuit in his mouth. 'Oh. I almost forgot. Abbie said she thought this belonged to you.'

He reached into his pocket and brought out a silver key, dangling from a blue plastic elephant key fob.

'Bloody hell. That's mine. Where did she find it?'

'On the floor of the changing rooms at school. She was sure it was yours.'

'Thanks. I don't know what's wrong with me.'

'Shall I write a list?' laughed Will.

'No, you haven't got time.' I kicked him under the table. 'At least I don't have to tell Mum and she won't have to have all the locks changed again.'

It was a relief to have got the key back but it was annoying that it was Abbie who had found it. She must have recognised my cheap kiddie key ring I'd won at the amusement arcade. Total humiliation. I had to start taking better care of my stuff.

'That's a coincidence. Look. By the arcade,' said Will.

I turned around. Abbie was heading up the promenade carrying a bright red umbrella. Despite the rain and cold she was wearing a cropped white t-shirt and faded denim shorts. On her feet were a pair of very high red wedged sandals. Her long blonde hair was usually straight, but today she had curled it and I couldn't imagine how early she must have got up to make herself look as glamorous as that. Especially when she had a hangover. She didn't look in the least bit ill, to be fair.

A small brown dog, which looked like a teddy bear, trotted along at her side. I didn't care that I looked a scruffy mess in my old jeans and hoody compared to her, but if we met she was bound to say something about my hair disaster. I also wasn't looking forward to thanking her for finding my key.

'Will, can we go?'

'Sure,' said Will. He lowered his voice, even though there was no possibility that she could hear us. 'Actually I wouldn't mind giving Abbie a miss after last night.'

'She probably won't remember most of it.'

17

'I hope not. Before she put her head in that bucket she asked me about joining the band. I didn't know what to say to her. She can't play anything and she definitely can't sing.'

'How about "No chance"? Come on. Don't let her see us.'

Abbie had stopped to talk to someone. We raced from the café and clambered down the old stone steps on to the beach. The breeze was a bit stronger as we neared the sea and spots of rain blew into our faces. Not surprisingly, there was no one else around.

'Abbie won't come down here,' I said, trying to get my breath back. 'Not with those shoes on.'

'She's alright really,' Will said. 'I think I may have been a bit mean about her.'

It was annoying that Will couldn't see what Abbie was really like. I had to let him know how manipulative she could be. 'She's been telling everyone at school that me and you are going out,' I said.

'Why would she do that?' he asked, his face suddenly serious.

'Dunno,' I said. 'She just likes to stir things.'

'You're not bothered are you?'

'Don't be stupid. Course not. I just thought you ought to know.'

'Cool. I don't really care about what people say about us. Do you?'

I shook my head. 'Abbie won't come down here. Not with those shoes on.'

'She's alright really. I think I may have been a bit mean about her.'

'Hang on. Haven't we just had this conversation?' I asked.

'When?'

'Just now?'

'Don't think so. Although I get that sometimes … Déjà vu. You think things have happened before when they haven't. Totally weird.'

I knew I shouldn't keep going on about Abbie. All I wanted was for Will to see through her nice girl act and I didn't want her worming her way into his band.

'Are you alright?' Will asked.

I nodded.

'Fine. I just don't want to talk about Abbie,' I said.

We carried on walking without saying anything. Small shells crunched under my feet and every so often my trainers sank a little deeper into the wet sand. I half expected to feel tentacles or something reaching up and grabbing my legs.

'Bloody hell. It's really starting to rain now. Maybe this wasn't such a good idea,' said Will. 'Race you to the next set of steps.'

He started running back up the beach, but I had to stop to rub some sand out of my eyes.

It was then that I heard it.

I thought it was the waves rolling on to the beach at first or perhaps one of the gulls but it didn't sound like either of those. More like a radio station when it's not quite tuned in. My name echoing in the wind.

Then nothing.

Will had almost reached the wall of the promenade so I hurried to catch up with him. He seemed to hesitate at the steps and instead of climbing up, he walked slowly around the side.

He crouched down.

I saw at once what he was looking at.

I was wrong about the girl being in Filey.

She was huddled into the corner, sitting right against the wall with her knees drawn up, a black bin bag at her side. Her long plait was coming undone, the ribbon was gone and bits of hair were sticking out all over the place. She was wearing one of my old Lion King nighties. Her feet were bare and I could see they were dirty and scratched.

'Hi,' I said hesitantly. 'Mirabel?'

She looked over at me but she didn't answer.

'You OK?' I asked. 'Everyone's been looking for you.'

'Not *everyone*,' she said. 'That would be impossible.'

Will laughed. 'She's right Meg. Not *everyone*. Think it through.'

I ignored him. 'You stayed at my house last night. My mum's …'

'I know who you are,' she said. 'It's taken you ages to find me. I was getting tired.'

'I wasn't … I mean we weren't … How come you know who I am?'

'Your mother showed me a picture of you. You were wearing a blazer. Your hair was different though.'

'Must have been my school photo,' I said. 'Before … Anyway, I look like a freak on that.'

'Meg is a freak actually,' whispered Will. 'But don't tell her I said so.'

She smiled.

'You seem nice,' she said. 'What's your name?'

'Will,' he said holding out his hand. 'Please to meet etc.'

Mirabel shook hands with him solemnly.

'I was trying to get home,' she said. 'But it all seems ... different somehow. I got lost.'

'You shouldn't have gone out by yourself,' I said. 'But look ... we've found you and we need to get back now. Are you sure you're OK?'

'I think so,' she said wistfully. 'But something's hurting here. On the back of my neck.'

She lifted up her hair and Will leaned over to have a look. 'I can't see much. There's a small lump. I think it might be a mole. Or a weasel.'

Mirabel laughed, lowering the plait again. 'You're funny,' she said. 'And a good sense of humour is important if it's kept in proportion. I think we are going to be friends.'

There was no mention of me. Everyone likes Will. There's nothing not to like.

'I'll ring Mum and get her to come and pick us up,' I said, pulling my phone out of my pocket. 'We'll have to meet her up on the main road though. Can you walk, Mirabel? It's not far?'

'Of course I can,' she snapped. 'But I hope she hurries. I'm very hungry.'

'What say we pick up some chips on the way back?' Will said.

Mirabel reached over and picked up her bag. 'Isn't that rather unhealthy?' she queried.

'I know,' said Will. 'But I like to live life on the edge.'

She got to her feet.

'Haven't you got any shoes?' I asked.

She shook her head and glared at me, as though it was my fault that I hadn't provided her with any for her escape mission.

21

'You'd better put these on,' Will said, taking off his trainers. 'They'll be a bit big but they're better than nothing.'

'What are you going to do?' I asked. 'You can't walk in just your socks.'

'Why not? What's wrong with my socks?'

'They're bright yellow for a start. Where do you even buy socks that colour?'

'If I told you that I'd have to kill you,' joked Will. 'Now hurry up. My feet are getting cold already.'

It took a few tries to get through to Mum but when I did I could tell that she was really relieved that we had found Mirabel. She said she would come straight away. It felt great to be in her good books for a change.

We climbed up the stone steps and walked along the promenade, towards the main road. It had suddenly got a lot busier and I knew people were staring at us as we passed. Mirabel was filthy and she looked ridiculous in my nightie and Will's trainers. They were way too big for her and she was walking like a demented duck. She'd refused Will's offer of help to carry the bin bag.

I looked around for any sign of Abbie but thankfully she was nowhere to be seen.

From the small fair on the seafront, the sickly smell of candy floss and fried onions filled the air. A few people were hanging out around the stalls but the rides were still and empty. Different music tracks clashed with one another as we walked past.

'That must be what I heard on the beach,' I said.

'What are you on about?' said Will.

'When we were walking on the sands before. I thought I heard … did you call me?'

'Call you what?'

'Funny.'

'She's hearing things now, Mirabel,' said Will. 'I told you she was a freak.'

'Will,' Mirabel said, her feet slapping on the pavement. 'You will help me, won't you?'

Her question reminded me of my dream but I didn't say anything.

'I can trust you, can't I, Will?' she asked.

'Absolutely,' he said.

'I'm finding it difficult to remember things,' she went on. 'But I have a feeling that I'm in some sort of danger.'

Will put his arm around her. 'I'll let you into a secret.' He lowered his voice. 'You'll be safe with us. Nothing exciting ever happens around here.'

Chapter 4

When I went downstairs on Sunday morning, I was surprised that Mum was sitting by herself in the kitchen. She was sifting through a pile of old letters and photographs.

'Where's Mirabel?' I asked.

'She hasn't woken up yet. And before you say anything, she is still there. I checked.'

'So glad,' I said sarcastically. 'For a minute I thought we were going to be on our own this summer.'

She stopped what she was doing, took off her glasses and looked at me. 'I know this is difficult for you Meg and I know we talked about not taking in any more kids, especially now Dad's got to work down in London for a bit. But this was an emergency. What could I do?'

Say no, I wanted to respond but thought better of it.

'And speaking of Dad,' she continued. 'He won't be able to come home at all for a few weeks. He seems to be getting a lot of work at the University. I told him we'll be fine.'

'Can we go down and see him?'

'Not at the moment.' She paused. 'I didn't say anything about your hair. With a bit of luck you'll have got rid of it before he gets back.'

'You said it was OK when I asked if I could do it.'

'Yes, but you didn't tell me it was against school rules and that it would double my washing bill.'

I ignored her and started rummaging about for something to eat. 'How long is Mirabel staying?' I asked without looking up.

'Only until tomorrow. Or Tuesday at the latest, I think.' Her voice softened. 'I have to say Meg, I was very proud of you yesterday, going out to look for her.'

I pretended that there was something very important in the cupboard that needed my attention and I didn't answer. I felt guilty now that I hadn't made any attempt to actually find Mirabel and that it was only luck that we'd seen her on the beach.

'And you've certainly got sharper eyes than the police because they told me they'd sent someone into Bridlington to check she hadn't gone there,' she went on. 'Well done. Now get yourself some breakfast. I need to get on with this.'

There wasn't much food in the fridge. I picked out some juice and closed the door. Mum put her glasses back on and picked up a bunch of photographs from the table.

'What are you doing?' I asked.

'Spring cleaning.'

'It's July.'

She laughed. 'OK. Summer cleaning. I can't believe some of the things I've kept. I should have done this years ago.'

'You haven't been throwing any of my stuff out, have you?'

'No. I haven't been near your room. Haven't had time. Why?'

'It doesn't matter.'

I wasn't going to tell her that when we got back yesterday, I had tried to find my diary but it wasn't there. And I was sure my watch and bracelet had been on the dressing table but they had gone too. The lid was open on my rock and shell collection but to be fair I could have left it like that.

Mirabel had been acting really oddly yesterday but she'd gone straight to her room on our return and refused to come out. She couldn't have taken my stuff.

I had to try to stop losing things.

Mum threw a handful of pictures into the bin by her side.

'You're not going to throw those photos out are you?' I said, rushing over and picking out a picture of a red brick cottage. A white wooden gate opened on to a beautiful garden, much bigger and nicer than ours.

'Isn't this where we used to live?' I asked. 'It was way cooler than here. Why did we move? It's …'

'You can't possibly remember it,' she snapped. 'You were only small when we left.'

'I remember sitting outside on the grass … crying or something or … maybe that was somewhere else.'

I stared at the photograph and tried to picture what the cottage looked like on the inside but I couldn't.

'Meg. Throw that away and leave this to me. Make yourself some toast and let me get on.'

Mum was getting mad again and I couldn't face a row. I pretended to put the photo in the bin but instead I slipped it into my pocket. There were probably a few more that I should save as well. Mum was obsessed with tidying up and turning our house into a show home. We'd have no memories left at this rate.

27

'There's no bread.' I said, peering into the bread bin.

'Oh for goodness sake … there's a brand new loaf by the toaster.'

'Fine.'

I reached over and grabbed it.

'Sorry, Meg. I'm a bit snappy this morning … It's not your fault … I'm just tired. I shouldn't have started this.'

She was right about that.

Just as I opened the bread bag, the toaster popped up.

'How did that just happen?' I asked.

Mum didn't seem to hear me. I didn't remember putting any in but I must have done. I was losing it big time.

'You are always so good with the children we take in, Meg. You really are,' said Mum. 'And I do understand it's not always easy for you when there are other kids around.' She sighed. 'You know, this Mirabel seems to me like a girl who is in real trouble,' she went on. 'She's not shouting or swearing like some of the others we've had but there's something about her that tells you things are not right.'

'She was talking a right load of gibberish yesterday on the way back from the beach,' I said.

'Like what?'

'Said she thought she was in danger.'

'From what?'

'Dunno.'

'Well that's a bit worrying. I'll mention it when they come to get her. Did she say anything else?'

'No. She just kept going on about that house in Filey. How come they haven't found anyone that can look after her?'

'I've no idea. They can't find any records about her at all at the moment. Go and have a chat to her now. Take her some toast and see if you can find out anything else. Ask her about this aunt she mentioned. Perhaps she'll tell you something now that she knows you better.'

'I'm not sure about that.' I remembered how she had totally ignored me and linked arms with Will on the way to the chip shop. 'I don't think she likes me very much at all.'

Chapter 5

On the landing I thought I could hear voices coming from Mirabel's room. I tried to listen through the door but there was nothing. I remembered the strange sounds I had heard on the beach yesterday. It must be the lack of sleep and all those bad dreams I kept having that were making me go a little crazy. Last night's had been the scariest yet. I was back on Filey beach but this time the sand was thick and oily. It ended the same way, with me being pulled under and almost drowning in the black slime.

I needed to get a grip.

I knocked.

There was no answer so I pushed the door open carefully just as I had yesterday, half expecting Mirabel to have gone. But she was there, sitting cross legged on the bed, her pale eyes staring into the distance.

'I brought you some food,' I said. It sounded more abrupt than I had intended but Mirabel didn't seem to notice.

She didn't move.

I put the toast down on the bedside cabinet. 'Were you watching TV?' I asked, struggling for something to say. 'Don't worry. It's OK. You didn't need to turn it off.'

Just as I said that, I realised that the one in this room was really old. It hadn't been working for months. 'I can get you something to listen to if you like music. Or are you into games and stuff?'

She didn't answer and I was about to give up and go when she turned her head towards me. 'Will's nice isn't he?' she said. 'Full of light.'

'Well he's full of something,' I said, smiling.

'I see.'

'See what?'

'I've noticed before that you use humour as a defence mechanism.'

'I do jujitsu as well,' I said. 'On Thursdays.'

She shook her head slowly. 'Sarcasm is your other weapon I see. It suggests insecurity. You should meditate. It helps to strengthen what is on the inside.'

Great. I'd only come up here to give her toast. I didn't need this. 'Look there's some food there,' I said, definitely wanting this conversation to come to an end. 'I have to go.'

'Please stay. I didn't mean to offend you.' She slid herself on to the end of the bed. 'It's just that I'm very skilled at reading people. I think you must be a good person. Deep down. It is possible that we could become friends.'

In my experience, making friends was never as simple as that but I didn't say anything. Just a few more seconds and I would make a run for it.

'What is strange is that you seem familiar,' she went on.

'Maybe you've seen me around. Where do you go to school?'

'I don't know,' she said. 'I don't think I go to any school.' Closing her eyes, she moved herself back into the centre of the bed and took up her meditating pose again.

'Look I'd better be off,' I said. 'Do you want this toast? Only ...'

'I seem to have lots of memories but they're all jumbled up,' she said.' Like a jigsaw puzzle.'

'It may take a bit of time to ...'

'There's a voice too. I need to concentrate if I'm to hear what it's saying.'

The girl was seriously disturbed. I was about to go when I remembered what Mum had asked me to do. I would be in bother if I went back downstairs so soon.

'You know how you told the police that you live with your aunt?' I asked. 'Do you remember that?'

She opened her eyes. 'Not really. But I do remember my aunt. We were on the beach by our house and then all I know ... all I know is that one minute she was there and the next she wasn't. No. It's no good. My head feels all sort of fuzzy.'

She started to hum. It was a bizarre noise and really annoying. 'I can teach you how to do this if you like,' she said. 'It helps things to clear.'

'You're OK.'

I took a step towards the door. I'd rather face Mum than stay here. I wasn't going to find out anything useful. 'I ... I should leave you to it,' I said.

'Let me show you something first.'

She reached for her black bin bag and pulled it on to the bed. She tipped out the contents. A ball of screwed up clothes covered in sand and mud and bits of what looked like seaweed tumbled out.

'Bloody hell, Mirabel,' I said, turning my face away. 'They absolutely stink.'

'I got so wet,' she said. 'On the beach.'

'What were you doing there?'

'I told you. My aunt … she was with me … then she wasn't.' She sighed. 'Do you think my clothes are ruined?'

'Put them back in the bag and I'll give them to Mum. She'll know what to do. Probably.'

Ignoring me, she delved into the pocket of a pair of black trousers. I could see now that the clothes were not just filthy, they were torn as well.

'This is it,' she said, pulling something out. 'Look.'

It was a pendant and she held it out, insisting that I took it.

I had never seen anything like it before. A golden oc-tagonal-shaped cage hung from a thick gold rope chain. Inside, lay an oval-shaped crystal which was perfectly clear.

'What kind of stone is this?' I asked, staring into the centre of it.

She didn't reply.

I held the pendant up and the crystal rattled a little against the sides of its prison. As I moved again, the light caught it and I saw what looked like ribbons of mist skim across its surface. They parted and lights started glinting, reds and yel-lows and purples from somewhere below its surface. Then Mirabel moved and I lost my concentration. The stone had cleared again.

I couldn't imagine what the crystal was or where you would even buy a pendant like this. It must have cost an absolute fortune. Where had Mirabel got it from?

'I don't think it's mine,' she said, as though she had read my thoughts.

'Whose is it then?'

'I haven't told anyone I've got it. Only you.'

'Right,' I said, a little flattered that she was confiding in me at last. 'It looks … well it looks expensive.'

I suddenly thought about the missing things from my room. Maybe I was wrong to trust her. Could she have gone in somehow without me seeing? 'You didn't … I mean you didn't take it from anyone did you?' I asked.

'I'm not a thief!' Her cheeks reddened.

'Sorry. No. Sorry. Of course you're not. Only you said it wasn't yours and … Look, I shouldn't have said that.'

'You can go now,' she muttered.

I felt so stupid. I genuinely hadn't meant to upset her. 'OK,' I said, trying to sound as friendly as I could. 'I will but look … why don't you come downstairs with me and show this pendant to Mum?'

'No. And you have to promise not to tell her either. It has to be a secret.'

The anger in her voice had gone and her eyes were filled with tears. I actually felt sorry for her for the first time. We'd had some weird kids in the past but nothing like this.

'I think it would be best if you gave it to Will,' she said. 'He's my friend and I know he'll look after it for me.'

'I'm not sure that's a good idea.'

'Please. Just until I remember things.'

I looked down at the pendant. I saw the crystal in the centre glimmer a little.

'It would be better if it stayed here,' I said firmly. 'I promise I'll take care of it and if you need it back then … well it would be easier than involving Will. Especially if it's a secret.'

'I suppose you're right. But are you sure you can be trusted?'

'Absolutely.'

Before she could say anything else, the message tone sounded on my phone.

Dad making me help out. Come down here and give me a hand? Gingerbread latte in it for you! ☺

'Sorry. I need to go but I'll see you later,' I said.

She didn't answer and she didn't say anything else about the pendant. She crossed her legs and stretched out her arms.

I closed the door and walked back down the corridor.

Behind me I thought I could hear the sounds of the TV again but it couldn't be that. It was probably just Mirabel's humming and I'd definitely heard enough of that to last the whole summer.

At the bottom of the stairs I stopped.

I could hear Mum talking on the phone. It sounded as though she was talking to Dad.

There was no way she was going to agree to me going to Will's. She would want me to stay here with Mirabel but I couldn't face spending any more time with that crazy kid. If I was quiet I could sneak out by the front door and get away before she noticed.

I still had the pendant though. I knew I needed to tell Mum but I couldn't face entering into a long discussion about it just at this moment.

I picked up one of Mum's scarves from the coat rack, carefully wrapped the pendant inside and opened my schoolbag. I tucked it away out of sight and placed my pencil case on top. I zipped up my bag and stowed it away under the hall table.

I'd show it to Mum later.

Walking as quietly as I could to the front door, I let myself out.

Chapter 6

At the entrance to the caravan park Will's dad was polishing his van.

'Ay up Meg, love. What do you think about this then?' he asked, smiling over at me.

I smiled back at him but I wasn't sure what to say. 'Will told me. It's … it's awful,' I managed.

'I thought it was very eye-catching,' he said, looking crushed. 'Really make me stand out.'

'Abbie's sick?'

He laughed. 'No … No. I cleaned that off. I meant the slogan. What do you think of the slogan? Just had it done.'

'*BAY VIEW CARAVAN PARK-WHERE THE FUN NEVER STOP'S*' was written in big red letters on the side.

'It's … it's very … nice,' I said.

It was the best I could manage. I wasn't sure what 'fun' was to be had on a site that had no swimming pool, no club and nothing to do. There also shouldn't have been an apostrophe on the 'STOP'S' bit. But I liked Mr Clarke and I didn't want to upset him. He was big and gruff with a booming voice and he always remembered my name. Will's mum had died when he was only a baby and Mr Clarke had moved Will all around the country, setting up lots of different businesses which had all been disastrous. They had moved to Bridlington six months ago to start up a caravan park and I just had to hope that they would be successful this time. I couldn't imagine life without Will now.

'It wasn't cheap but it'll be worth the investment,' said Mr Clarke.

'It's ... a good idea,' I said. 'Get you noticed.'

He beamed. 'We need to drum up more trade. It's been a bit slow but it's only our first year. Things'll pick up'

I nodded and smiled at him. I had to hope he was right.

'Anyway. To what do we owe the pleasure of your visit?' he asked.

'Is Will around?'

Mr Clarke's expression changed. 'It's a pity you weren't here the other night,' he grumbled. 'You'd have kept control of things. You're the only one of his pals with any sense.'

'I had to stay in,' I said. 'We had a girl arriving and ...'

'Don't you worry yourself, love. You missed nothing. How's your mam?'

'Fine,' I said.

I didn't want to talk about Mum. I had never snuck out of the house before without telling her and even though I knew I was in the right, I felt guilty now. I should send her a text in a minute to let her know I was OK.

'Will's in the shop doing jobs for me,' said Mr Clarke. 'He's in the dog house.'

He turned back to his polishing.

The shop seemed empty at first but then I heard some scuffling from behind the counter and I peered over. 'I'll have a caramel mocha with extra cream please,' I said. 'No actually. Change that. I'll have something I like.'

Will stood up and brushed the dust from his jeans. 'Dad's making me sort out all these cupboards under here,' he said. 'Apparently I have to work in the shop for the rest of my life to make up for one rubbish party.' He laughed and passed me a chocolate bar.

'You might as well have one. They're all out of date but I don't think that matters. It won't kill you or anything.'

He peeled the wrapper off his bar and took a huge bite. The next minute he was clutching his throat. 'AHHHHHH!' He screamed making huge melodramatic gestures. 'Tell Dad I love him. I leave all my worldly possessions to my hamster … AHHHH!!!'

He pretended to fall behind the counter.

'Will, pack it in. You're not funny. You haven't even got a hamster. And if you keep doing things like that, one day when you are actually choking, we'll just ignore you. The boy who cried wolf? Ever heard of him?'

'Is Will alright?'

I swung around and to my dismay I saw Mirabel standing in the doorway. She was dressed in the black leggings I had given her and my 'Come to the Dark Side, We have Cookies' t-shirt. On her feet were a pair of Mum's old trainers which were way too big. The bin bag she was holding was looking really tatty now and some of her things were sticking out of the sides. I thought about the pendant she had given me. I should have shown that to Mum straight away. And I definitely shouldn't have come here without telling her.

'Mirabel! What are you doing? Where's Mum?'

She shrugged. 'It's not important,' she said.

'What do you mean?'

Mirabel ignored me and looked directly at Will. 'I need to go to my house. I want you to take me there.'

'You can't ask Will that,' I said. 'We …'

Just at that moment the bottom of her bin liner gave way. Everything in it scattered on to the floor. I noticed that a few of my things, like my hairbrush and an old doll of mine seemed to have found their way into her possessions.

Will leapt over the counter. 'Hang on. Let's start by putting your stuff in here,' he said. He grabbed a roll of bin liners from the counter and ripped off a new one.

He bent down and started to help her to retrieve everything.

'And then we can go, yes?' she said.

'Yeah. Home. Mum is going to kill both of us,' I said.

'How come?' asked Will.

'She doesn't know I'm here. And now Mirabel has followed me. This day can't get any worse.'

'I didn't follow you,' said Mirabel. 'I don't care where you are. I'm not going to your house. I want to go to mine.'

'But will there be anyone there?' asked Will.

Mirabel nodded. 'Of course,' she said. 'But I can't go by myself. I have no means of transport.'

'If Dad's finished cleaning his van he can give you a lift,' said Will. 'I'll go and ask him.'

'Will!' I said angrily. 'We can't take her anywhere. Mum'll go into meltdown. We …'

'Meg, why are you finding this so difficult to understand?'

she interrupted. 'I can go home now. I had a message. From my grandfather. It's all been explained to me and I need to get back as quickly as possible!'

She stopped. Her face was bright red and she was breathing heavily. She stared at me without blinking.

The girl was nuts. 'You never mentioned you had a granddad,' I said.

'You never asked. Everyone has a grandfather, Meg. Mine is at the house waiting for me. He wanted me to come on my own but that would take ages. So I thought you two could help. I thought you were my friends.'

'Yeah but we can't take you home. Not without …'

'I don't see why there has to be all this fuss,' she snapped. 'Will seems to think it will be alright.'

This kid was a major pain and she was totally ruining my holidays.

'You promised to help me, Will,' she went on. 'You can't go back on that now.'

'Absolutely,' he said. 'What do you think, Meg? If her granddad's back, that's OK isn't it? And my dad won't mind running her up there.'

I hesitated. 'Why don't we just ring your granddad and ask him to come and get you later?' I asked. 'That way Mum can …'

'This is wasting time,' she said angrily. 'I live at Wyndrift House, near Filey. We need to hurry.'

'Just let Meg ring her mum and ask her if it's OK,' said Will. 'I'll bet she'll be cool about it.'

I wasn't sure about that but Mum was always banging on about how much red tape there was in this fostering business. If there was an easy solution to Mirabel's problems then she could be out of our hair by tonight and we could go back to normal.

'OK you two,' I said. 'I'll ask her to meet us there. But if she says no, then that's it, right?'

I waited for Mirabel to agree but she turned away from me.

I walked out of the shop to get away from her and rang Mum. She answered straight away and I had to listen to her throwing a fit over me disappearing. She didn't believe that I hadn't taken Mirabel with me as well.

'Why would I do that?'

'It's totally irresponsible. You can't go gallivanting off with her.'

'I didn't! But she says her granddad's back now. She seems pretty sure of where she lives.'

'The police tried and there was no one there. They didn't mention a grandfather. I haven't got time for this, Meg. I have to …'

'Mum, it's fine. I know what I'm doing. Mr Clarke's taking us and we can meet you there.'

'This is typical of you, Meg. You don't listen to what anyone says. You …'

She carried on ranting for a bit and I stopped listening. There was no point.

'Alright, alright. I hear you! We'll bring her back.' I clicked my phone off. 'After we've checked if her granddad is at Wyndrift House,' I added.

After all, Will was right. If everything could be sorted quickly, then we could get rid. I couldn't deal with this aggravation for the whole of my summer holidays.

I went back to Will and Mirabel. 'She says it's not a problem as long as we're quick,' I said.

It was a bit stifling in the van. The rain had stopped and the sun was beginning to emerge from the clouds. Mirabel sat up at the front with Mr Clarke but Will and I had to make do with the floor in the back. There was a pungent smell coming from somewhere. It was all I could do not to be sick.

I was surprised at how animated Mirabel had suddenly become. Mr Clarke was pointing out all of the features of his new van and she seemed really fascinated by what he was saying.

'Now where is it we're going again?' he asked her.

'Wyndrift House … It's …'

'Yeah, I know it. I think I know how to get there. I wondered if anyone had taken on that house,' he said. 'It's right near the beach isn't it? Lovely spot. I expect your folks will be setting about doing it up. If they need any help …'

'Dad! Can you slow down!' shouted Will.

Mr Clarke ignored him and as he turned a sharp right, Will and I smacked into each other.

'Watch it Dad!'

'Nearly there,' he said.

I felt the van draw to a stop and we both tried to pull ourselves upright again.

'Dad! You almost killed us! There's no seat belts in the back you know!'

Mr Clarke laughed. 'You kids. You're all soft these days. Never had seat belts when I was a lad.'

'You didn't have cars, did you?' said Will. 'Wasn't it all horses and carts?'

'Or walking,' said Mr Clarke. 'Which is what you'll be doing if I have any more lip.'

I could tell by the tone of his voice that Will was forgiven. Mr Clarke was too nice to be mad for very long. Not like Mum. I tried not to think about how crazy she was going to be when she figured out what I had done.

Mr Clarke slid open the door to let us out and to my surprise we were in the middle of a large caravan site. I recognised it at once.

'Happy Valley,' I said.

'Yep,' he said. 'Biggest caravan site for miles. This is grand. It's what ours'll be like one day.'

I couldn't help thinking that Mr Clarke was a little optimistic if he thought his park could ever match this one. It had a funfair for one thing and a swimming pool. Just around the corner from where we were standing there was a pub, a mini supermarket and a cafe. The only food Mr Clarke seemed to sell on his caravan park was out of date crisps and chocolate.

'What are we doing here?' Will asked emerging from the van and rubbing his neck. 'I thought we were supposed to be taking Mirabel to her house.'

'I've parked here because Mirabel's place is down that private road, clever clogs. It's a bit narrow for the van and there's not much room to turn round at the bottom.'

'You could go on to the beach,' Will said. 'Loadsa space.'

'Not if the tide's in, you idiot. This van's a beauty, Will, but she can't swim. Now hurry up. I'll wait here for you. I'm going to eye up the competition.'

'Well at least the caravans on your site don't look as bad as that one,' I said. 'Why's it got all those wires hanging from the roof?'

Mr Clarke turned. 'Which one love?' he asked.

'That.' I pointed to a caravan that was on its own, near to the edge of the cliff. 'The green one with all the paint flaking off.'

'I can't see …'

'I don't live here,' Mirabel interrupted.

'Wyndrift House, yeah?' asked Mr Clarke. 'The big place near the beach? You can just see the top of it from here. You'll need to go down that road there.'

She nodded. 'Yes. Yes of course. I am grateful to you, Mr Clarke. I don't think I'll need your services any more. My grandfather will take care of me. But thank you anyway. You have a pure heart.'

She marched off towards the road.

'Well she's a strange one and no mistake, Meg.' Mr Clarke laughed. 'Nice enough though. Don't be long will you?'

Chapter 7

'Bloody hell,' said Will. 'She doesn't really live there does she?'

'It's what she keeps saying.'

I had seen the house that Mirabel was heading towards before of course, but Dad had told me that it was empty. It was three storeys high and it reminded me of a white wedding cake. A massive box formed the ground floor then slightly smaller ones had been placed on top of each other for the second and third levels, leaving room for balconies edged with glass. It was surrounded by a low white wall.

'WILL! HURRY UP!' Mirabel yelled, racing ahead.

'Well, she seems sure enough that it's her place,' said Will. 'Come on.'

He sped off but I didn't chase after him. If anything, I slowed down. Mirabel was clearly a mixed up kid and I shouldn't have let Will talk me into bringing her here. If she had made up this stuff about the house and her grand-dad then what would I do? Take her home with me again? I couldn't imagine her agreeing to that, or how mad Mum was going to be with me for lying to her.

I glanced at my phone but there were no messages yet. How long would it be before she figured out what I had done?

She was going to kill me.

Ribbons of sea mist drifted up from the path, swirling in front of me now and making it difficult to see far ahead. I quickened my step. I had experienced sea frets before, when the fog rolls off the sea and the air becomes thick and drizzly. It was much colder all of a sudden and my clothes were already feeling damp.

'Wait, you two!' I shouted.

But the clouds had come in so quickly that I couldn't see either of them.

'WILL?' I called. 'MIRABEL?'

I couldn't even see the house now. Everywhere had gone eerily quiet.

I stopped.

This was ridiculous.

'WILL!' I shouted. 'WILL, I …'

The mist lifted for a moment and I saw that I had reached the low wall surrounding the house. Sitting on it was an old man. He was hunched over, his long grey hair lank and matted. I wondered if he was asleep or ill or something because as I got nearer to him he didn't move. He was wearing a black leather coat with a fur collar over some very scruffy track suit bottoms. The slippers on his feet had holes in and I saw that there was a large bandage wrapped around one of his ankles. The dressing was filthy.

'Are you … are you OK?' I asked cautiously.

He looked up. It was all I could do not to gasp. One side of his face was bright purple and covered in lumps and swellings. Flaps of skin sagged down and I could see some of them were bleeding slightly.

He suddenly became very agitated. He stood up, grabbed his walking stick and started waving it. Whatever he was saying, it wasn't in English.

I backed away.

The fog was still thick behind him and there was no sign of Will or Mirabel.

He shouted over to me again, but this time I understood him.

'Don't take another step!' he yelled. 'DON'T MOVE!'

He was pointing the stick at me as though it was a machine gun or something.

I stopped.

'I don't know how you did it,' he said. 'But you needn't think I'm afraid of you. I ... I ...'

He started coughing uncontrollably and slumped back on to the wall, unable to say any more.

'Shall I get you some help?' I asked.

He shook his head and waved the walking cane towards an old tartan shopping bag that lay just out of his reach.

'Don't just stand there gawping. Get me a drink out of that,' he barked. 'Quick.'

I thought about pointing out that he had told me not to move.

I didn't. I walked over slowly and picked up the bag. It seemed to be full of bottles of whisky. 'You sure this is a good idea?' I asked. 'Maybe water would be better. I could go and ...'

'Give it here.'

He held out his hand and I passed one of the bottles to

him. Unscrewing the top, he took some big gulps before a coughing fit forced him to stop. Eventually he seemed to recover and his breathing became more steady.

'If you're OK now, I need to find my friends,' I said.

Narrowing his eyes, he peered at me. His breath was full of whistles and even from a distance I could smell something dead and rotting. I tried not to flinch or to stare at the ripped bits of skin hanging down from the side of his face.

'Take that hood off,' he said. 'Let me look at you properly.'

I was about to refuse when there was a blast of wind and my hood fell down anyway.

He leaned forward and really stared at me. His eyes were blinking and streaming like mad and I wondered if he was able to see anything at all.

Then for some reason he leaned back and smiled. I caught a glimpse of his teeth, yellow and crooked and broken. He shook his head and started to chuckle to himself. 'Just for a minute there,' he said. 'Just for a minute you had me fooled.'

He sighed and looked away from me. 'Old age,' he went on. 'Old eyesight. Brain going to mush.'

'I don't know what you're talking about,' I said.

'Meg,' he said. 'Meg Rowlands.'

'Do you know me?'

I had definitely never seen the old man before. There was no way I would have forgotten.

'You always had that orange stuff in your hair?'

Just at that moment my phone started to ring and I pulled it out of my pocket. There was a sharp flash and a stinging pain ran up my arm. My phone flew out of my hand and spun through the air.

The next second the old man was holding it.

'How the hell … give me my phone back!'

I tried to step forward but for some reason I didn't seem able to move.

He didn't say anything but placed my phone on the wall. He took another swig from the bottle and it seemed to revive him a bit more.

I really didn't know what to do next. It was ridiculous that I couldn't just run away but I seemed rooted to the spot.

'Do you know who I am, Meg Rowlands?' he said, his voice much stronger now.

'No.'

'But you're afraid of me, right?'

I shook my head but in truth he was totally freaking me out. I noticed that his pale eyes were mottled like the shells of birds' eggs.

'What do you make of Mirabel?' he asked.

'How … how do you know her?' My voice was not much more than a whisper.

'You're a bit slow on the uptake, aren't you? She's gone inside hasn't she? Who's that with her?'

A terrible thought occurred to me. 'You're not … are you Mirabel's grandfather?' I asked, not being able to hide the shock in my voice.

'What's up? Disappointed?'

I didn't answer.

He didn't blink or look away, as though he was trying to tell just by looking at me whether I was being straight with him.

'Meg,' he said at last. 'Meg Rowlands. From Bridlington.' He took another drink from the bottle and wiped his mouth with the back of his hand. 'For a minute there I thought you were someone else.'

'I ... I don't know what you mean.'

'You can leave Mirabel with me now, any-road,' he said, picking up my phone and turning it over in his hands. 'I'll take care of her.'

'You'll need to talk to my mum first. She's coming down here and ...'

'No need. I think my granddaughter will be safe with me don't you? Name's Ward. Alfred Ward.'

He touched his cheek where one of the sores had started bleeding a little. I wondered what on earth could have happened to his face to have damaged it so much.

'Just ... just give me my phone back and ...'

'Try where you normally keep it.'

I slipped my hand into the pocket of my hoodie and it was there. 'How ...?'

'I can see that we've got off on the wrong foot but not to worry. Why don't you go in? Get Mirabel to show you round the house. She'll like that. You'll see everything's ship shape.'

His voice was much softer now and he attempted a smile. I hadn't imagined Mirabel's granddad to be anything like this.

No wonder the kid was messed up.

The mist started to lift. I could see the path that I had walked down. I felt able to move again and I glanced over towards Wyndrift House which was emerging from the fog. It looked even more impressive close up than it had from the top of the cliff.

The front door was open. 'I'll just call Mum and ...'

I turned around but the old man had gone.

Chapter 8

Will was standing in the lounge.

'Are you alright?' he said. 'Where've you been?'

'Talking to Mirabel's granddad. He … did he come in?'

'When?'

'Just now?'

'Nope.'

'He's … well he's … I don't know where he went. Anyway we can't leave Mirabel with him. He's horrible.'

I knew that was an understatement but I didn't know how to explain to Will what had just happened outside. I glanced around but I couldn't see Mirabel anywhere.

'Tell me you haven't lost her,' I said, suddenly worried that she had run off again.

'Course not. She's upstairs. I thought I'd wait for you but … you know we were talking about déjà vu yesterday?'

'Maybe. Will, we need to …'

'Only I really feel like I've been here before.'

We were standing in the lounge and I looked around properly for the first time. I couldn't see anything remarkable about it. A brown sofa stretched out against one of the white walls. There was a wicker chair with yellow cushions on it and next to that a round battered-looking coffee table.

'You must be imagining things,' I said. 'Unless you came here once and forgot.'

'No. Deffo not. But it's really like somewhere Dad and I used to live,' said Will. 'And the kitchen looks familiar too only … well there's nothing in the cupboards or the fridge. It's freaking me out.'

He looked genuinely worried and I had to admit I was feeling really uncomfortable inside this house too.

'We should go and find Mirabel,' I said. 'And get out of here.'

'And there's a load of cookbooks on the shelves,' he went on.

'What?'

'But there's nothing in them. All the pages are blank. The same with the ones in the front room.'

'They must be just for show,' I said. 'Or … look … let's go and get Mirabel. We can't leave her with her granddad. He's well old and he was drinking whisky outside. He seems more confused than her. We have to get her back to mine and let Mum sort this mess out.'

Will didn't say anything. He ran his hands through his hair and looked around the room again.

'Will!' I snapped. 'Are you listening? We have to go.'

'Yeah. Fine. You're right,' he said. 'We shouldn't have come. This is my fault.'

'You were only trying to help.'

'This place is giving me the creeps. I can feel the hairs on the back of my neck standing up.'

I knew exactly what he meant.

We found her on the top floor in one of the bedrooms. Mirabel was very different from me, it was true, but I didn't expect her room to look the way it did. She was supposed to be my age but either it hadn't been decorated for years or she was still into fantasy in a big way. The wallpaper had a bright pink background. Fairies with lacy wings sat on flower heads whilst butterflies danced around their heads. The bedspread was covered in fairytale castles and in the centre a unicorn was pulling a pink coach shaped like a pumpkin. Most surfaces on the white furniture seemed to have a stuffed animal of some kind on them.

Mirabel had opened the wardrobe door and was peering in.

'Mirabel. You OK?' asked Will.

She didn't answer.

'We were just saying we should go back,' he said. 'Go and find my dad. I bet he'd let us go and grab some ice cream if you want?'

'Something's wrong,' Mirabel said, ignoring him.

'Like what?' I asked.

She closed the door of the wardrobe carefully.

'I can't explain it,' she said. 'I just know this isn't right. I need to go and find my grandfather.'

'Meg says ...'

'He's not here,' I said, jumping in quickly before Will could finish. 'And we can't leave you on your own. Will's right. You'd better come back with us.'

'This is definitely like my room,' she went on. 'But it doesn't *feel* the same. And downstairs is different somehow. I ... I wish I could remember things more clearly.'

She started searching through the drawers of her dressing table, throwing stuff out on to the floor.

'What are you doing?' I asked.

'I want to find my key. I like to fasten my door. It makes me feel safe.'

I wondered what she'd think about the way Mum kept spare keys on top of door frames, but I didn't say anything.

'Is that it?' asked Will, pointing to a large keyring hanging in the lock. It was in the shape of a silver teddy bear wearing a fluffy pink tutu. Truly hideous. Even worse than my blue plastic elephant.

'Thanks,' said Mirabel, racing over and turning the key. She put it into her pocket. 'Now come and see my balcony.'

'Mirabel! There's no point in you locking the door. We need to go!' I was getting really anxious now. Mirabel looked at me for a second and then walked over to the patio doors and slid them open.

'Please talk to her, Will,' I said. 'This has gone far enough.'

'Let's just humour her and look at the view. I bet she'll be ready to leave after that.'

I followed him outside, not convinced that Mirabel was going to be ready to do anything she didn't want to.

The sides of the balcony were made of glass and you could see for miles along the beach. It was definitely an amazing place to live and the house must have cost a fortune. So how come she had turned up at our place in a scraggy old pair of pyjamas carrying a bin bag? Why had she been found wandering around on the beach so near to this place and yet no one could find any relatives to take care of her? Especially if her granddad lived right here? It didn't make any sense.

'Mirabel,' I said, trying again. 'You know you can't stay here, don't you?'

'Why not?' she snapped. 'I'm home now.'

'I need you to come back with me. Talk to Mum.'

'Your mum is very nice,' she said. 'But my grandfather will look after me now. Until my aunt returns. There must be something important she has had to do, but she'll be back soon.'

'I think it might be better if you waited until your aunt actually appears,' I said. 'She ...'

'She's called Rhiannon,' she said. 'Rhiannon Kendrick. I just remembered. You see. I'm better already now that I'm here.'

'The thing is ...' started Will.

'We have to go back,' I said. 'Your grandfather isn't ...'

A strong smell of whisky and cigarettes hit me. Someone coughed. I swung round and saw the old man sitting on a chair in the corner of the balcony. How could he have come up here without us noticing? And hadn't Mirabel locked the door?

His cane was resting against the arm of the chair but when he saw me looking at it, he picked it up.

'Isn't it time you were going?' he said.

Will looked over at me in astonishment. Perhaps he believed me now about the problem of leaving her with the old man.

'You've not introduced me to your boyfriend,' he said. 'Does he always gawp like a fish?'

'This is ...'

I was interrupted by a loud knocking from downstairs. 'HELLO! ANYONE THERE?'

Someone was shouting to us from the ground floor. I leaned over the balcony and saw a policeman and a policewoman waving up at me.

'That'll be the law, I expect,' said Mr Ward. 'I rang them. They're coming over to check Mirabel's safe. Which of course she is. You'll be fine with your old granddad won't you, Mirabel?'

She didn't reply but she nodded slowly.

'There you are then. Be a good girl, Meg. Run down and let the coppers in. And then you and your boyfriend can be on your way.'

Chapter 9

After three failed attempts I managed to call Mum. I expected her to go crazy but even though the line was bad, her voice sounded way calmer than I had expected.

'I hope Dad's waited for us,' said Will, after I had finished. 'I don't fancy walking all the way back to mine.'

I was still thinking about Mum and I didn't answer. We were heading up to the cliff top but I couldn't resist turning around to have another look at the house.

Nothing felt right about the whole thing.

'You OK?' asked Will.

'Not really.'

'You don't need to worry. I mean I know her granddad looks … well … he is a bit old and that but that's not his fault is it?'

'I'm not that shallow, Will. It's just …'

'That policewoman we chatted to seemed cool. She said they were sorting it out. They wouldn't let Mirabel stay there if they think she's not safe, would they?'

'No. I know.'

'And your mum's OK with it all now. Happy days I say.'

'That's what's bothering me, Will. On the phone just now. She sounded … weird.'

'What do you mean?'

'Well her voice was so soft I could hardly hear her.'

'Yeah, but the signal's crap round here. It comes and goes.'

'Will. If Mum was mad with me, I'd be able to hear her shouting at me without her even using the phone. But she … she didn't even sound a little bit annoyed and she didn't say anything about me going out without telling her or coming down here. She actually thanked me for taking Mirabel back to her granddad. That can't be right.'

He laughed. 'Your mum's cool. I think you're making too big a deal of it. And talking about mad parents, I don't think I want to upset Dad any more. I think he's forgiven me now but I don't want to push it.'

We had reached the top of the cliff but as we neared the van we could see it was empty. There was no sign of Mr Clarke.

'He can't be still looking around the caravan site,' said Will.

'I'm not. I'm fixing this bloody thing,' a familiar voice boomed out.

I couldn't see where he was at first. We walked around the other side and there was Mr Clarke, hard at work changing a tyre. A couple of men were helping him. They looked up when they saw us.

'Must have driven over some nails,' he said. 'Shouldn't be too long. Go and get yourselves a drink. There's a cafe over there.'

He dug into his pockets and threw some money over to Will.

'Four quid!' shouted Will. 'Result! Perhaps I should arrange another party while my luck's in.'

Mr Clarke looked stern for a moment but then he smiled. 'I'll text you when I'm done,' he said.

'You mean you've actually got your phone on?'

'I'll have that money back …'

'You're OK,' Will said hastily. 'Come on, Meg.'

We headed towards the cafe. Will rattled on about the plans for the band but I was only half listening. I was still thinking about Mirabel and that weird conversation I'd had with her granddad, when something caught my eye. We were passing the green, peeling caravan I had seen before but now there was a man on the decking, dressed in a flowery jacket and bright red trousers. He was flashing a torch around as though he was looking for something. A large plaque had been screwed to the side of the caravan at an odd angle.

He looked up, and when he saw us he waved. When I waved back he looked shocked and scurried back inside the caravan.

Everyone was acting mad today.

'So what do you think?' asked Will.

'About what?'

'The band. The name for the band.'

'Do caravans have names?'

'What are you on about?'

'Like when people call their house something like Dunroamin'. Is it the same with caravans?'

'I suppose,' he said. 'Actually, Dad's letting me use one of the old ones on the site for the band. You can name it if you like.'

'How about Dunsinging? Or Dunplayingaguitar? Or …'

'OK. OK. Enough. Very funny. You're forgetting something though.'

'What?'

'I'm the one with the money so you'd better be careful. Any more sarcasm and I might order you an Egg Nog latte.'

'I might like it.'

'No one likes Egg Nog Latte. Not even with twenty sugars in it. Come on.'

Chapter 10

When I arrived home Mum was sitting at the kitchen table again. She had gone back to sifting through the papers and old photos. I had expected her to give me a proper roasting but she was calmer than I'd ever seen her. She told me that Mirabel had gone home, as though I didn't know already, and asked me to make her a cup of tea. She didn't say a word about anything else. Maybe she was saving it all up for later.

Or for when Dad came home.

I made my escape to my bedroom.

What I needed to do was to forget all about Mirabel, who was nothing to do with me, and to concentrate on more important things, real things. Like seeing how much festival tickets cost and how I was going to persuade Mum and Dad to let me go to one. I must have been messing about on the computer for about an hour or so when there was a soft knock on my door.

Mum popped her head around. 'I thought you might be hungry.'

She came in and put down a glass of coke and some chocolate biscuits on to my table. Surely this was the calm before the storm. Now I would get the rant about how irresponsible I was and her list of things that 'might' have happened because of 'what I had done'.

She smiled at me. 'Have a drink,' she said. 'You must be thirsty.'

Mum had filled it right to the top and I had to drink some before I picked up the glass. She watched me as I gulped about half of it down.

'Is something wrong?' I asked. She was making me nervous.

'I thought you might be hungry,' she said again, handing me a biscuit.

'You said that before. And I'm fine. Are you sure you're OK?'

'It's raining,' Mum said, ignoring my question and strolling over to the window. 'You look very busy up here.'

I couldn't stand much more of this. 'Look Mum. About before. I …'

'I had a telephone call this afternoon,' she said. 'Such a nice man. I thanked him of course, for what he did.'

'Mr Clarke's great.'

'No … no.' She was looking wistfully out of the window. 'I didn't mean him. I'm talking about Mirabel's grandfather.'

'You talked to him?'

'Good to know that Mirabel's in safe hands.'

Her voice sounded far away and I wondered if she had been drinking. She didn't usually. I thought about the smell of Mr Ward's whisky and winced. He hadn't struck me as 'nice' or 'good' but he had certainly turned on the charm when the police arrived. They didn't react to him in the way I had and they even apologised for not finding him sooner.

Mum started to hum a tune. She never sings.

'Mum … what's going on?'

She was staring into space. Perhaps she wasn't well.

'Mr Ward,' she said. 'I've remembered. Mr Ward. That was his name! He rang just after the policewoman. Such a gentleman. And the whole thing a misunderstanding.' She paused. 'You know I think I may be coming down with a cold. I can't … I can't quite remember what he said now. Anyway it's all turned out for the best. Not often you can say that, is it?'

I was about to launch in with what I thought of Mr Ward and tell her about the weird things that had happened but I thought better of it. No one else seemed to have a problem with the old man. They obviously all thought that Mirabel was safe with him. I had to leave it.

It was up to other people to worry about Mirabel now. I was done.

Mum sank down on my bed and looked around. 'I was thinking about doing a bit of decorating. This room could do with brightening up and the one Mirabel stayed in is even worse. Perhaps you could help out this summer, just while you're waiting for a job. Nothing too major. Just a lick of paint. What do you think?'

I turned away from the computer screen. 'Only if I get to choose the colours and I get paid.'

She laughed. 'What happened to just being satisfied with a job well done?'

'I'm too skint for that.'

'Well, we'll see. I thought of maybe a lemon colour?'

'What is it with you and yellow?'

'Lemon's not too bright though. I thought it would look fresh.'

'Mum. No one likes yellow.'

'I do. It's a happy colour. The colour of sunshine and flowers and …'

'Vomit,' I said,

'Meg!'

My phone sounded and lit up. It was a text from Will.

Any news on Mirabel? ☺

Bloody hell. Not him as well. I texted back that she was fine. I wanted there to be no more conversations about that girl.

'Look, I'll leave you to it,' said Mum. 'How about I nip out and get us some chips?'

She really was unwell. Chocolate biscuits and chips? What happened to her going on about healthy eating?

'OK,' I said, before she changed her mind. 'Can I have curry sauce with mine?'

'Really? I don't know how you can eat that stuff.'

'You'd like it. It's yellow.'

I picked up my glass of coke and almost spilled it again. It was full to the brim.

I opened my window a little to see if Mum was coming back from the chippy. The street was normally quiet at night but I could hear something now – a voice whispering in the growing darkness.

SHHHHHH

I shivered and was about to close the window when I looked down and saw a figure standing on the driveway.

There was no mistaking who it was. She was wearing the big pyjamas and clinging on to the bin bag.

'Mirabel?' I said. 'Mirabel! Wait. I'm coming.'

I raced down the stairs and flung open the front door.

There was no one there.

'Sorry I've been so long,' shouted Mum, walking towards me up the drive. 'There was a massive queue. Are you alright? You look like you've seen a ghost.'

Chapter 11

'I am absolutely starving!' Will bit into his toast. Butter and jam splattered on to his top.

'Bloody hell. Soz, Meg. This is going everywhere.'

'Are you even listening to me?'

'Sure. No problem. You saw Mirabel last night.'

'Yes.'

'Under your window.'

'Yes.'

'But she wasn't there when you went to look for her.'

'No.'

'And you told your mum and …'

'She's still in Wyndrift House. Mum checked.'

'So … you couldn't have seen her?'

'Well … yes and no.'

'I don't get it.'

This wasn't going well. I tried to tell him about the voice I'd heard but it just sounded stupid. Mum had thought I was going mad last night, especially when I refused to go to bed until she had made some calls. She was adamant that Mirabel couldn't have been outside our house and anyway, when I had time to think, why would she be dressed like the first time I'd seen her? With no shoes?

'Look, sit down and have some food,' he said, as though he was the one that lived here. 'You must have been dreaming or something.'

'Maybe.' My dreams had been very vivid lately. Maybe I was starting to lose sense of what was real. I flopped down on to the chair opposite him. 'How much breakfast do you actually eat?' I asked as he reached for more bread.

'I don't normally. No time. This is great. I bloody love the holidays.'

Mum came in with a load of washing in her arms. She'd had a right go at me about the state of my room earlier so things were definitely getting back to normal in some ways.

'Oh, hi Will. I didn't realise you were here,' she said, smiling. 'Enjoying your holiday?'

'Not really Mrs R. I take my education very seriously. Opportunities for learning missed as far as I'm concerned.'

Mum looked a bit bemused.

'Only joking Mrs R. Holidays are well cool. Anyway, I'm up to date with most stuff even if it's not very good. I'm not a brainbox like Meg.'

Mum smiled. 'She's clever enough Will, but ask her to do a few simple jobs and …'

'Did you hand in that Shakespeare assignment on Friday?' I interrupted Mum before she started showing me up. 'Mr Andrews said it had to be in before the holidays. I bet you forgot.'

Will picked up the bread knife. 'That is where ye is wrongeth. I did indeed handeth it in. I'm an expert on Hamlet now in fact. *Is this a dagger I see before me …?*'

He waved the knife about in the air.

'Brilliant, Will. Only that's Macbeth and we're doing The Tempest.'

Will placed the knife down carefully and lowered his voice.

'"*Be cheerful, Meg.*

Our revels now are ended. These our actors,

As I foretold you, were all spirits and

Are melted into air." Ta-dah. I thank you.'

'That's brilliant Will,' said Mum. 'You should be an actor. More toast?'

'Sound, Mrs R.' He paused and looked over at me. 'We were just wondering about Mirabel, actually. She was pretty cool. Do you think she'll be alright with her granddad only he was … well old.'

'Has Meg been pestering you? Look you two. She's perfectly safe. They would not have let her stay with just anyone. Not if they had any doubts. We can't interfere.' She looked over at me. 'And anyway I spoke to Mr Ward on the phone about ten minutes ago. He told me things are fine and Mirabel's happy.'

'He rang you again?' I asked.

'Yes. I think he just wanted to reassure me that everything was alright. Oh, and he asked if we'd found a necklace belonging to Mirabel. A gold pendant? I've turned the room inside out but there's definitely not anything there. You haven't seen it have you?'

I had completely forgotten about that. It was still in my bag. 'I can't keep a track of my own stuff, let alone anyone else's,' I said.

I don't know why I lied. Maybe something about last

night was still haunting me or maybe I thought I was going to get into even more bother. Whatever it was, the mention of Mr Ward had made me uneasy again. I didn't like that he was asking for the pendant. I just didn't trust him and there was no way I wanted to hand it over. Mum might be happy about the way things had turned out but I wasn't. I couldn't get the thought of Mirabel out of my head.

No.

The pendant could stay in my bag for now.

'Never mind,' said Mum. 'I'll have to tell him that …'

Her phone rang. She pulled it out of the pocket of her apron. 'Who's this now?' She stared at the screen. 'Oh, it's social services. Give me a minute.'

She went out into the hall.

'OK. So what shall we do today?" asked Will.

I sprang to my feet. 'Grab your coat.'

'What? Now? I haven't finished …'

'Hurry up.'

'Why?'

'JUST MOVE!'

Shoving a last piece of toast into his mouth, Will grabbed his jacket from the back of the chair. 'Well it's a lovely day for … erm what exactly?'

'An adventure. You're the one who keeps saying nothing happens around here.'

'Absolutely. An adventure. Totally up for that.'

'Mum! We're going … We're going to Will's,' I shouted into the hall. 'See you later.'

'Just a minute,' she called.

I thought for a moment she was going to make me stay in. 'I'm in Scarborough all day today. I can give you a lift back at about four if that's any good? I could do with some help with the shopping.'

'I don't need a lift … I …'

'See you at four. Keep your phone on and …'

'Fine,' I said as I closed the door. How annoying could one woman be?

I strode ahead of Will up the path. Mum was always banging on about not getting too involved with the kids we fostered, but that wasn't easy. I didn't seem able to forget about Mirabel, however much I wanted to.

Chapter 12

The bus station was crowded. Holiday makers were arriving into Bridlington armed with the usual windbreaks, buckets, spades and cool boxes. There were also quite a few kids hanging around and I hoped that we didn't bump into anyone we knew.

Especially Abbie.

'Meg, I'm not going any further until you tell me what's going on. Is this still about Mirabel?'

I ignored Will and strode off towards one of the stands. Despite what he said I knew he was still following me.

'You've just charged ahead and you haven't said a word all the way down here. What's happening?'

'Are you going to Filey?' I asked a driver, who was having a cigarette in front of a bus. 'We need to get off near Happy Valley.'

'I knew it!' said Will.

The bus driver nodded. 'School holidays eh? Them teachers have the life of Riley.'

Will found a seat. 'So we're going to see Mirabel which is cool but …'

'I need to be sure she's OK.'

'But your mum checked and …'

'You're going to have to trust me.'

'Absolutely. One hundred percent.'

He took his phone out of his pocket. He didn't say anything for a while and I was glad. The bus started up and we pulled out of the station.

'Am I allowed to ask just one thing?' he asked at last.

'Go on.'

'How long do you think we'll be?'

'Not long. We could walk up to that beach cafe at Hunmanby Gap after, if you like. Mum's not picking me up until four. There's plenty of time.'

'Cool.'

'Is that OK?'

'Yeah. Totally. Only... I kinda asked Tom and Chris round this afternoon – band stuff. You could help us if you like.'

'With what?'

'Listening to some of our new songs. Give us your opinion. You see Tom's found out that Abbie's got this uncle who's some big music producer up in London and ...'

'You're going to be rich and famous.'

'No. But I think it's genuine, Meg. She told Tom that this guy might come and see us. I think we were just lacking a bit of motivation before. This is just the kind of thing we need to get us noticed.'

'You don't actually believe Abbie, do you?'

'Well Tom seems pretty convinced. He says she can get us a gig and then her uncle ...'

'Who doesn't exist ...'

'Her uncle can come down and listen and maybe ... well we can decide all that later.'

'And by "we" you mean …'

'I thought you might fancy tagging along. Abbie's invited us all over to hers next week and we need to be ready. She lives on that farm up at …'

'I know where she lives, thanks.'

'She says she has some good ideas.'

I couldn't believe that she had managed to worm her way in after all that Will had said. And I was even more certain that she wouldn't want me 'tagging along'.

'I thought you didn't want her in the band anyway,' I said. 'Voice like a mangled rabbit were your exact words.'

Will didn't answer and was silent for the rest of the journey. When I rang the bell for our stop, he put his phone in his pocket but he didn't even look at me. The door opened and I stepped down. My foot sank into a deep puddle on the side of the road. The dark muddy water slapped into my trainers.

'Excellent. Today really can't get any better,' I muttered.

The sun was just beginning to appear and a lot of the holiday makers were sitting outside their caravans enjoying the sun. A young boy on a bike way too big for him almost ran into us. We still weren't talking and when we turned into the road to Mirabel's house, I almost suggested going back.

What was I doing?

I couldn't have seen Mirabel last night and now that I was here it seemed like a very bad idea to meet up with her again. I should have given the pendant to Mum when I had the chance.

I was acting like a crazy person. No wonder Will was planning to get some new friends.

Wyndrift House came into view.

Will stopped.

'Meg, look, I am really sorry,' he said. 'I know I can be a prat sometimes. It's just I really want this band thing to work, you know. But if it means …'

I turned to look at him. 'It doesn't matter. Let's just forget it, shall we? I'm in a bad mood that's all.'

Will smiled. 'Let's just say hi to Mirabel and then get back to civilization.'

'I was thinking that maybe we should just forget about it.'

'You're joking me now.'

'Maybe you were right. I think … well … I must have been dreaming last night. Mum said …'

'Meg. It's fine. To be honest I'm not sure about her grand-dad either if that's what you're worrying about. I know your mum said it was all sorted but there's no harm in checking is there? We did promise Mirabel we'd be there for her.'

'True.'

'And anyway, I thought we were going on an adventure. So far the only exciting thing we've done is got on a bus. Not much there for my first novel.'

'You're writing a novel?'

'Started it last week. It's set in Bridlington.'

'Not much happens then.'

'Now that is where you are wrong. It's about …'

'You can tell me the plot later. Let's just do this.'

'OK. If it's a no go on the adventure front then I'll treat you to a Ristretto at that beach cafe.'

'I don't even know what that is. And I don't think–'

'Is that Mirabel?' he asked interrupting me. 'Up there?'

I turned and saw her standing on the glass balcony of Wyndrift House, her arms raised in the air. She suddenly began to twist and stretch, like she was performing some kind of bizarre dance. Will waved but Mirabel wasn't looking in our direction.

'Come on,' he said. 'Let's go and say hi.'

'Wait, Will.' I grabbed his jacket and pulled him back. Ahead of us on the tarmac, small wisps of mist were emerging.

It had suddenly become very cold.

'What are you doing?'

'Come off the road!'

We stumbled on to the grass and into a group of trees.

'What the hell is going on now?'

I didn't answer.

'Meg, would you mind enlightening me here, only one minute we're seeing Mirabel, then we're not and ...'

'I made a mistake,' I whispered.

'What about?'

'Being here. Everything.'

'Bloody hell, Meg. You're really freaking me out today. What's going on?'

On the breeze I was suddenly aware of a sickly mix of cigarettes and whisky.

I turned around.

I was staring right into the face of Mr Ward.

Chapter 13

I froze.

I was unable to look away from the purple sags of skin which formed one side of Mr Ward's face.

He swayed a little and Will managed to catch him before he fell. His cane dropped to the ground. I picked it up. It was surprisingly heavy and had several scorch marks on the pale wood, particularly near the bottom edge. An odd looking bird was carved on to the top; its feathers splayed up into a sort of ruff around its head and its strong thick beak slightly crossed over at the end. Purple stones had been inserted to look like eyes and these glinted as I moved it.

'Whoa. Steady Mr W. Are you alright?' asked Will.

'My ... my cane,' he managed.

I handed it to him and he leaned on it again.

I didn't say anything. I was sure that this frail old man thing was just an act.

Will was still holding on to him. 'If we can find some-where to sit you down, I'll call for an ambulance,' he said. 'Just ...'

'Just nothing ... Help me get back.'

'Will you be able to make it to the house?' I said.

'It's not far,' said Will. 'If you lean on me, I think we can manage it.'

'No … No. Not there. Got another place. Down here. Quicker.' He nodded towards a small track between the trees. 'Please.'

I wasn't aware that there were any houses in the woods. Dad and I had walked all around Happy Valley but there were no buildings on this side, I was sure of it.

'OK. You're the boss,' said Will. 'Steady as you go.'

I caught the old man glancing up at me and I was even more convinced that he was faking. Will had started to steer him down the track though and I had no choice but to follow.

The path turned right towards the beach again and to my surprise I saw we were heading for a small bungalow. Maybe I hadn't been this way before because this place had certainly been here a long time. It was almost derelict and everything about it looked awkward and lopsided, the roof in a state of collapse. Several windows were broken; looking as if they might drop from their frames at any moment.

The old man seemed to revive all of a sudden. He let go of Will. 'That'll do,' he said. 'I'm alright now. Come on in.'

The hallway was dark and cluttered. Several suitcases lay stacked on top of one another, covered with long silky cobwebs. An old faded evening gown hung from one of the picture rails and it fluttered a little as we entered. I supposed that Mr Ward must have been married once but it was hard to imagine. Photographs in cracked frames lined the walls but were so dusty it was impossible to see who they were of. The air was damp and stale with old cigarette smoke. Water dripped into a bucket from a hole in the ceiling.

Curled up on a stack of old books was a cat with no fur. Its head looked too big for its body and its pink skin was so thin it was almost transparent. It raised its head as we entered but I looked away quickly.

I glimpsed a kitchen, the sink piled high with dirty dishes and every surface covered with empty cans, jars and bottles. We entered into a small sitting room that was in the same sort of chaos. There were some large boxes piled up against one wall, as though Mr Ward had once thought of moving out but then changed his mind.

The old man flopped down into an arm chair.

'I thought you lived in Wyndrift House,' said Will.

'No, no,' Mr Ward said. 'This place was left to me by some friends. I let the kid and her aunt have the run of the big house. Prefer it here.'

'If you're Mirabel's granddad … then is her aunt your daughter?' Will asked.

'There are no flies on you, are there?' Mr Ward said. 'And they say the schools today are no good.'

'What happened to Mirabel's parents?' I asked.

'You're nosy buggers. Do you need a family history? Her mam and dad are both dead.'

'How did …?'

'Car accident. I'd give you the details but they're not pretty.'

'No … I didn't mean …'

'Enough … enough said on that.'

He fell into another fit of coughing which was so severe

he could hardly get his breath. I had to admit he didn't look like he was pretending now.

'I think I should ring for a doctor, Mr W,' said Will.

Mr Ward shook his head. 'Tea,' he rasped. 'Just make me some tea then you can bugger off.'

'Rightio. If you're sure. I mean …'

'Look, I'm alright.'

Will disappeared into the kitchen and I walked over to the window. It was so dirty it was hard to see out. I rubbed my hand over the glass to clear a small section. The view from here was towards the beach, but as I looked, I realised that only about a couple of metres of earth and a flimsy barbed wire fence separated us from the edge of the cliff. I stepped back carefully, as though my weight would cause the house to topple over.

The old man had leaned back in his chair and closed his eyes. He did seem genuinely tired. In the light from the window the folds of skin on his face looked sore and cracked. I noticed that there were blue lines embedded into the purple blotches, like little snakes that appeared to be twisting and moving. He had placed the cane by his chair. I saw the bird's eyes glint for a moment and I moved nearer to get a better look. Without opening his eyes he grabbed it.

'We keep bumping into each other, don't we? he said. 'Can't be a coincidence, can it?'

'What do you mean?'

He opened his eyes and stared at me in the same way he had when I had first met him.

'This place is a death trap Mr W,' said Will, interrupting us as he came back from the kitchen. 'Just put your kettle

on the stove and the gas flame almost singed my eyebrows.'
He held up a plastic container and shook it. The milk had
congealed into solid lumps. 'And this is a little bit off if you
don't mind me saying.'

The old man stopped looking at me and I backed away.
'Don't need milk. Just need the brew,' he said, 'and some of
this.'

He reached down to the side of his chair and I recognised
the tartan shopping bag. He lifted out a bottle of whisky.
'This'll bring me round.'

'Tea'll be a few minutes anyway,' said Will, tossing the milk
carton into a bin that was already full. 'That stove's a bit slow.'

Will walked over to the table, moved a few dirty newspapers off a wooden chair and sat down. I perched on the end
of the chair on the opposite side. I didn't want to touch anything. As soon as the kettle was boiled we would make our
excuses and leave. I needed to get back out into the fresh air.

'You've got a lot of stuff, Mr W,' said Will, picking up
some leaflets. Dust danced around us into the air and I
wondered how much longer we would have to stay.

'It's not all mine. I inherited this place years ago. Keep
meaning to have a clear out. Pass me one of the yellow
sheets. On the top of that pile nearest your girlfriend.'

I flinched but Will smiled. 'Sure,' he said, getting up and
handing it over.

Mr Ward grabbed it. 'See that. "The Great Mancello".
You'll know him of course.'

'Nope.'

Mr Ward snorted. 'Don't they teach you anything nowa-
days? He was only the best magician there's ever been.'

'I've never heard of him,' said Will.

'Well he was a bit before your time. But he was very famous in his day. I worked with him and his wife in the good old days.'

'Do you know how to do some tricks then?'

'Not tricks, lad.' said Mr Ward, lowering his voice. 'Magic.'

'There's no such thing,' I said.

'You don't believe me?'

I shook my head.

Mr Ward sighed. 'Travelled everywhere with them shows, we did. Even went to London once. Talk of going to America but it never came off. See … I've not always been like this. You look at me and you see some old bloke who knows nothing … and then there's this.' He pointed to his face. 'I'm a wreck now but I was young and beautiful once.'

I blushed. I didn't like the man but I didn't want him to think it was because of the way he looked. The bald cat padded into the room and leapt on to Mr Ward's knee. He rubbed its wrinkly head and I shuddered.

'Where's that tea?' he asked, his voice gruff again. 'That whistle's blowing and I'm parched.'

'On its way, Mr W,' said Will racing off into the kitchen.

Mr Ward lifted his head and stared at me again. His eyes looked bloodshot and one of them was weeping. He wiped it with the back of his hand. There was silence between us for a moment. I could hear Will moving around in the kitchen and I wished he would hurry up.

'You haven't told me what you're doing back here anyway,' Mr Ward said at last.

'We came to see if Mirabel's OK.'

'She's fine. Why wouldn't she be?'

I didn't say anything.

'You think I can't look after her,' he sneered. 'You're checking up on me.'

'Where's Mirabel now then?' I asked, not caring if he thought I was.

'She's at the house. She's not a baby,' he snarled. 'She'll be fine for ten minutes.'

'So where's her aunt?'

It was his turn to be quiet. When he did speak his voice was a lot calmer. 'There's nowt to worry about, lass. That's what I'm saying to you.' He paused. 'Her aunt Rhiannon will be back tonight and everything will be right as rain.'

'Where's she been?'

Again he didn't answer the question.

'There is something you can do for me though. Now that I've run into you. Something for Mirabel actually.'

'What?'

'Mirabel lost summat at your house, Meg. A pendant. Gold chain, nice little dropper on the end. Anyway she's been mithering me to get it back for her. You know where it is?'

I shook my head.

'You're a difficult one to read, Meg.' he continued. 'I can normally make sense of people but you … Anyroad up. I expect she showed it to you. It's got a sparkly stone in the middle. The kind of thing you girlies love.'

I winced but tried to keep my cool. 'I don't know what you're talking about,' I said. 'But I don't understand why Mirabel's aunt …'

'You probably picked it up by accident,' he went on before I had finished my question. 'Forgot about it. Easy done.'

He was staring intently at me again now and I felt very uncomfortable.

'It can't have disappeared,' he said irritably. 'You said yourself. There's no such thing as magic.'

'I'm not a thief.'

'No ... No Meg. You've got the wrong end of the stick there. I just ... Mirabel is upset, you see. I don't like seeing her like that.'

'Why don't you just buy her another one?'

He glared at me. 'You youngsters. You think money grows on trees. Anyroad, the one she lost. Sentimental value. You understand?'

'You should talk to my mum,' I said calmly.

'I did. She seems like a nice woman. It would be a shame if she got into trouble over this. You see I don't want to go to the authorities and report it; make an official complaint.'

He lowered his voice. 'The truth is ... well, it's a family heirloom, like. Irreplaceable.'

'I haven't got it,' I said.

'Not on you. No. But I think you know where it is and I think you're preying on my good nature.'

'I'm not doing anything.'

'I'm just saying ... best all round if it turned up. I have a feeling that you'll find it,' said Mr Ward. 'If you look hard enough.'

I was fuming but I didn't want to give him the satisfaction of knowing he had rattled me.

'I'll call at yours tonight,' he said. 'Around seven. Pay my respects to your mother. Have it ready.'

Before he could say anything else, Will came in with the tea. 'Grab one of these, Meg,' he said. 'They're burning my hands off.'

I took one of the mugs from him. It was old and cracked and I had no intention of drinking from it.

'Here you are, Mr W.' He put the mug down beside the old man.

'Chuck some of that whisky into it, Will, there's a good lad. Don't be mean with it. It'll cool it down a bit. You have some if you like. Better than milk.'

'Alright,' said Will, picking up the bottle. He poured some into Mr Ward's tea and then his own. 'Bloody hell. That's strong,' he said, sniffing the steam that was rising.

'You get used to it,' rasped Mr Ward.

He picked up his mug and began to slurp his tea noisily.

'I wanted to be a magician when I was little,' said Will. 'I used to do card tricks. They were rubbish. I wasn't quick enough.'

Mr Ward smiled. 'Your girlfriend doesn't believe in magic, Will. Else I'd show you one of the tricks Mancello taught me.'

'Go on then. Please.'

'Yeah,' I said. 'Don't mind me.'

'Alright. Have you got a coin I could borrow?'

Will fumbled in his pocket and brought out a fifty pence piece. 'You're not going to lose it or anything are you, Mr W? Otherwise I'm not going to have enough for the bus back.'

'No, no lad. Let me put this mug down and … right. Now. Hand it over.'

Will gave him the coin.

He laid it flat on the palm of his hand for a moment and stared at it. Then he picked it up and placed it on his tongue.

He closed his mouth and swallowed.

After a few seconds he opened it again and leaned over towards Will, showing him that his money really had gone.

'Mr W–' began Will.

Mr Ward signalled for him to be quiet. Suddenly, he blew. A pale yellow butterfly flew out of his mouth and into the air. Its almost translucent wings opened slowly but before it could escape Mr Ward held out his hand and it fluttered down on to his outstretched palm. He brought down his other hand and slammed it as hard as he could.

I flinched and let out a cry.

Will looked over at me and tried to speak. 'I … I don't think we …'

'Now. Tap on my knuckles three times. Go on, lad.'

Will reached over hesitantly but he did as he was told. Mr Ward opened his hands. I expected to see the squished butterfly but it had gone.

In its place was the fifty pence piece.

'That was brilliant!' shouted Will. 'How the hell did you do that? Where's the butterfly?'

'Disappeared,' said Mr Ward. 'Like magic.'

He looked over at me and I could tell he was hoping I'd seen the significance of the moment he'd squashed the butterfly.

'It's not magic though is it, Mr Ward? You see what you want to see,' I said, annoyed with myself for having reacted to his trick.

'Very wise, Meg. I said you were clever. I'll have to be sharp around you.'

He took another sip of his drink.

'Show us another one, Mr W.'

Mr Ward shook his head. 'Not now, Will. Not now.' He gazed around the room. 'Mancello left me all of this when he … when him and his wife passed away. Remember it like it was yesterday.'

'This was the magician's house?' asked Will. 'Cool. And you've kept everything the same? All this time?'

'Sentimental, I suppose,' Mr Ward said. 'I like to come over here. Remember the good times. She was a lovely woman, his missus. Pity she went so young.'

Will nodded in a sympathetic way. 'What happened to her?' he asked.

'No one knows for sure. An accident,' he said pointedly. 'They do happen.'

The cat suddenly arched its back and spat at me.

Will put down his cup. 'I'm not sure I'm going to get used to this whisky, Mr W. It feels like it's burning my mouth out. If you're OK we'll be going. Is it alright if we call in on Mirabel?'

'That won't be happening,' he said.

The cat shot off Mr Ward's knee, sprang on to the table and knocked my cup flying. It shattered, spraying hot tea everywhere.

I leapt to my feet.

'Steady Bess. Steady,' said Mr Ward.

The cat hissed again and jumped on to one of the piles of books.

I wiped at my jeans with my hand.

'You need to go home,' said Mr Ward. 'Before you make any more mess.'

'We came to see Mirabel,' I said, looking at him. 'I don't get why we can't. Especially if she's been left on her own.'

He ran one hand over the raised purple skin on his cheek and then he picked up his cane.

'I … I should have been straight with you, Meg. And you, Will. About our Mirabel … well she's … she's not like other kids. I expect you've seen that for yourself.'

He was certainly right about that.

'Yeah,' Will said, 'but she's …'

'What do you know about it? You're only a kid yourself. I'm telling you that we've got our work cut out trying to look after her. Rhiannon's got her job at the Science Institute over in Scarborough and she has to lean on me a lot. But look at me. What can I do?'

'Mirabel seems like a great kid,' Will said.

'She is. Most of the time but … don't know what the fancy term is for it. She's had all the tests but they haven't come up with anything definite. She lives in a world of her own, see. Total fantasy land. There's no getting through to her.'

'She was OK with us,' Will said, although I wasn't sure he was right there.

'You wouldn't want to cause them any trouble would you?' He paused and coughed a little. 'I mean the authorities. You know what they're like. Next thing you know she'll be taken away from us.'

'We didn't mean to interfere,' said Will. 'We …'

'When Rhiannon comes back I need to have another talk with her. Get Mirabel some proper help,' Mr Ward interrupted. 'Even if it means moving right away and starting again.'

'Yeah sure,' Will said. 'But what if …?'

'Best to let her and her aunt get on with their lives eh?'

He let go of his cane, raised himself up a little more on his chair and looked directly at me. 'Anyroad up, I can let you know what's happening when I see you later.'

'What do you mean?' asked Will.

'Meg and I have made a little arrangement. I'll be calling to see her mam and well, there's no need for me to say anything more, is there, Meg?'

I stood up. 'We have to go,' I said.

There was a faint judder from under the floorboards. Nothing here felt right. If we didn't hurry this whole bungalow would be sliding down the cliff and into the sea.

The bald cat raised its head and glared at me as we headed towards the door.

Chapter 14

The sun had come out and it felt much warmer outside. I took off my jacket and breathed deeply. I hated the old man even more now. I knew he was lying to us about Mirabel although I couldn't figure out why. How come the police and everyone couldn't see through him? And where was Mirabel's mysterious aunt?

I had to get Mum to see what he was really like. She'd have to do something then. I needed to talk to her about everything before he came round for the pendant.

'You OK?' asked Will.

'Yeah, yeah. I am so sorry to have got you into all of this,' I said when we were clear of the house. 'But that man …'

A sharp pain seared across my forehead.

'Meg! Are you alright? You're really pale.'

'I just need to talk to Mum.'

'Can't you text her or something?'

'No. I need to speak to her properly. I can get a bus to Scarborough from the end of the road. I know where she'll be.'

'This is mad,' said Will. 'You're acting like a crazy person today.'

'Thanks.'

'No. Sorry. I didn't mean that. But I thought we'd straightened things out coming down here. I mean, I was worried about Mr Ward but I think he's harmless and he said Mirabel's aunt will be back soon. I think it's all OK.'

I didn't say anything. I couldn't see how he had come to that conclusion after our visit to the bungalow.

I started walking up the track, staring at the ground. Bits of conversation from the previous two days were whirling round in my head and making me dizzy. I could have sworn that someone was calling my name again but there was no one around. My head throbbed now even though I hadn't drunk any of Mr Ward's tea or his whisky. Perhaps it was the terrible smell of damp and mould in his bungalow that had got to me.

'I do feel sorry for Mirabel,' Will went on. 'But I understand what Mr Ward meant. We don't want to upset her and make things worse, do we? She ... you know you really don't look well at all, Meg. I'll see if I can get a signal and ask Dad to come and fetch us.'

'I told you. I'm going to Scarborough.'

Another voice cut through the air before he could reply. 'Alice! Alice! Come back!'

A little girl was running towards us along the track from the beach carrying a bucket and spade. A black and white dog chased after her, barking like mad. The spade was scraping along the ground but it seemed to catch on something. The next second she fell face down on to the tarmac. There was a slight pause before she realised what had happened and then she started to scream. Will rushed over and helped her up.

A woman wearing a pink floppy hat and sunglasses came dashing over to us.

'Oh thank you, love. Thank you. We've been down to the beach but she just ran off.' She lifted up the sobbing girl. 'You're OK now, Alice. You're OK. No damage done.'

The dog was leaping about and barking wildly.

'Get down, Ben,' the woman shouted. 'What with dogs and kids …'

'We … we have to go,' I said.

'Of course. Thank you so much for helping. These people have been very kind, Alice. What do you say?'

Alice turned towards us, her face red and blotchy from crying.

'She dropped these,' said Will, picking up the bucket and spade. He pretended to hand them over and then pulled them away. The girl stared at him, and when he did it again she smiled.

'Come on, Alice, Thanks again, you two.'

Will stuck his tongue out at her. She copied him. He did it again and the girl giggled.

'Oh no. Ben! What's that dog doing now?'

Ben had found something hidden on the opposite side of the path and he was digging furiously. Grass and mud and stones were flying into the air.

The woman plonked Alice back on the path.

'I'll get him,' said Will, dashing off.

Alice's mother followed but the little girl turned towards me. Her nose was running. She didn't attempt to wipe it.

SHHHHH

'What? What's …?'

The girl was standing completely still, staring at me intently. Her eyes were wide and unfocused. 'We need to say this,' she said. 'You have to listen.'

'No time.'

There were two voices now, coming out of the girl's mouth.

Both women.

I was totally freaked out but I couldn't speak or move.

'He must be stopped.'

Through the corner of my eye I could still see Will and the girl's mother with the dog but they seemed far away and I couldn't call to them or anything. All I could do was to look into the little girl's face.

'Go to Mirabel.'

'At the house.'

'Get her away.'

'Get her away now.'

'You must stop him.'

'Stop him.'

'Before it's too late.'

'The dog found a dead bird. Or at least I think that's what it was,' said Will, jogging back to me. 'You OK?'

Alice turned and stuck her tongue out again and the spell seemed to break. I could move again and I turned to Will. He was busy pulling faces at the girl and they were both giggling.

'Alice …' I started, my voice cracking. 'Alice … she said something … she …'

'What are you on about?'

A wave of nausea swept over me and I tried to concentrate on my breathing.

'Bloody hell, Meg,' said Will. 'You're as white as a sheet.'

'Something happened,' I started. 'Just then … I … We have to find Mirabel.'

'What? You're kidding! Meg, you are acting really weird. We promised we wouldn't go near her.'

'She's in trouble.'

'How do you know that?'

'I just do.'

'Look, why don't we phone your mum and …'

'There isn't time,' I said, trying to pull myself together. 'We have to go and find Mirabel right now.'

Chapter 15

There wasn't time to think about what had just happened. I raced off towards the house as quickly as I could. I didn't even look round to see if Will was following me. Somehow I knew that I was doing the right thing.

I was certain now that Mirabel was in danger.

When I reached the wall of the house, I stopped for a moment. It was all very quiet. There wasn't even anyone on the path from the beach.

I looked up. There was no one on the balcony. In fact there was no sign of life at all.

'What now?' Will had caught up with me. His voice sounded strained. He clearly thought I was going mad.

'We *have* to find her,' I said.

I pushed open the gate and walked up to the front door. I knocked loudly. There was no answer.

Will went over to the window and tried to peer into the front room. 'All the curtains are drawn,' he said. 'Can't see anything.'

'Let's try round the back.'

'You don't think she's run off again?'

'She's here somewhere. I know it.'

'Perhaps she's too scared to open the door.'

'Maybe.'

The house had been built very close to the cliff so there was not much of a garden at the back. Yesterday, in the mist, I hadn't really noticed the state it was in. Where the lawn ended, the ground became a tangle of weeds clambering around bits of broken bricks and rubble. The walls were faded and peeling and some of the windows were cracked. An old rusty fire escape ran up to the first floor but the last step had broken off completely so it didn't reach all the way to the ground.

A herring gull squawked loudly overhead and made me jump. It landed on a broken upturned wheelbarrow, tilting its head to one side.

I leaned forward and tried to see in through the back door. The glass was frosted and filthy but it didn't look as though there was anyone moving inside. 'No one there,' I said. 'I'll try the window.'

The curtains were drawn, just as they were at the front, but it was possible to see through a gap in the middle.

The room was empty.

'What can you see?'

'All their stuff's gone.'

Will went up to the window and peered in.

'How can you tell? It's too dark to see anything. And the gap's not big enough. You couldn't possibly ...'

'It's all gone,' I said, although when I looked in again I realised that Will was right. It was pitch black. I couldn't think what had made me so certain that there was nothing in the room when I had looked before.

'Now what?' asked Will.

'There's a window open at the top of that fire escape,' I said.

'You're not thinking …?'

'I'm just going to take a look.'

'No way. This has gone far enough.'

'I just want to check she's there,' I said. 'And that she's OK. You keep watch down here.'

'You're not … this is stupid. You can't climb up there. That thing's not safe.'

'I'll be fine.'

The fire escape creaked as I pulled myself up and I felt it judder. I wasn't sure if it would bear my weight but there was no going back now. I kicked off my trainers to get a better grip and they tumbled to the ground, almost hitting Will.

'What are you doing?' he called. 'Get down off there!'

'I'm OK. I'll be quick.'

The metal steps were cold against my bare feet. I climbed quickly without looking down. The whole contraption groaned as I moved and I tried not to think about what would happen if it gave way.

There was another step missing near the top and I had to heave myself up on to the small platform. I stared in through the window but there was so much dirt and mould on the glass that I couldn't see in.

I had to take a closer look.

Ignoring Will's shouts from below, I pulled at the window. It was stiff but I managed to open it wide enough so that I could climb in. I stood on the windowsill for a moment and then I lowered myself over the sink and on to the tiled floor. The door to the bathroom was half open.

There was a loud banging noise and I heard someone shouting on the floor above.

Mirabel.

I was right.

She was in trouble.

Out on the landing, I was about to head up the stairs, when I heard someone coughing just above me.

The familiar smell of whisky and cigarettes drifted down and I bolted back into the bathroom and hid behind the door. Mr Ward. How had he got here so quickly? And why hadn't Will spotted him?

'Alright alright. I'm here. Stop your yelling.'

At Mr Ward's voice, I glanced to the window wondering if I should race over and climb back out but my legs were shaking so much I wasn't sure I could move at all.

Mirabel pounded on her door.

'PLEASE! LET ME GO!'

'Soon,' he said. 'Soon. Now pipe down.'

I heard him coughing again but then everything went quiet.

It was too risky to move. If he found me, I wouldn't be much help to Mirabel.

'I just want to talk to you,' Mirabel said. 'I want you to tell me what's happening.'

There was no answer.

'WHAT IS HAPPENING?' Mirabel screamed.

'Stop making such a fuss,' Mr Ward growled. 'You won't be in there for long. Trust me. I don't know how you got out on to the balcony but you're locked in tight now. Them friends of yours. Have they been here?'

Mirabel didn't answer but she banged on the door again.

'No. I thought not. They won't be coming,' he said. 'Not after what I told them.'

'I'll keep screaming until you let me go,' said Mirabel.

'There's no one to hear you round here and even if they do – what are you going to say? How are you going to tell them who you are?'

'I don't … I don't understand,' said Mirabel. 'What … what do you want with me?' Her voice was shakier now and I could sense her fear. I didn't blame her. I was so afraid I could hear my own heartbeat thundering in my ear.

Especially when I realised that Mr Ward was starting to come down the stairs.

'We'll talk about all this later,' he said.

He was getting nearer.

'You'll have to stay put for now,' he went on. 'Until I've sorted some things out. Then we'll be leaving. The shouting and banging won't do you any good. When I … when I come back …'

He didn't finish what he was saying but I knew he was right outside the bathroom door now. I could hear the rasps and whistles in his breath.

'This had … this had better be worth it,' he muttered. 'Need to get away from here and be rid of her.'

I heard him shuffle towards the door. If he came into the bathroom I was finished. I needed to get help. I pulled out my phone but it was no use.

No connection.

The terrible smell that surrounded Mr Ward got stronger and he walked in.

'Why's that window open?' he snapped, pulling it shut.

It didn't close properly and he tried again. The catch came off in his hand.

'Gah!' he exclaimed. 'Useless! Like everything round here.'

I closed my eyes and squeezed myself as far behind the door as I could. If only something would happen to distract him.

SHHHHHH

That noise again. The one I had heard last night and again on the cliffs when the little girl spoke to me.

SHHHHHH

He slammed the catch on to the windowsill and swung round. I cowered but he didn't even glance in my direction as he stomped out of the bathroom.

'You have got to be kidding me,' he muttered as he left. 'That had better not be who I think it is.'

The house fell silent.

I waited for a few seconds more but couldn't hear anything. I closed the bathroom door slowly and quietly and then I crept over to the window, shoving it wide open. I had to get to Will before Mr Ward came back and we could ring the police.

I had just started to climb on to the windowsill when I heard Mirabel scream. I nearly jumped out of my skin.

I couldn't leave her. I got back down.

The bathroom door creaked a little as I pulled it open. There was a pain in my chest and I realised it was because I was forgetting to breathe.

Everything downstairs seemed quiet.

I turned and crept up the stairs, every squeak sounding like a firework exploding.

Mirabel had stopped screaming but I could hear her crying on the other side of the door. 'Mirabel,' I hissed, as loud as I dared. 'Mirabel! It's me, Meg.'

There was no answer.

'I'm going to try to get you out of there,' I said.

I looked around wildly. Where was the key?

I was standing in an empty space. I remembered furniture and carpet up here from yesterday but that had all gone. There wasn't anywhere to look. I pulled my hands through my hair in despair and as I did so I looked back at the door.

Of course. I thought of Mum and the way she kept the cellar key on top of the door frame. Perhaps Mr Ward had done the same. I reached up.

Nothing.

I was frantic. I didn't want to leave her with that madman but if I tried to barge the door he would hear me and we'd both be done for.

'Meg,'

Someone was speaking but it wasn't Mirabel.

SHHHHHH

'Look again.'

I swung round.

No one there.

It was a woman's voice, calm and soft.

'Look again.'

I stared at the door.

Then something caught my eye.

I ran my hand along the top of the door one more time.

The silver teddy with the pink tutu.

There was no time to think about how it had got there.

I unlocked the door quickly and saw Mirabel standing in the middle of an empty room. She was wearing the same clothes that she had left our house in the day before but her long blonde plait was loose and her hair looked like wild straw. She had nothing on her feet.

'Where … where is everything?' I asked in a whisper. 'How …?'

'I don't understand. I don't understand any of it,' she said quietly. She was shivering and her eyes were red and swollen.

'We have to get out of here, OK?' I asked, trying to speak as quietly as I could. 'Right now.'

She didn't move. 'My shoes,' she said, looking up at me directly for the first time. 'He took my shoes.'

'It's fine. I haven't got any on either. Come on.'

She stared at me and she planted her feet more firmly on to the floor. 'You have to tell me what's happening.'

I glanced out of the door but there was no sign of anyone. 'There isn't time. You have to trust me.'

I raced over and grabbed her hand. Without saying anything more, I pulled her down the stairs to the bathroom. I eased the door closed and snapped the bolt shut.

At least we were safe in there for a moment.

'Look I know this is scary,' I whispered, 'But …'

'You didn't have to pull me,' she said. 'You hurt my arm.'

'Sorry. But we can't talk now. I have to get you out of here.'

'He locked me in my room.'

'I know. He shouldn't have done that. Let's get back to Mum and you can explain. Now listen. I came in through this window. There's a fire escape. Can you climb up?'

She hesitated and then nodded.

I helped her on to the window ledge.

'Now step across on to the platform. The first step's missing so you may have to sit down and lower yourself on to the next one. Quick as you can. It's not far.'

She looked back at me. I could see she was frightened. 'I don't like heights,' she said.

'Then don't look down.'

I thought she was going to refuse point blank and I was just trying to calculate our chances of running through the house and out of the front door when there was the sound of a door banging shut downstairs.

'Please,' I pleaded. 'Just go.'

'I can't. I'm scared.'

'Will's down there,' I said. 'You'll see him as soon as you climb out. He won't let anything bad happen to you. Neither of us will.'

Someone coughed from somewhere below us and this helped her to make up her mind. She gripped hard to the window frame with one hand and gingerly stepped out on to the fire escape.

I heard it creak and I thought she might change her mind but she didn't.

'Go on,' I hissed at her. 'Climb down as quickly as you can.'

'I can see Will,' she said.

'I told you. Now go!'

This time she did as she was told and as soon as she was down, I stepped on to the rickety contraption. I raced down the steps and leapt off. My feet seemed to make a loud thud on the ground even without shoes on. I landed on something sharp and I almost cried out. Looking down, I could see my foot was bleeding but there was no time to do anything about it.

'What the hell's happening?' demanded Will. 'What …?'

'No time,' I managed, feeling breathless. 'We … we have to get out of here.'

'Why?' Will's eyes widened.

'Mr Ward.'

'He's not around. I've been watching. No one's …'

'He's here. He'd locked her in her room.'

'No way.'

'We have to go now.'

I took Mirabel's hand and pulled her forward towards the muddy slopes.

'Run as fast as you can,' I said to Mirabel. 'And don't look back. OK?'

She nodded and we sprinted up the first part of the slope where stones were jagged and sharp underfoot. I was annoyed at leaving my trainers but there was no way I could go back for them now.

Chapter 16

A short way down the cliff path, a stitch in my side forced me to a halt. I felt dizzy, especially when I looked down at my foot and saw it was covered in blood.

I let go of Mirabel's hand.

'Are you alright?' Will asked. He put his arm on my shoulder.

'You two … you go ahead,' I spluttered. 'I just need a minute.'

Everything that had happened was whirring round in my head and I couldn't make sense of any of it. How long would it take Mr Ward to realise what we had done? And how the hell was I going to explain it all to Mum?'

'We're not leaving you!' said Will. 'If you can just manage a few more steps we'll be at the cafe and …'

'What cafe?' I said glancing up.

'We're almost at Hunmanby Gap.'

'We can't be,' I said, still clutching my side.

There was no direct path from Happy Valley to Hunmanby. Dad had brought us here loads and I knew that you had to go down on the beach in the places where the cliff had been worn away. Besides, it was over a mile away.

I glanced up though and saw that Will was right.

I could see the cafe clearly now. 'How is that possible?'

'Shall I give you a piggy back or something?'

I took a deep breath.

'No … No I'm fine. Let's get moving. We can't afford to stop now.'

I limped on, glad when we reached the main path but still confused as to how we had got here at all. Mirabel was just strolling beside Will and chatting to him. There was no sign of the panic behind the screams I had heard through that locked door in Wyndrift House. It was as though nothing had happened.

It didn't matter. I knew we had done the right thing and at least we were among people again. It seemed normal and that was good.

'Over here!'

Someone was waving at us from one of the picnic tables.

'Oh no,' I groaned. 'This really can't get any worse.'

'Who is it?' asked Mirabel, stopping to let me catch up.

'No one.' I said. 'Pretend you haven't seen her.'

But it was too late.

The small brown teddy dog I had seen her with the other day bounded up to us and started barking ferociously. It was wearing a fluorescent pink collar with diamond studs. Abbie's bright red wedges made her wobble slightly on the uneven ground as she dashed towards us. She wore a blue and white strapless dress which she was having trouble keeping up. I noticed that she had put some pale pink streaks in her hair.

'JASON! JASON!' she yelled. 'Get down.'

The dog was still barking and growling. Mirabel waved her arms about, a bit like a ballet dancer and the dog watched her mesmerised. He gave a little whimper and then rolled over.

'Hey Meg. Hi Will,' said Abbie.

'Hi,' said Mirabel. 'Is this your dog?'

'Yeah … he's such a babe. Are you one of Meg's foster kids?'

I winced but Mirabel didn't seemed to react at all. 'I'm Mirabel. We're just having an adventure,' she said.

'You have got to be kidding me!' I said. 'Look we need …'

'I like dogs,' Mirabel said. She knelt down and started to tickle Jason's tummy.

'Me too,' said Abbie. 'But it's boring having to take them for walks. It's Simon's turn really but he made me come down here with him and he's wandered off.'

'I know someone called Simon,' said Mirabel. 'He works with my aunt.'

'My brother hasn't got a job,' Abbie said. She lowered her voice. 'He doesn't do anything actually. He's such a loser. He's on the beach smoking a cigarette. Mum would go mad if she knew. He could give you a lift back in a bit if you like.'

'We're OK, thanks,' I snapped.

'He won't mind. He's always liked *you*, Meg.' She grinned. 'Come and wait with me.'

'Thanks,' said Mirabel, straightening up. 'Can I still play with the dog?'

'Sure. No problem.'

I was clearly going mad. Less than an hour ago, Mirabel was screaming out in fear but all that seemed forgotten.

She couldn't have been playing some sort of game, could she? But what about the empty room? And Mr Ward?

'Meg. We may as well do as Abbie says,' said Will. 'If her bro could take us back that would be a lot quicker and easier and we can let people know what's happened.'

He was right. There was no signal here, not until we reached the main road. Before I could say anything, Will and Mirabel walked off with Abbie and left me to limp along behind them. My side was still hurting a little and the stones on the road were making my injured foot sting like mad.

'Your foot's bleeding,' Abbie said, stating the obvious as I reached the picnic bench. 'What happened to your shoes?'

'I need to go into the cafe,' I said, ignoring her and looking over at Will who seemed to be settling himself down at the table with Mirabel. 'Use their phone.'

'You can't. It's closed.'

'You're joking,' I said.

'No. Simon said someone broke in and the police have been here.' She laughed. 'How hilarious. Is that why you look so guilty, Meg?'

'What are you on about?' I asked.

Abbie leaned over and lowered her voice. 'You can tell me. Was it you?'

'Don't be stupid,' I snapped. 'Of course it wasn't. We need to go back right now. Can you go and get your brother?'

'Sure. I *hate* it round here anyway. It is sooo boring. I *hate* this beach actually.' She turned to Will. 'I'm sad the cafe's closed. I could have bought you all a drink or an ice cream or something.'

114

'We need to go,' I repeated, standing up. 'We don't have time for this.'

'I like your hair,' Mirabel said, smiling at Abbie.

Abbie giggled. 'She's *adorable*,' she said, as though Mirabel was another of her pets.

I was about to say something but I stopped. We really had no choice but to go back with Abbie and although it pained me, I realised that I might have to be nicer if I wasn't going to blow the chance of a lift. I tried to sound a bit less annoyed.

'We … if Simon could take us back that would be great,' I said, forcing a smile.

'We should head back to mine,' said Will. 'It's nearer anyway.'

He was right. Mum would still be out. We could talk to Mr Clarke at the caravan site.

'It *so* great to meet you, Mirabel. Has Will told you about the party? I was soooo hung-over. Honestly. Wrecked. It was the best party *ever*.'

How did she work that out? She'd spent most of the night with her face in a bucket before spewing all over Mr Clarke's car!

I didn't say anything.

'Oh! I have something. I just remembered.' She delved into her bag and fished out a pair of pink flip flops with enormous yellow flowers. 'Aren't they just the best? I bought them from here last time we came,' she giggled.

Will laughed. 'They're your colour Meg,' he said. 'They match your eyes.'

I scowled at him.

'Mirabel,' Abbie said. 'Would you like these? You can

keep them if you like. I can't believe that these two are letting you walk about with no shoes on. I thought Meg was supposed to be looking after you.'

Mirabel beamed over at her. 'Thank you *so* much,' she said, copying Abbie's way of speaking. 'They are so lovely.'

Abbie laughed. 'She's a treasure! I love her! I wish I had some to give you, Meg, but my feet are so much smaller than yours.'

'It's fine,' I said. 'Really.'

'Fab,' said Abbie. 'Will, is it alright to drop you off and then come back later?'

'Sorry?'

'With Tom and Chris, dummy. To practise?'

'Bloody hell. I forgot about that.'

He looked away from me.

He had obviously also forgotten to explain that Abbie was definitely part of the band now.

'You said to come about four but I need to get changed first,' she said. 'I am so excited about the band Will …'

She droned on and I tried to block out her babble. Will seemed to be hanging on her every word though, and I wondered if he was starting to think that choosing to be friends with me had been a mistake. After all, he hadn't been at the school long and I just happened to be the first person he sat with. Even Mirabel was laughing with Abbie now and for someone who had just been rescued from a terrible situation she seemed remarkably happy.

I bent down and tried to brush some of the dirt from my feet. The cut was agony and I still had to walk over the stony ground to the car. It seemed like I was the only one who understood the enormity of what had happened.

'ABBIE! I said I'm going,' came a shout from behind us. 'If you want a lift …'

'Simon! Can't you see I'm talking with my friends? You're a complete animal.'

If Simon was an animal it would have to be some sort of bear because he was seriously huge. He had that way of bending his head down constantly like some tall people do to try and convince you they are smaller than they are. On Simon this had the effect of making his lank dark hair drip down around his face and you couldn't really see his features at all. It was hard to believe that he was related to Abbie but then again, I didn't have any brothers or sisters and I couldn't imagine what they would look like if I did.

The dog started barking.

'I said we'd give my friends a lift back to Brid,' Abbie said, unfastening Jason's lead from the bench and starting to walk up to the car park. 'I …'

'SIMON! 'shouted Mirabel, jumping up. 'SIMON! It's me!'

I've never seen anyone look so shocked in all of my life. Simon bent his head even further down and shuffled backwards a little. Mirabel ran towards him and flung her arms around him.

'Get this nutter off of me!' Simon shouted. 'What the hell is going on?' He pushed Mirabel away. 'If this is your idea of a joke …'

'Simon, I think she's just being friendly. And you're such a …'

'I'm going back to the car,' he said. 'And then I'm off. You can come if you want but leave these morons behind. Especially that one.'

He pointed towards Mirabel.

'Simon! You're being really horrible and Mirabel's … I promised them all a lift and …'

'I'm not a bloody taxi!' he shouted, turning round and heading off up the hill with a barking Jason nipping at his heels.

Chapter 17

'Is everything OK?' asked Will, as I came out of the caravan.

I stared at him. 'You're joking, right?'

Simon had eventually agreed to bring us back to Bridlington but only because I said I would sit in the front and talk to him.

At Will's caravan site, Mr Clarke was nowhere to be found. Will had suggested that Mirabel should have a lie down in the caravan his Dad let him use. It was in a bit of a state. The horrible sludgy brown exterior was badly scratched and there was a massive dent on the side. One of the windows was missing completely. Inside had not been much better but at least Mirabel would be safe there while we waited for help.

She was exhausted and as soon as she had lain down on an old sofa, she had gone to sleep.

'How long are the police going to be do you think?' asked Will.

'They said they would come as fast as they could.'

'It's been a while since you rang.'

'Do you think I should call them again?'

'Give it a few more minutes,' he said.

I sat down on the caravan steps. 'To be honest, I'm not sure that the man I spoke to totally believed me,' I said. 'I told him Mum rang the other day when Mirabel went missing but he didn't seem to know what I was talking about.'

'They're definitely sending someone out though?'

'He said so.'

'And nothing from your mum?'

I shook my head. 'Her phone's not even on.'

'Neither is Dad's but that's not surprising.' He laughed. 'We're on our own, kid. It's just you, me and Mirabel against the world.'

'Will! It's not funny. We're in a real mess here.'

'Yeah. Sorry. But I think everything's going to be OK now. Mirabel's safe here. I don't know where Dad's gone but he shouldn't be long. Oh. I found you a plaster.'

'Thanks.'

My foot was still stinging. I was pretty sure that I should clean the cut but I didn't want to move. If I put the plaster on at least that would stop me from making it worse.

It was good to have something practical to do, even if it was only something small. It was impossible to even try to make sense of everything that had happened and I wasn't confident that sorting things out was going to be as easy as Will seemed to think.

'What do you think Mirabel was going on about before? When she said she knew Simon?' Will asked.

'I've no idea. She told me he's a technician in her aunt's department.'

'That can't be right. Simon spends all his time in the arcades. The only technicianing he knows about is how to work the one-armed bandit. She must have made a mistake about him.'

'It's hard to understand Mirabel at all,' I said. 'And why can't they find her aunt? It can't be that hard.'

'Mr Ward told us she was expected back.'

'I don't believe anything he says. And the house. I mean … what is going on there?'

'What do you mean?'

'Her room. The bed, the furniture, the pink wallpaper … Where did everything go?'

'Are you sure you were in the same place?'

'What? Yeah. At the top of the stairs.'

'What if there's more than one set of stairs though? It's a big house and we went in through the back, remember. Maybe you were in a different part of the house.'

That couldn't be right, could it?

We fell silent for a moment and while I fixed my plaster, I tried to picture the way the rooms worked. I had to admit that I hadn't seen round the whole place the day before but I had been confident that Mirabel had been in her own room.

'I found the key though,' I said. 'Mirabel's key.'

'Yeah, but a key can open more than one door.'

'Maybe.'

I thought about how the key had suddenly appeared from nowhere but I decided not to mention that. Will thought I was crazy as it was. He wasn't looking at me and I could tell that he wasn't convinced about everything I had told him. To be honest, the things that had happened in Wyndrift House seemed to be getting more twisted in my head the more I tried to straighten them out.

'Anyway, while you were talking to Simon, Mirabel asked me when she would be able to see her granddad again,' Will said.

'You're kidding.'

'Nope.'

'Bloody hell.'

'She won't be allowed, will she?'

'No way. She can't go back there. Not after I tell them what's happened.'

There was silence between us for a moment.

'Will she get to stay with you again?' asked Will at last.

I hadn't thought of that. Mum would be keen to keep her on but that wouldn't be happening, surely?

'No,' I said. 'Mum promised that we would stop fostering for a while.'

'Why?'

'Dad's away and … I don't really want to talk about it, Will.'

'Fair enough.'

Will looked a bit disappointed, but he had no idea how hard it had been for me over the years with different kids in the house. I really wanted us to be on our own from now on.

'The police need to find Mirabel's aunt … she's the key to all of this,' I said.

'You don't think … you don't think Mr Ward'll go to the police as well, do you?' asked Will. 'Give them some sob story about you kidnapping his granddaughter?'

'That isn't what I did.'

'No. I know.'

'She was locked in, Will!'

'Yeah but what if he denies it? I'm not sure that Mirabel is going to back you up. She's already saying she can't remember stuff. I mean you shouldn't have been in there really.'

'Bloody hell, Will. Whose side are you on?'

'Yours, you idiot. I was just thinking how it might look.'

'Well don't.'

'Sorry. You did the right thing, deffo.'

'What's that supposed to mean?'

'Nothing. If you thought Mirabel wasn't safe there, then you had to get her out.'

I was astounded at Will. I had told him what had happened in the house and I didn't think for one minute that he would doubt me.

'It was me who went up there, remember? I heard everything.'

'I know. But maybe … I'm just saying that maybe things looked worse than they actually were.'

I couldn't believe it.

I stared down at my foot again. My eyes were starting to fill with tears but I didn't want to start crying. Will was being a complete idiot. I just had to tell the police that Mirabel had been in danger. I knew that and I had got her out.

Obviously I wasn't going to mention the little kid, Alice, or the way the key just seemed to appear or that everything in the room had disappeared since yesterday. Could I have been wrong about those things after all? The stress had definitely got to me since Mirabel had arrived. I thought about the wild dreams I had been having and the voices I had heard in my head.

Was I sure that I knew exactly what had happened back

at Wyndrift House? Or was this what it felt like if you were going mad?

I tried to push those thoughts away.

We sat in silence again for a few minutes.

Why were the police taking so long?

'Bloody hell,' said Will. 'What time is it?'

'Nearly four. Why?'

'Abbie and the boys will be here soon.'

'Can't you cancel them?' I mumbled.

'Yeah. Yeah, sure. But they'll probably be on their way now. And after Mirabel's gone we can …'

'Don't worry,' I said, getting to my feet. 'I'll get everything sorted by the time they get here.'

I rubbed my hand across my eyes.

'In fact I might go and wake Mirabel up,' I continued. 'Mum must have forgotten she was picking me up. We can't mess about any longer. I'll take her to the police station myself. They're obviously not coming.'

'Meg! Don't … don't be like that. I am on your side. Honest. Stay here, please. The police will be here any second. I just meant … Everything will be sorted.' He leapt up. 'Hey. Had an idea. Stay there.'

He went over to the caravan, opened the door carefully and crept inside. I sat down on the grass again. Will's phone suddenly whirred into life. I glanced over and saw a message. It was from Abbie, of course.

Hey Will. See you later alligator? ☺ **xxx**

I was tempted to send a witty remark back, something about biting her head off, but I didn't think Will would be too happy that I had messed with his phone.

'Thought we'd do a bit of sleuthing while we're waiting,'

Will whispered, carrying a laptop that looked just as old and decrepit as the caravan. 'Just might need to wait for this baby to fire up.'

'What are you doing?'

He ignored me.

'I'm piggybacking on Mr Jones' wi-fi from just behind the van and it doesn't always work,' he said. 'But it's worth a try.'

The computer screen flickered.

'What are you doing?' I repeated.

'You said that finding Mirabel's aunt was the key. So … we know she works at a Science Institute and we might be able to look something up about her.'

It wasn't a bad idea, to be fair.

'I've never heard of an Institute,' I said. 'But Mr Ward mentioned Scarborough?'

'Blast,' said Will, smacking the side. 'The screen's going weird.'

It took several more seconds for the search engine to emerge but when it did he typed in 'Science Institute.'

The screen went blank. He hit the side of the computer again and lights flashed.

'Ah. Here we are. Just some weird places in America I think.'

'Try putting in Scarborough UK, you fool.'

'OK. Yeah.'

He quickly typed in the name again.

'Right. That's better. But … no Institute. Not on the first page. It's just brought up Scarborough University. Science and engineering department. Do you think that's it?'

'Mr Ward definitely said Institute and that was the word Mirabel used too.'

'Same thing, isn't it?'

'I'm not sure it is. I never heard Dad talk about anywhere called an Institute and he's done loads of work with the Uni over there.'

'Maybe I'll just type in her name and try that. What was it?'

'Rhiannon Kendrick.'

It seemed to take forever to work but when it did I couldn't believe how many entries there were.

'Bloody hell,' said Will. 'I didn't expect that.'

'Me neither. The top ones are links to newspapers.'

He clicked on the first one.

'Some sort of awards thing … blah blah. Hold on. Rhiannon Kendrick. Applied physics. That must be her.'

'Is there anything about her?'

'No just a list of names … wait, no– There's a picture.'

Straight away, I could see a family resemblance. The woman had the same piercing eyes as Mirabel, eyes that went right through you. She was sitting at a table holding some kind of plaque.

'Give me the laptop. Maybe there's something else,' I said.

'OK, boss. But …'

I grabbed it from him and clicked back to the search engine.

'What you doing?'

'Finding out if there's an address or an email or something. You're too slow. If we can contact her direct it might save time and …' I stopped. 'No … no. This can't be right.'

Without me touching anything, another screen flashed

up. It was an article from Filey News. I scanned it quickly. 'Will,' I said. 'I think you'd better take a look at this.'

He leaned over and read out the headline.

'July 29th 2014. Famous physicist and her niece feared dead after freak storm hits Yorkshire Beach ... Bloody hell.'

He stopped.

We had both seen the names in the next sentence.

The missing people were Rhiannon and Mirabel Kendrick.

Chapter 18

'*The search has been called off for the famous scientist Ms Rhiannon Kendrick and her niece, twelve-year-old Mirabel Kendrick, who both went missing from Filey beach two days ago. It is feared that they were swept into the sea after an unexpected storm hit the area. Coastguard, Brian Philips, told us, 'Storms of this magnitude are rare on the east coast, especially at this time of year, but today we have made the decision to ...'*

The screen went blank. 'Blast,' said Will, 'Come back you idiot.' He banged the laptop again but there was no response. 'I think it might really have died this time,' he said.

'Make it work! We've got to finish that article.'

'Just give it a second. Sometimes it comes back on without me doing anything.'

We both sat very still, staring at the empty screen.

I took a deep breath. 'Nothing's happening. Bloody hell, Will ...'

'It can't be about our Mirabel can it? She's in my caravan, unless you've forgotten. Not in a watery grave.'

'It doesn't say definitely that they died; only that they were missing. They must have been found.'

Will paused and looked deadly serious. 'Unless … she's one of the undead sent to roam the earth and to wreak havoc through the whole of the East Riding.'

'I very much doubt it.'

'It is a bit weird that the names are the same though, isn't it? And they are aunt and niece as well?'

'Well, I'm certain Mirabel's not a ghost. We need to see if there's anything else. We only read the first bit.'

'Why don't we just wait until Mirabel wakes up and ask her?'

'No way. It might freak her out even more. We just need to get to the end of that story. If it is just a coincidence then … can't you get this machine to work?' I said, giving the laptop a whack.

'It's sometimes better when it's plugged in. I'll get the power cable from the house.'

'Well hurry up. This is important.'

'Aye Aye, Cap'n.'

Will raced off. I pressed a few buttons but there was no response. I realised I could see my face in the screen. I looked a wreck. My hair was a tangled bush on the top of my head and I had black circles under my eyes. I looked more like a ghost than Mirabel did.

'Meg! Meg!'

I got to my feet and pressed my ear against the door of the caravan. I didn't want Mirabel waking up yet. Not until we'd had a chance to look at the newspaper articles again.

'Meg!'

She must have heard us talking.

Damn.

I opened the door but Mirabel was still stretched out on

the sofa fast asleep. She was breathing very noisily. I was pretty sure that spirits didn't take naps or snore. I was tempted to go and wake her up and ask a few questions but I knew I wouldn't get a straight answer. Maybe she had been involved in a terrible accident a few years ago and somehow she had been rescued. It might help to explain her strange behaviour.

It must have been Will who called but I couldn't see him. Back outside I checked my phone again.

Still nothing from Mum.

What if Mr Ward had contacted her and she'd gone home to meet with him? But then surely she would have called me?

I tried the landline but there was no answer.

I sat down and dragged Will's laptop on to my knee but there was definitely no sign of life. In frustration I banged the side hard with my hand and just for a moment a tiny light flickered on the screen.

'Yes!' I said. 'There's still some power! Come on. Switch on.'

As though it were answering, the machine made a sort of grating noise but immediately went silent. 'Work, you stupid thing.' I said, hitting it again.

SHHHHHH

That sound was familiar.

Only this time it was coming from the laptop.

I bent nearer to it.

SHHHHHH

A light flashed just for a second and made me jump. Then a word appeared on the screen, white against the dark background.

MEG

Must be Will's screensaver, I thought as my name vanished.

'Please work,' I said aloud, trying to bash it in the same spot as before.

My name reappeared.

MEG.

I gave it a shake. Another message popped up almost straight away.

Find Erasmus

What the hell was that?

The message faded.

'Will?' I called. 'If you're trying to freak me out it's not working.'

There was no reply and absolutely no sign of Will.

The screen was still blank and no matter what I did I couldn't get anything to work.

Maybe I had imagined it.

Anyhow, it wouldn't be Will. Practical jokes were not really his style and I couldn't believe he even knew how to do something like that. He wasn't that good with computers.

'Find Erasmus,' I muttered to myself.

The name did seem to strike some kind of chord but I couldn't remember where I'd heard it before. I didn't remember Will talking about anyone of that name.

I put the laptop back on the step and stood up.

'Got it! Well I think this is the right one,' Will shouted running towards me. 'Sorry I was so long. Dad's mixed all the leads up. There's about a million …'

There was a loud whirring noise and the laptop came to

life. Another message flicked back on to the screen but this time it was blinking wildly. I could only just read what it said.

F ... IND
ERAS ... MUS.

Chapter 19

'I promise you I didn't do anything,' insisted Will. 'And I've never heard of anyone called Erasmus so why would I …?'

'Who's Erasmus?' Mirabel had crept out of the caravan so quietly we hadn't heard her at all.

'Oh, hi. Are you alright?' asked Will. 'We were just coming in to check on you.'

'You didn't answer my question,' she said.

'The name just flicked up on my screen,' said Will. 'But then this laptop's always doing weird stuff. Looks like it's died again now.'

She yawned. She looked tired and her clothes were badly creased. There was dried mud on her leggings from where we had been scrabbling about on the cliffs earlier and her top was splattered with dirt as well. Mum was going to have a fit when she saw her.

She pushed her matted hair out of her eyes and flopped down on the step. I noticed she was still wearing the bright pink flip flops.

'Your computer's very old,' she said.

'Actually it's a time machine,' said Will. 'If it worked I could take you anywhere you wanted to go.'

'Will, stop it,' I said.

'Sorry Mirabel,' Will said. 'Ignore me.'

Mirabel rubbed her eyes. 'I thought I was dreaming,' she said. 'But you're both still here.'

'Well, don't worry,' said Will. 'Meg's phoned ...'

'Mum should be here any minute to pick us up.'

I glared at him. When we had got back from the cliffs I had suggested that we didn't mention contacting the police. Mirabel had been brought to us by the authorities a few days ago and she had seemed really afraid of them. I didn't want to scare her and risk her running off. I was desperate to ask her about the newspaper article but that would have to wait, too.

'Yeah. Yeah. Sure,' said Will.

I looked at my phone again. Mum must have got my messages by now.

'I'm hungry, Meg' said Mirabel. 'Can we have a picnic?'

I stared at her in amazement. She looked as though she had been through a terrible experience but she sounded as though she had forgotten about it all already.

'There's not time,' I said. 'We'll be going in a minute.'

'Meg, you're a very nice person and everything,' said Mirabel. 'But sometimes you can be rather annoying.'

'MIRABEL! WILL! OVER HERE!'

I turned and saw Abbie walking up the path with Kathryn. There was no sign of Tom or Chris. She waved some bags of bright pink candy floss at us.

'Bloody hell,' I muttered. 'Please. Not now.'

As she came nearer I noticed that she had changed since we had seen her at the cafe. She was wearing silver shorts and a t-shirt with 'Heartbreaker' written across it in neon pink. Her jewelled sandals glinted in the afternoon sun.

Kathryn walked beside her. I wondered how she could see anything through her long black hair which fell over her eyes. Her t-shirt was dark grey and it had a picture of a bleeding skull on it.

I groaned.

'We got loads of free candyfloss at the fair,' Abbie said, as she reached us. 'I just love it.' She hugged Mirabel as though she hadn't seen her for years. 'You're *so* adorable Mirabel! I've missed you sooooo much. Have some of this.'

Mirabel beamed at her.

'You're still all muddy,' she said. 'Meg doesn't take very good care of you, does she?'

I glared at her but I didn't say anything.

'I *love* Will's caravan,' she went on.

'Do you want to have a picnic?' Mirabel asked.

'Oh I'd love, love, *love* that. Can we have some food, Will?' She batted her eyelashes at Will and to my complete disbelief he blushed. 'I might need to say sorry to your dad, first. He's such a babe. He'll forgive me, won't he?'

'He's gone out somewhere but he'll be fine. He doesn't bear grudges,' said Will. 'What if we order some pizza or something?'

'Fab. Come on Mirabel,' she said, holding out her hand. 'You look a fright. Let's get you cleaned up.'

She helped Mirabel to her feet, and they went inside the caravan. Kathryn glared at me for a moment and then followed

'You need to get rid of them,' I said, when they had all gone. 'I don't want them involved in this.'

'Relax. When the police come we want Mirabel to stay really calm don't we? Tell her side of the story.'

'What do you mean?'

'Only that … look she seems more settled now. And she really likes Abbie.'

'But she hates me?'

'No. No. It's just that Abbie might be able to talk to her and …'

'And tell her I'm a lunatic?'

'That isn't what I said. I just think …'

'What?'

'Well, you have been like really stressed over this and I'm not saying you were wrong to get Mirabel out if you thought she was in trouble but …'

'Do you really think that I made the whole thing up, forced her out of her granddad's and made her come with me. That I've lost my mind?'

'No. Of course not. I mean … you did what you thought was right. But I was thinking. Before. Could Mirabel have locked herself in? I remembered how she said it made her feel safer? You don't think …'

'This is ridiculous. She was screaming her head off.'

'Yeah. But she may have just been upset.'

'The key was on the outside.'

'Maybe there's more than one. I mean you wouldn't let a kid lock the door and not have any way to get in, would you?'

'And Mr Ward? What I heard him say?'

'I dunno. But Mr Ward seemed to be genuinely bothered about her when we were at his bungalow. I just think … look, you were totally right to get the police if you thought something was wrong.'

I picked up my phone and stuffed it in my pocket.

'What are you doing?' he asked.

'Leaving,' I said. 'I'm guessing that Mr Ward has got to Mum before me and now she's not going to believe me either.'

'Meg! Please I …'

'I'll go and find her and tell her what really happened. Then I'll bring her here. If you can manage to hold on to Mirabel until I get back that would be good.'

'Don't be like this. I'm not saying that I don't believe you. I just …'

There was a shriek of laughter from the caravan and Abbie appeared at the door.

'Will,' she screamed. 'This caravan is *too* perfect. Please say we can stay in it tonight? You promised we could at the party. Please, please, *please*. It will be *such* a laugh.'

'Sure,' Will said.

'Woo,' said Abbie raising her hand in the air. 'This is going to be brilliant!'

She dashed back inside.

I felt sick.

'I'm going,' I said.

'You're being stupid,' said Will.

'All you have to do is make sure that Mirabel stays here. She's got no reason to run away now, has she? And if the police do come, then … well, I won't be long.'

'Just stay until they get here. Your mum …'

'Don't worry about her. I'll tell Mum that it's all my fault that we got into this mess. You had nothing to do with it, so you can just go and play with your new friends,' I said as spitefully as I could manage.

Will looked crushed.

I could feel tears welling up in my eyes.

'I don't understand why you're being like this,' he said.

I wanted to add something about loyalty but I knew that if I spoke now I would probably burst into tears at the unfairness of it all.

I started walking away and I knew Will wasn't following me.

I heard Abbie calling. 'Will! Will! Come on! Tom just texted. He's bringing cider!'

Chapter 20

The sickly smell of wet paint hit me as soon as I entered the kitchen. I had calmed down a bit on the way home and now my own doubts were getting to me. Will was right about me being stressed recently and the nightmares I had been having had meant I hadn't slept well in ages. Now that I thought about it, none of it added up. I was already finding it hard to remember what Mr Ward had actually said to Mirabel when he was outside her room. It had sounded threatening and Mirabel had been frightened. But now she seemed fine and she had actually asked to visit him again.

What was also worrying me was that I had been hearing voices coming from nowhere and even seeing things. I had thought Mirabel had appeared below my window last night but that definitely wasn't true.

Could I have got things horribly wrong?

One thing *was* certain.

I definitely shouldn't have left Mirabel at Will's. What had I been thinking?

And what was I going to say to Mum?

The back door was open; the kitchen empty. The radio

was going full blast from upstairs. No wonder she hadn't answered my calls. 'Mum? MUM!' I yelled.

No answer.

Her phone lay on the table and I picked it up. Twenty missed calls. All from me. Trust her not to carry it around with her.

There was a note beside it.

'*Gone to shop. Back in five minutes.*'

'Bloody hell,' I said aloud. 'You didn't even lock the door.'

What if Mr Ward had been and gone?

A terrible thought struck me. I raced into the hallway and emptied my backpack on to the floor. Books, pens and pencils spilled out and finally the scarf holding the pendant. I unwrapped it carefully, relieved that it was still there. I had forgotten how fabulous it was, especially the amazing crystal hanging in its golden cage. If Mr Ward had been here already then he hadn't found this at least. I needed to show it to Mum when she came back.

I slipped it into my pocket and headed back towards the kitchen.

Everything had gone quiet. The radio had stopped. Maybe Mum had been here all the time.

'MUM!' I shouted, as I raced upstairs. 'Are you there?'

The door to the room Mirabel had slept in was open and I walked in. Mum was not there, but I could see she had started decorating. A patch of wall had been painted canary yellow. I went over to the window.

No sign of her but the note said she wouldn't be long.

The radio was tuning in and out now and I went over and switched it off.

Turning around I caught sight of myself in the bedroom

mirror. For a moment I didn't even recognise who was looking back at me. There wasn't a millimetre of me that wasn't covered in some sort of mud, sand, dried blood and general grime. Bloody hell.

Maybe I should clean myself up before she got back and then just explain calmly what had happened. At least if I looked vaguely human she might be prepared to listen to my side of the story.

The only thing was that I wasn't even sure what my version of events was.

I would think it through while I got ready.

It was a relief to get into a hot shower even though my foot hurt like crazy. It hadn't helped that I had walked all the way back home with bare feet. I found several other cuts and scratches on my arms and legs from scrambling up the cliff.

I dried myself and took a proper look at my face in the mirror. My hair was wet and standing on end like a toilet brush. Even in this light I could tell that my 'cool' streak was getting more orange by the minute. My skin was deathly pale and my eyes with their freaky green colour, made me look like something you would see on Halloween. I slipped into my dressing gown, wrapped a towel around my head and sighed. No wonder Will preferred Abbie's company. Even Mirabel thought Abbie was a better friend than me.

I went back into my bedroom and plonked myself on the chair by my desk. A message appeared on my phone and I grabbed it thinking it was from Mum. It wasn't. It was from Will.

I'm sorry. Mirabel's fine. Please talk to me. ☹ *X*

I tried to think of a good reply but everything I typed seemed either sarcastic or naff so I didn't send anything.

I glanced out of the window. I half expected to see the disfigured face of Mr Ward looking up at me, or a police car drawing up. This was all getting too much and I needed Mum to come back. A wave of sickness came over me and when I tried to stand up I felt really dizzy. I was not feeling well at all.

My wet hair dampened my pillow as I flopped down on the bed, but I couldn't be bothered to move. It was hard to see how all of this had started. A few days ago I had been excited about the summer holidays and had been best friends with Will. Now … well now I wasn't sure what was happening.

The smell of paint seemed to be getting stronger. I didn't want to think about anything any more. I closed my eyes but images from the last few days kept floating into my head. The open window in Mirabel's room. Will and me finding her on the beach crouching against the wall. Her long blonde plait and the Lion King t-shirt. Will's yellow socks. The sand stinging my face and the sound of the sea. Wyndrift House.

Mr Ward.

I opened my eyes but I wasn't in my room any more. I was down on the beach. My feet were bare and the sand was getting into my cuts. The pain was unbearable.

Suddenly, I saw Mirabel not far away from me.

I tried to call out to her, but I had no voice.

She was talking to someone.

There was a figure, leaning against one of the concrete huts on the beach. I wanted to move nearer to them but I couldn't.

'They are called pillboxes actually,' Mirabel was saying. 'They were built in the war to watch out for the invaders. To stop them landing on the beaches. People thought they looked like the boxes they put medicine in.'

The stranger didn't reply. Whoever it was wore a grey hoodie which was really baggy. They had pulled the hood right over their face and I couldn't even tell whether it was a boy or a girl.

As though she read my thoughts, Mirabel turned towards me for the first time. 'Sometimes they don't want to show their faces,' she said. 'Sometimes ghosts have no faces.'

There was a loud crack and a streak of purple light flashed past me.

'RUN!' shouted Mirabel. 'RUN!'

I tried to move but something was happening beneath my feet. Hundreds, thousands of small crabs were clawing their way to the surface. I felt them nipping and pinching and biting and I tried to move forward. With each step I could hear the cracking of shells and now pitiful screams were emerging from somewhere deep and dark and terrible under the sand.

'I CAN'T DO THIS!' I yelled. 'I can't do this! Just let me go … I can't …'

I sprang up.

I was in bed.

In my room.

Another dream.

It was getting dark and I realised I must have been asleep for a while.

'Bloody hell,' I said, leaping up. 'I can't believe I …'

My phone started ringing. 'Mum?'

'Meg? Meg?'

It was Will. 'I can hardly hear you. Did you get my text?' he asked.

'Yeah … yeah.'

'I just wanted to say that it's all fine here. Mirabel's enjoying herself. Abbie's been making her up and she's gone a weird sort of orange colour. She looks like an Oompa Lumpa.'

'OK,' I muttered, my head pounding. 'I … we'll be there as soon as we can.'

'No problem. Mirabel's fine. The police never came though. Should I ring them or something?'

'No. No. It's OK. Wait until we get there. Mum will know what to do.'

'Right.' There was a long pause. Neither of us knew what to say. There was a crash in the background and someone screamed. 'Look, I'd better go. I'll see you later, yeah?' he asked.

'Yeah.' I took a deep breath.

'And I'm sorry. About before,' he said.

There was a noise downstairs.

'Mum's back,' I said. 'We'll be at yours soon.'

I threw my phone down and raced towards the stairs in the dark but as I passed Mirabel's bedroom I realised that the radio had started playing again.

'MUM?' I shouted. 'MUM!'

There was no answer.

I flicked on the light switch.

There was something I hadn't noticed before. Blobs of paint splattered on the carpet. I turned around and saw a trail of yellow spots leading down the stairs. I followed them all the way into the kitchen.

Everything there looked the same. The phone and the note were still on the table. I picked up the piece of paper but then I realised something. I had seen it before. Mum had left that message a few days ago.

The back door clicked and slowly swung open.

'Mum?' I said nervously. 'Mum …'

I took a step back, looking for something, anything to protect myself. The blunt bread knife was the best I could do.

I waited but nothing happened.

No one appeared.

I edged towards the door and as I got there I saw there was something on the step. A brown paper parcel, tied with a ribbon.

Without me touching it the ribbon started to untie and the paper fell away.

Inside were my trainers. The ones I had left at Mr Ward's. Something was sticking out of one of the shoes.

A photograph of Mum. I ran over and grabbed it. A message had been written on the back in black ink.

It read:

*Tomorrow. 8 sharp. Wyndrift House. Bring Mirabel **and** the pendant.*

*Your mam's safe with me but tell **anyone** and you'll never see her again.*

You're a bright girl, Meg.

Do as I say.

A. W.

Chapter 21

I'd been standing at the entrance to Happy Valley for what seemed like hours. The sky was a dull grey and the rain fell like a soft mist. I was shivering, partly from the cold but mainly because I was absolutely terrified. I'd had no sleep and I'd spent the last few hours tying myself in knots about what to do for the best.

There seemed no way out, other than to do exactly what Mr Ward wanted.

Last night, even though I knew Mum wasn't there, I'd hunted for her frantically through every inch of the house, fooling myself that the note from Mr Ward was a lie or another hoax. Maybe she'd been taken ill, or collapsed somewhere? I'd searched the garden, the shed and her car. I'd even walked to the corner shop but they said she hadn't been in.

She really had gone.

When I picked up her phone I went through the missed calls and realised that the last one was from an unknown number.

It wasn't too late to ring Dad, I knew that. I had thought about it many times in the night and almost given in. But he'd want to get the police involved and I couldn't let that happen. As soon as Mirabel was handed over and Mum was safe, I would make sure the police were told then.

I could handle this myself.

I wouldn't let Mr Ward harm Mum or Mirabel.

I shivered again and stuck my hands into my pockets.

There was no sign of Will yet and it was already a quarter to eight. He couldn't be late. Not today.

I checked again that the pendant was safe. I wished I had told Mum about it straight away instead of hiding it. And I shouldn't have gone charging off to find Mirabel myself. Mr Ward was a much more dangerous character than I had ever imagined.

This mess was my fault.

I closed my eyes. These same thoughts had been whirling around in my head all night but I couldn't find a way to make everything alright. I'd rehearsed what I was going to say to Will and Mirabel and now I needed to concentrate if my plan was to work.

I had to make them believe me.

'We have to stop meeting like this,' joked Mr Clarke, as he pulled up. 'I'm spending more time here than on my own site. Why so early?'

He beamed at me and I tried to smile. He didn't seem to notice that anything was wrong. 'I … I …'

For a split second I almost caved in and told him every-thing.

But I knew I couldn't.

'I … Mirabel's aunt is back,' I said, trying not to look at him. 'Mirabel's going home.'

'Will told me. Good news that. Is your mum here?'

'Yeah, of course. She's … she gone on ahead.' My voice was wavering and it was hard to keep it together.

'You know I'm glad we came here the other day,' he went on. 'I was thinking about some improvements to my site and …'

'We're in a bit of a hurry,' I said, interrupting him.

'Fair enough,' he said, getting out and walking over to the van door. 'I can go on a bit I'm afraid. Look, I've got to be in Scarborough early today. There's a big sale on. You and Will can come if you want. I'll square it with your mum and …'

'No … No … We … Mum said she would take us out for breakfast after. As it's early. But thanks.'

'OK. Up to you.'

He didn't look at me and I could tell he was a bit annoyed with the way I had spoken to him. I hated to think that I'd upset him but I needed him to leave.

Things were off to a bad start.

He opened the door and Will and Mirabel clambered out. 'Aren't you impressed?' said Will. 'We're not late.'

I didn't answer. My attention had been taken by Mirabel. I couldn't believe what she looked like. She was bright orange, and glittery blue eye-shadow had been badly smeared over her lids. Her nails had been painted blood red.

'Hi, Meg,' she said. 'You look cold.'

I didn't say anything.

Mr Clarke climbed back into the driver's seat and rolled down the window.

'See you laters, alligators!' he shouted.

'She doesn't know what you're talking about, Dad,' laughed Will.

'I do,' said Mirabel. 'After a while crocodile, Mr Clarke.'

151

'You see, Will. She knows what cool is all about.' He waved his hand to us as he drove away. I'd let my last chance of help go but I couldn't afford to be weak now.

I swallowed hard and tried to smile.

'What's the matter, Meg?' Mirabel asked. 'You seem different.'

'I'm fine,' I said, trying to hold it together. 'Like I told you last night on the phone, your aunt's back and everything's alright.'

'Where did they find her?' Will asked.

'Scarborough. She … was working at the university.'

'Then how come no one could trace her before? I mean …'

'Just a mix up. It's all sorted now.'

'OK. Cool. Let's go then.'

'No. You can't. Mum told me to bring Mirabel down to the house but she said you'd better stay out of it.'

'Why?'

'You're not needed. I'm not staying long either. If you wait here, I'll take Mirabel and then come back for you.'

I hadn't expected it to be this difficult. I took a deep breath and tried to look more relaxed. Will was staring at me and I could tell that he thought I had gone completely mad.

'I don't get this,' he went on. 'You've been acting weird for ages now, Meg. And none of this is adding up. On the phone last night … well it didn't make any sense and now it's quarter to eight in the morning and suddenly Mirabel's aunt has appeared from nowhere and your mum's …'

'This has nothing to do with you now,' I said, aware that tears were starting to well up.

'I want Will to come,' said Mirabel.

'Well, he can't. Not this time.'

152

'That seems a bit unfair,' Will said. 'I mean …'

'Which part of "you're not coming" are you not getting?' I snapped.

'Meg! I …'

'All you've done is make me feel terrible and as though I've done something wrong. You don't believe a word I say! You keep telling me you're my friend and you care but the only person you're really bothered about is yourself! It would be better if you just went home.'

'I can't believe you said that.'

'JUST GO, WILL!'

My voice echoed around the campsite and for a moment all I could hear was the sound of my heavy breathing.

Will stared at me. He looked really hurt.

'Meg? What are you doing?' asked Mirabel. 'Why are you being like this?'

I brushed away the tears that were now rolling down my cheeks. I couldn't afford to frighten Mirabel. She had to come with me.

'Sorry, Mirabel. Sorry. We need to find your aunt.'

'Why would you say that stuff?' asked Will. He looked pretty devastated. 'I never …'

'We have to go,' I said. 'If you ring your dad he'll probably turn round and come and pick you up.'

He didn't say anything else and I didn't look at him. It was all I could do not to break into sobs. To my surprise Mirabel slipped her arm through mine.

'I don't like this argument,' she said. 'But there is something upsetting you Meg and you should tell us what it is.'

'I'm fine.'

'That isn't true but if you won't tell us the problem then we can't help you.'

'There's no problem. We need to go and find your aunt.'

'Yes,' she said. 'I agree. But are you sure that Will is not invited?'

I nodded.

'That is a pity but if your mother thinks we should go alone then we shall,' she said. 'Goodbye Will. I'm not sure that I will see you again but you have been a true friend.'

'I hope we can keep in touch,' he said. 'Good luck with it all. Say hi to your aunt for me.'

He was smiling but I could tell that really he was very upset by everything. He turned away from us and started walking back to the gate.

I couldn't think of anything else to say and I didn't know whether to feel relieved or guilty that Mirabel had agreed to come with me so easily. What I had said to Will was unforgivable but I had no choice. He couldn't come with us.

As we started walking through the caravan site, I did glance back for a second. Will hadn't gone. He had sat down on the floor by the gate and had taken out his phone.

When this was all over I couldn't see how we were going to be friends again.

We reached the path that led to Wyndrift House. There was no one around. Not even at the old battered green caravan on the top of the cliffs.

I think I was waiting for someone to suddenly come and rescue us but instead, whispers of white mist started curling across the path.

Mr Ward was already here.

My nerve was failing me.

'Why have we stopped?' asked Mirabel.

I didn't answer. My mouth was so dry I wasn't even sure that I could say anything.

'Meg. You're very pale and Will's right. You are acting very strangely. Are you unwell?'

'I'm fine,' I managed. 'We … we have to go.'

'Of course,' she said. 'But I don't think you were very nice to Will, and I think …'

'I know. I … I'll say sorry. Later.'

As we started walking again I noticed the mist thickening a little and I knew it would only be moments before we were plunged into the fog and were out of sight and at the mercy of Mr Ward. There was a pain in my head and I felt like I was about to throw up. It was bad enough that I had been vile to Will and probably lost his friendship forever, but now I had to hand Mirabel over to a monster. I knew she trusted me but I didn't know what else to do.

'Do you think my aunt will like my new look?' asked Mirabel.

I didn't answer.

'I had such fun last night,' she said. 'Abbie is a great person. She's my friend.'

A better friend than I am, I thought, trying not to look at her.

'She asked me where I came from.' she went on. 'And I seemed to remember more than when I was with you.'

'Like what?'

'I remembered about being on the beach … and what my aunt said.'

'Good for you.'

'And I remembered Erasmus.'

I stopped walking. 'Sorry? Wait. What are you talking about?'

She stopped too and turned to look at me. 'You and Will said the name Erasmus. When we were at his caravan.'

'If this is a joke …'

'No. Of course not. My aunt and I were heading down to the beach and she … she was looking really cross and she said … she said … "You must find Erasmus," and I said, "Who?" and then …'

'Find Erasmus. Mirabel. Are you making this up?'

'No! I remember it. When you asked me before, I'd been asleep in Will's caravan and …'

'Bloody hell.'

'What's wrong?'

'The caravan.'

'What about it?'

My heart seemed to miss a beat.

Erasmus.

It couldn't be.

'Mirabel.' I said. 'You are brilliant. Come on. We'll have to run!'

I grabbed Mirabel's hand and pulled her back up the path.

'What's happening now?'

'Quick!' I yelled. 'We have to hurry. Get out of this mist!'

'Why? Where are we going? I thought …'

'We're going to find Erasmus. I know where he is.'

Now I realised where I had seen that name before. The plaque on the old green caravan at the top of the cliff. The one that kept attracting my attention.

The name on it was Erasmus.

Chapter 22

'Will!' shouted Mirabel, letting go of my hand. 'I thought you'd gone.'

Will had, of course, followed us. He was standing at the top of the path and after he had hugged Mirabel he stared at me.

'What the hell's going on Meg?' said Will. 'You have to tell me now.'

'I'm so sorry, Will,' I said, trying to catch my breath. 'There's no time. Erasmus. I know what the message means.'

'What message? You mean the one on the screen? I …'

'Come on. We have to hurry.'

He was still saying something as I raced on but I didn't stop to listen. There had to be a connection and I wasn't going to be told that I was wrong.

A few metres away from the caravan I stopped and waited for the others to catch up. The door was open but there was no sign of anyone. There were wires trailing to what looked like an old fruit machine on the veranda. I could definitely smell bacon.

'This has to be it,' I said.

'I don't understand,' said Will.

'What's happening?' asked Mirabel. 'I thought my aunt was waiting for me. I …'

'Someone was telling us to find Erasmus,' I said, ignoring her. 'Now look on the plaque by the door. It says "Erasmus". That can't be a coincidence.'

'This is mad,' said Will, running his hands through his hair. 'Have I been on the cider? I can't see anything …'

'She's right, Will. It does say that,' said Mirabel.

'There. In front of us,' I said. 'Look.'

'At what?'

'The old green caravan. The one I pointed out the other day. That must be where he lives.'

'I don't think Will can see it,' said Mirabel. 'There's some sort of optical illusion being used. Not a very sophisticated one. They mustn't think they are in much danger of being seen.'

'What are you on about?' I asked.

'It's why Will can't see the caravan. Only really gifted people can see through this kind of trick. I'm not surprised I can see it but I don't know why you can, Meg. It doesn't make sense.'

I had no idea what she was babbling on about but there was no time to think about that now.

I walked forwards but with each step the caravan seemed to be moving further away. It felt like I was treading water. I tried to slow down but it made no difference.

'What's happening?' I said.

'You won't get anywhere like that,' said Mirabel. 'I told you. Whoever lives there doesn't want visitors. They've tried to stop people seeing it, or getting anywhere near it.'

'So what do we do?' I asked.

'Stand perfectly still,' said Mirabel, confidently.

'But …'

'Meg. You wanted me to trust you before but now you have to trust me.'

I hesitated for a second and then nodded. 'OK.'

'You can still see it right?'

'Yeah … but …'

'Look more carefully. Notice the details. See where it is in relation to the edge of the cliff. Take it all in and then close your eyes.'

I hadn't the strength to argue with her.

'Can you see anything at all, Will?' she asked.

'Of course not. This is mental,' said Will. 'What the hell are we doing?'

'You'll have to hold my hand then, but you must close your eyes and I will pull you through. You can move forward when you are ready, Meg, but you have to keep the image of the caravan firmly in your mind or …'

She stopped.

'Or what?' asked Will.

'Or she may walk off the edge of the cliff by mistake. Now let's go.'

'This is …'

'Shut up, Will! Just close your eyes and do as Mirabel says,' I snapped.

However crazy Mirabel sounded, I was willing to try anything now to get to that caravan.

'If this is some sort of wind up, it's not funny,' said Will.

'Let's just get on with it,' I said. 'We have to hurry.'

I glanced at my phone again. Quarter to eight. I must have misread it before. We still had fifteen minutes.

Will held his hand out to Mirabel. She grabbed it and he closed his eyes.

I closed mine. I tried to picture the old green caravan, the strange looking wires and the telescope on the roof, the guy waving at me from the steps. I remembered the smell of bacon from a few minutes ago. It was so real now I could almost taste it.

I walked forward tentatively, expecting the ground beneath me to disappear at any moment. I had no idea how near I was to the edge of the cliff.

'Can I help you?' a voice said.

I stopped and opened my eyes.

I was standing at the bottom of the steps that led up to the caravan. The man I had seen yesterday was in the doorway with a frying pan in his hand. He was wearing baggy yellow pyjama bottoms which had large red roses printed on them. On the top he wore a bright blue and green sweater that was way too big for him. Even though he had tried to roll up the sleeves, they kept falling over his hands. A pair of gold rimmed glasses rested on the end of his nose.

'Bloody hell,' said Will, opening his eyes. 'There's a caravan right in front of me. Why couldn't I see it before?'

'How did you get here?' asked the man.

'It wasn't difficult,' said Mirabel. 'You didn't hide your caravan very well.'

'Can someone tell me what the hell is happening?' asked Will.

'What impertinence! Really. Who are you?'

'He's Will. That's Meg. My name's Mirabel. I think you've dropped something.'

The man looked down and picked up a bacon rasher that had fallen on to the veranda. He wiped it quickly on his jumper and then put it back in the pan.

'At the risk of sounding ill mannered, I must ask you to leave,' he said. 'This is private property.'

'Please listen,' I said. 'We had a message. To come and find Erasmus. We think you can help us.'

I pointed to the black plaque on the side of the caravan.

The man looked at us all steadily for a moment. He held the pan in front of the sign in an attempt to hide it. The bacon fell to the floor again. 'Nonsense,' he said. 'No one of that name here.'

'There has to be.'

He stared at us again and then scowled. 'Who are you, exactly?'

'Meg ... Meg Rowlands. You see ...'

'This is really most annoying.'

'Someone told us to find you,' I said desperately.

'Who?'

'I ... I don't know.'

'Well that's that then. Now I have no idea what you are doing here nor do I care. I am sure that you feel a great sense of achievement for having broken through my invisibility shield. Perhaps science in schools is not so badly taught as I feared ... but you must go. I have nothing to say to you.'

'But we've been told to find you,' I repeated. 'It's a long story but if you would just listen ...'

The man turned around and dashed into the caravan. He slammed the door firmly shut. I ran up the steps and tried to open it but he'd locked it. I hammered with all my might.

There was no answer.

'Meg!' said Will. 'He's not going to come. He doesn't want us here. We've made a mistake.'

I carried on pounding on the door. My last chance had gone and I couldn't think of anything else to do. Tears were streaming down my face now.

'Let's just go home,' said Will. 'We can ...'

I stepped away from the door and wiped my eyes with the back of my hand.

'I have to go to Wyndrift House,' I said quietly, trying to pull myself together. 'Take Mirabel.'

'Not that again. No way, Meg. Look, what's going on? What are you doing?'

'I ... I can't tell you.'

'Well, let's go and find your mum and ...'

'We can't,' I stuttered.

'Why not? She's cool and I'm sure ...'

'HE'S GOT HER!' I blurted out. 'Mr Ward's taken her. He wants Mirabel back in exchange. That's why we're here. I lied. I'm sorry. I didn't know what to do.'

The two of them just stared at me for a moment and then Will laid his hand on my shoulder. 'It's alright,' he said.

'No, it isn't,' I sobbed. 'I lied. Mirabel's aunt ... she isn't there. I've made a huge mess of things. I'm so sorry.'

'You were using me?' asked Mirabel, looking at me in disbelief. 'And you lied?'

'No ... well I had to. I wasn't going to abandon you, I promise. I should have told you what was going on,' I said. 'But Mr Ward threatened me. He said he would hurt Mum if ... if ... I told anyone.'

'OK. This has gone far enough. We need to tell the police,' said Will.

'No. I'll go and talk to Mr Ward. Perhaps …'

'No way,' said Will. 'This is madness. We need to get some proper help now. Mr Howard, the site manager will know what to do.'

'But Mr Ward told me not to say anything.'

'Of course he did. He's trying to scare you into doing what he wants.'

'Will! He's got my mum! If we don't do as he says … I think he's capable of anything.'

'Maybe. But what's to say that if you just pile down there with Mirabel that Mr Ward will keep his word and just hand your mum over like he says? You can't handle this on your own any more. It's too dangerous. We have to get someone. Mr Howard will contact the police and I'll make sure Dad comes back as soon as he can. Do you know how to get hold of your dad?'

I nodded but he had already started walking away.

I glanced back hopefully at the caravan but there was no one there.

Will was right.

I was way out of my depth and I couldn't see how I could make a happy ending out of this however hard I tried.

Chapter 23

Reception was closed. Mirabel and I followed Will around the other side of the building. We passed a pub, a launderette, a small amusement arcade, a shop and the coffee bar, all of which were locked and in darkness.

I had no idea whether I had done the right thing by telling Will the truth but the relief was enormous. Mirabel had not said a word to either of us since she'd found out I had lied to her. I didn't know if she would ever be able to forgive me but at least the decision about what was going to happen would soon be out of my hands. I should never have tried to cope by myself.

'I didn't know they had a diner here,' said Will, as we reached a small brightly coloured restaurant. Its neon sign read 'OPEN'.

'It looks new,' I said.

'Me and my dad went into one of these in Scarborough. Must be a chain. Come on. Someone in here might tell us where Mr Howard is.'

The door swung open before he had time to try it and we followed him inside.

There was no one around.

The diner had been made to look as though it was from the fifties. The walls were painted a candyfloss pink and there were photographs of fifties icons everywhere. I recognised Marilyn Monroe and James Dean, but only because my dad goes on about them such a lot.

The floor was covered in a checked pattern of shiny black and white tiles which reflected the soft glow of the pink neon lighting. At a long white bar there were high silver stools with bright red seats. As we moved further inside, a juke box started up and blared out some Elvis Presley song.

'Ok. So this is weird,' said Will. 'It's *exactly* like the one I went to in Scarborough. I swear it's even the same music and …'

'There's no one here,' I said interrupting him. 'Maybe we should try somewhere else?'

'The sign said open. They must be in the back.'

He walked towards the bar but I didn't follow him. I sank on to a chair. My legs felt like they couldn't even bear my weight any more. I felt exhausted and I was starting to shiver. Mirabel looked at me with disgust and then went over to Will. I didn't blame her for hating me.

There was a bell on the bar and Will rang it. Immediately a young girl came out of the back room, dressed in a pink polka dot dress. A white apron with printed pictures of ice cream sundaes was tied around her waist.

'Yes?' she said.

'Is Mr Howard around?' Will asked. 'It's urgent.'

She didn't seem to understand what he had said. 'Can I take your order?'

'No,' Will said. 'We're not eating. I'm Will Clarke. We

need to talk to Mr Howard or at least tell us where we can find him. It's …'

He stopped.

The waitress turned her head towards me. She blinked and I thought I saw a glimmer of yellow light from behind her eyes.

Will glanced at me. He had noticed it too.

'Are you alright?' he said. 'Only …'

She didn't reply. In fact she didn't move at all. The door to the cafe slammed shut.

'I think we ought to get out of here,' I said, jumping off my chair.

'You're right,' Will said. 'Come on Mirabel.'

'What's happening?' she asked.

'We need to go,' I said.

Will grabbed her hand and we all raced to the door. I got there first but realised straight away that it was locked. I tugged and tugged at the handle but it wouldn't budge.

Will hammered on the window. 'Hey! Hey!' he yelled.

But there was no one outside to hear him.

The music had stopped and everything went eerily quiet. I turned.

The waitress had disappeared and now a cat with no fur was sitting on the bar washing its paws.

'Fancy meeting you here.' The voice came from somewhere inside the juke box.

'I don't like this,' said Mirabel.

'Me neither,' said Will. 'Stay together.'

He pulled out his phone but then shook his head.

'It's completely dead,' he said.

A door at the back of the cafe opened slowly and out of

the darkness emerged the familiar figure of Mr Ward. All of us stood as if frozen to the spot, watching him edge forwards, leaning on his stick.

He reached the cat and he stopped, bending forward to stroke its bald head. The light caught his face now and made the purple patch of skin seem shinier than ever. There was a new mark too, on his opposite cheek which was weeping blood a little.

As though he was reading my thoughts, he wiped at it with his hand.

'How do you like my new venture?' he asked, looking directly at me.

There was an intensity in his face that I had not seen before.

'What's going on?' Will asked, glancing back at the door.

'You're not very grateful,' wheezed Mr Ward. 'This diner was a very clear memory of yours, Will. Look how carefully I've recreated it.'

'How … what do you mean?'

'I told you I worked with magic. It's one of my best party tricks. Borrowing people's memories, their thoughts … gives me the edge if you see what I mean.'

'That's impossible,' said Will. 'You can't …'

'Where's my mum,' I interrupted. 'If you've done anything to her …'

'Meg. Meg. There's no need to get upset. Your mam is perfectly well. For the moment. I thought I'd made it clear that I wanted you to come to Wyndrift House. And on your own. I'm not happy that I've had to come and find you.'

'We're not just going to hand Mirabel over to you,' said

Will. 'Who are you, anyway? Really. You're not her grand-dad are you.'

'This is between me and your girlfriend, lad. I don't know why you're here.'

He glared at Will and I looked desperately around the room for another way out. There wasn't one.

'You can't get away,' said Mr Ward. 'You should have just done what I asked the first time, Meg.'

'Look, people know we're here,' I said, trying to sound braver than I felt.

'What people?' asked Mr Ward, contemptuously. 'You're on your own. And you're going to do exactly as I say.'

'We're not going to let you harm Mirabel,' said Will.

He laughed.

'You're a bunch of idiots. You really are. Now, Meg. Let me talk to the organ grinder, not the monkey. You're brighter than that boyfriend of yours by miles. You'll understand. I won't be harming the girl, will I? There are people trying to find her, more important people than you can imagine. I'm going to be the one to claim any reward that's going. She's no good to me dead. Does that satisfy you?'

'You're lying,' I said. 'Or you've got the wrong girl. Mirabel's just a kid …'

'Oh no,' said Mr Ward. 'She's not just any kid. Anything besides. She's my ticket out of here. Even you must admit she's a bit different.'

'She's fine.'

'Has she told you anything? About her life before she came to you?'

I didn't respond.

He snorted. 'I bet she hasn't. Mirabel. Tell your friends how you got here.'

'I don't know. They found me on the sand,' she mumbled.

'Don't answer him, Mirabel,' said Will. 'Don't say anything.'

'Yeah, but before that,' snarled Mr Ward, ignoring him. 'Where is it that you came from? Tell us all that.'

'I … I live in Wyndrift House,' she said. 'With my … with my aunt.'

It obviously wasn't the answer that he was expecting and he started shouting. Whatever he was saying it wasn't in English and he swept his cane across the bar angrily. The cat let out a cry and leapt down. A water glass flew towards us, shattering on the tiled floor.

We all flinched but none of us had been hurt. I glanced out of the window again, hoping that someone, anyone would appear and help us.

There was no one.

Mr Ward fell into a coughing fit and it took several seconds for him to stop.

'Just let us go,' said Will, when it had gone quiet again. 'Please.'

'I haven't … got time … for this rubbish!' he said, his breath shallow and rattly. 'Now … now … you've brought me Mirabel so I'll keep my end of the bargain. I'll let you go in a minute and your mam will be released. All I need is the pendant and we're all square.'

'What pendant?' asked Will. 'We haven't …'

'I haven't got it,' interrupted Mirabel. 'And I'm not lying. I can't remember where it is.'

'I know you haven't got it. Meg has had it for quite a while now.'

'What's everyone talking about?' asked Will, running his hands through his hair. 'This is insane.'

'We're on about honesty,' said Mr Ward. 'And how some people can't keep their thieving hands to theirselves.'

'Like you, you mean,' I said angrily. 'The pendant belongs to Mirabel. And I won't be handing anything over until you show me that Mum's alright.'

'I don't think you're in a bargaining position. Now be a sensible girl and do what I say.'

'I need to see Mum. You have to ...'

'I don't have to do anything. I'm the one in control here unless you've forgotten.'

Mr Ward raised his cane. A purple streak of light shot across the diner and Will was hurled into the air. He cried out and then there was a loud crack. He had been flung against the juke box and he crumpled like a puppet on to the floor.

'Will!' Mirabel screamed.

We both tried to race over to him but there was another flash of light and a blasting sound and we were both knocked off our feet.

'Are you listening to me now, Meg?' said Mr Ward. His voice was a lot stronger and much more threatening. 'You can't win against me. I know you have the pendant on you and if I have to kill you to get it I will. Make no mistake about that. Now I'm going to count to three. One ...'

I put my hand into my pocket and felt the cool metal of the pendant. If I handed this over there would be no bargaining point any more.

'I want to see my mum first.'

'Two …'

'Let my mum go! You don't need her. I've done what you asked.'

'Thre–'

There was a huge crash. Before I could do anything I was thrown through the air and I landed again with a thud on the floor in front of the window. I saw the glass in the window crack and split into shards which all pointed towards me. As they started to move I instinctively curled into a ball to wait for the sharp stabbing to begin.

Instead, icy cold raindrops splashed on to the floor beside me.

When I looked again, the diner had completely disappeared. We were lying on the floor of an empty shop. Old furniture lay scattered around us and we were covered in dust and debris.

There was no sign of Mr Ward.

'What … what happened?' mumbled Will, raising himself up a little. 'Where are we? Where's Mr Ward?'

'Will!' I said, scrambling to my feet. 'Are you alright?'

'I hate to be a bore but it really would be expedient if we could leave now.'

I turned around and saw the man from the caravan standing in the hole where the window had been. He was still wearing his rose print pyjamas and he was carrying a walking stick. Although it was darker in colour than Mr Ward's, it had the same carving of a bird on the handle.

'I'm afraid I was a little short with you earlier,' he said, when we didn't move. 'Let me introduce myself. Name's Erasmus.'

None of us spoke.

'I'm afraid I didn't have time to change. My apologies. And as it seems that no one is badly injured, I suggest we retreat to my humble abode? Before we attract any more unwanted attention.'

Chapter 24

'Ah Diggleby,' said Erasmus. 'These are the young people I told you about. How are you getting along with updating our security systems?'

A man with a wild nest of orange hair was standing at the top of the caravan steps. He was wearing a white lab coat, rubber gloves and massive black goggles which he raised up when he saw us.

'Just finished,' he said. 'I still don't understand how they got through in the first place.'

He directed a suspicious glance towards me.

'Yes. Puzzling, I admit,' said Erasmus. 'But I am sure it was not due to any negligence on your part. Besides we have other things to concern ourselves with now. Please let me introduce you. This is …

'What are we going to do?' I interrupted impatiently. 'You said …'

'If you would be so kind, Diggleby,' said Erasmus. 'I think a nice pot of tea might be in order.'

'What? You have to be kidding!' I shouted. 'I told you on the way here. My mum is in danger. We have to go and get her!'

Erasmus looked over towards Diggleby.

'I'll put plenty of sugar in, sir,' he said. 'Good for shock.'

He opened the door and went inside.

'What is wrong with you people?' I said, my voice almost a screech. 'I don't need tea. I'm not in shock. Either tell me what you plan to do or I'll go after Mr Ward myself!'

Erasmus sighed. 'You are obviously a very brave and a very gifted young woman,' he said. 'But I think that you have seen that it is foolhardy to charge after a Kelve without careful consideration. They are not known for their ability to listen to reason. Indeed they seldom show mercy when there is something that they want.'

'What are you talking about?' I asked.

'What's a Kelve?' asked Will.

'Not what, young man. Who. According to Diggleby there are several of them that have made their permanent home on earth at the moment, which is most disconcerting. He had an altercation with one in Whitby just recently and managed to acquire this rather grand looking walking cane. The bird at the top is a Mondosal, I believe, from the ancient Helosian system. Symbol of the protector. They are rather sophisticated pieces of equipment and they can be persuaded to attack as well as defend. They are managed by the power of the mind and ... well I think I am doing rather well with this one, if I do say so myself.'

'Is that how you smashed the window and scared Mr Ward off?' asked Will. 'With that?'

'Indeed. I destroyed the illusion he had created. I beat him at his own game as it were.'

'Mr Ward told you,' said Mirabel. 'The diner wasn't real, Will. He stole one of your memories.'

'Yeah but … he wasn't telling the truth, was he,' said Will. 'That's impossible.'

'I'm afraid not,' said Erasmus. 'He took an image of it from you, my young chap, and recreated it. It is a rather clever skill, I have to admit.'

'My aunt told me that the Kelves are extinct though,' Mirabel said. 'They used to be able to make themselves invisible and even travel through time. They all died, she said.'

Will and I both looked over at her in astonishment. I was certainly losing the thread of this conversation and I was fed up of this nonsense. I wasn't sure how much more of it I could take.

'Look,' I said. 'This fantasy talk is all very well but …'

'Indeed, my dear, Mirabel,' said Erasmus, ignoring me. 'Your analysis of their considerable skills is very accurate. Although … I am afraid that I have to correct you in your belief that they are no more. No one knows for certain what happened to their planet. But it was destroyed many centuries ago. It was understood that they had all perished but it seems that they merely scattered themselves all over the universe. This cane is proof that they are still alive and well.'

'Are you saying what I think you're saying?' I asked. 'Mr Ward's an alien?'

'That's mad,' said Will. 'He can't be.'

'A crude definition. I do not like that expression, Meg. But if it helps you to understand my point, then it will have to do for now.'

'Bloody hell,' said Will, rubbing his head. 'This can't be happening.'

'Kelves are dangerous, but only in the sense of venomous snakes,' continued Erasmus.

'What do you mean?' I asked.

'They usually won't harm you if you leave them alone. No. The Kelves prefer to blend in, as it were. That's why many believed they had died out. Which makes me wonder even more why the Kelve in Whitby was so troublesome and why Mr Ward has chosen to attack you.'

'This is mad,' I said, 'You're all mad. Will, Mirabel, you need to come with me. We made a massive mistake coming here.'

I looked over at Will but he was deathly pale and he was starting to sway.

'Will!' I shouted. Mirabel and I grabbed hold of him just in time before his legs gave way.

'I … I'm fine,' he mumbled.

'We need to get you to a hospital or …'

'Bring him inside the caravan,' said Erasmus. 'I can assure you that Diggleby will check that he is back to tip top condition in no time.'

'Is he a doctor?' I asked.

Erasmus laughed.

'Indeed. He can even perform minor surgery if the need arises,' he said. 'Not that it will come to that,' he added quickly. 'I can assure you that he is totally reliable. I upgraded him myself.'

'I don't know what you're talking about.'

'Diggleby's one of the A4025 models.' He lowered his voice. 'He's not the top of the range I'm afraid but we should probably keep that to ourselves.'

I looked at him blankly.

'Diggleby,' he repeated. 'My assistant. Technically he's what you might understand as a robot but I am quite sure that he won't thank you for using that term. Now shall we go in and see if tea is ready?'

Chapter 25

The inside of the caravan was more surprising than the outside. The whole thing had been knocked through into one big room and it was filled with various kinds of machines, some which were easily recognisable and some that were not. Everything seemed to be whirring and blinking and flashing. It was unbearably hot.

Six massive computers were lined up on a bench all along the far wall, joined together by bright red and yellow twisted wires, They were all on, their screens flickering in unison. Further along, some one-armed bandits were spewing out thin strips of paper and playing the tune which usually indicated that someone had won a prize. There was a Penny Falls right next to me which had been converted into a printer. Inside, brightly coloured maps were being created but when I leaned over to take a closer look, I couldn't recognise anywhere I knew. Boxes of files were strewn about everywhere and there were pieces of paper and photographs pinned to every spare centimetre of wall space. Tangles of wires dangled from the ceiling and they threaded their way all over the floor. We had to tread carefully as we helped Will inside.

At the far end I noticed a trap door that was open and next to that a ladder leading up through the roof. There must be more rooms somewhere. Why on earth would someone build something like this? What were they doing here?

Erasmus quickly cleared some space and set up a deck chair. He helped us to lower Will down on to it.

Will didn't say anything.

He looked dreadful and he closed his eyes.

'Will!' I said desperately. 'Will. Please.'

He didn't move.

Diggleby came over and placed his hand on the top of Will's head.

'What's he doing?' I asked.

'Let him do his work!' said Erasmus cheerily. 'Absolutely nothing to worry about. There has been a lot to take in. I am aware of that. But I can assure you that ...'

'There is no lasting damage to Mr William,' interrupted Diggleby. 'My scanners do indicate he is a little dehydrated and of course the shock may have contributed to a temporary malfunction of the autonomic nervous system but otherwise he just requires rest. With your permission I could prepare him a hot beverage that might prove advantageous to his current condition?'

'Of course Diggleby, thank you. Excellent work as always.' He turned to me. 'You see, Meg. You do not need to be concerned about your friend. Now if I can find some more chairs.'

'Might I suggest these,' said Diggleby, pulling a couple of wooden stools out from under the bench of computers.

'Ahh! Excellent. Excellent. Resourceful as always. Please, Meg, Mirabel ... Sit.'

I was too weak to argue. I had given up expecting to wake up and find that none of this was real.

'Now, Meg,' said Erasmus. 'Now we are inside and calmer, let us analyse the situation more carefully and ...'

Diggleby coughed.

'There is ... I hate to intrude on your conversation, sir but I fear there is a matter of some urgency.'

'Of course Diggleby. You have my full permission to prepare young Will whatever he ...'

'No, Sir. I refer to an important matter concerning the young lady.'

'She is naturally upset about her mother. I think ...'

'No. No.' said the robot. 'The other one.'

He pointed towards Mirabel.

She looked over at me in alarm. 'What does he mean, Meg?'

'Nothing,' I said. 'You're fine.'

To be fair, she looked a bit tired and dirty and maybe all that makeup Abbie had applied was a bit smeary now. But she seemed to have dealt with the shock of meeting Mr Ward better than I had.

'You had better explain quickly Diggleby,' said Erasmus. 'You are causing some distress. Is she in danger?'

'Oh no sir. At least ... I have been detecting a faint signal ever since the young people approached our research facility.'

'A tracking device perhaps?'

'Impossible to be sure at this point. I have ascertained that the young lady in question has had a device implanted into the back of her neck. I came across a very similar scenario when I was working for ...' He stopped. 'Should I remove it?'

'What … what are you talking about? asked Mirabel.

'My dear,' said Erasmus. 'Please. I am sure there is nothing to worry about. But if Diggleby can take a look …'

'No,' said Mirabel. 'Meg. I want to go home.'

'Not yet,' I said. 'I've just remembered something. When Will and I found you on the beach that time you said the back of your neck was sore, didn't you?'

She nodded. 'It itches now,' she said. 'Sometimes.'

'Can I look?' I asked.

She hesitated for a moment and then she lifted up her plait.

'Can you see anything?' asked Erasmus.

'Yes,' I said, leaning nearer to her. 'But it's more swollen than when I saw it before. Maybe you should let Diggleby take a look at it, Mirabel.'

'No,' she said. 'I think we should go.'

She was really frightened now I could tell.

'Look, I know what I did before was wrong,' I said. 'But I wouldn't have let Mr Ward hurt you and I won't let anything happen to you now.'

I nodded to Diggleby and he stepped nearer.

Mirabel's pale eyes were full of tears. She didn't say anything but she let the robot take hold of her plait. He stared at the back of her neck for quite a time before allowing her hair to fall back into place.

To my surprise he actually sighed. 'As I mentioned. I was asked to implant such a device many moons ago,' he said, 'when I was working as a butler in the palaces of …'

'Diggleby!' said Erasmus sharply. 'Just tell us what it is.'

Diggleby looked a little shamefaced but he continued. 'The device is a memory suppressant,' he said. 'It was originally designed to help cases of post-traumatic stress. Patients found that with this device they could eventually forget what they had seen but of course some people found … well, other uses for it.'

'So … what is it doing in Mirabel's neck?' I asked.

'It filters out certain parts of a person's memories so I presume someone wanted her to forget particular aspects of her life.'

'But why? Who would do that to her?'

'I cannot tell,' said Diggleby. 'But there has been some damage to the device which has caused the swelling. Normally one would not even see it. It may mean that elements of her former life are starting to seep through as it were. It … it seems to be emitting signals too, which is rather unusual and I fear… somewhat dangerous.'

'What do you mean?' asked Mirabel. 'Why is he saying these things, Meg?'

'Try to stay calm,' I said. 'I'm sure it's nothing.'

'I did not mean to alarm you, Miss. But I have to let you know that if Mr Ward, the Kelve, is in search of you, or anyone else for that matter, they may very well be able to trace these signals as I did,' said the robot.

'Well, can we turn it off?' I asked.

Diggleby looked worried. 'Impossible. I dare only make slight adjustments. I am afraid any further intervention might prove too much for the young lady.'

'Is this … is this why I can't remember things properly?' Mirabel said. Her voice was almost a whisper.

'I am afraid so,' said Diggleby. 'You may of course be familiar with some things, the device does not obliterate memory completely. You still know who you are, certain important details as it were but much of what you have been through has been suppressed.'

'And can you … can you get her memories back?' I asked.

Diggleby did not answer my question. 'May I? he asked.

Mirabel nodded and lifted up her hair again.

He leaned over and placed his hand over the device. 'I have run a preliminary scan through my systems but they may take a little time to process,' he said at last. 'I can jam the signal at least so she will be safe here for a while. As will we. I have updated all security systems also to deter intruders.'

Tears were flowing down Mirabel's face now but when I tried to put my arm around her she pulled away. She had turned to me a moment ago when she was frightened but she hadn't forgiven me yet for what I had done earlier.

'I will prepare something for the young man and might I suggest tea could be a useful beverage at this point for everyone else?' asked Diggleby.

'Splendid,' said Erasmus. 'I am sorry that you are experiencing such things my dear Mirabel but it seems to me you have good friends and …'

'We're not having tea,' I said, taking a deep breath. 'I came here to get help. My mum …'

'Of course. Of course. And I can assure you I will do all in my power to assist you. But one cannot rush into things.'

'If you're not going to do anything then tell me because I'm going out to look for my mum right now.'

'I can assure you that your mother will be perfectly safe for the time being.'

'You can't know that … you …'

'Mr Ward is not going to harm your mother. Not yet. He is enjoying his hold over you and he thinks he has a bargaining chip.'

'This isn't a game!' I said, raising my voice. 'Don't you get it?'

My voice rang around the caravan.

'Please Meg. Your strong emotions are admirable but I fear they are not helpful in this situation. Now let us look at the facts. My understanding is that for some reason Mr Ward has taken it upon himself to kidnap your mother. Why? Not the usual ransom of money but rather an exchange. He wants Mirabel. If we can ascertain the reason behind his demands then perhaps we will have some leverage.'

'I just want Mum back!'

Will moved for the first time. 'What … what's happening?' he asked.

'Nothing, my dear boy,' said Erasmus. 'Now Diggleby will find us all some refreshment. Mirabel will be given the task of looking after you while I am away. And Meg, you come with me.'

'Where are we going?'

'Perhaps you would … perhaps if I show you what we've been working on, things might be a little clearer for you and you can see exactly what it is we are dealing with here.'

Chapter 26

We climbed the ladder which led out on to the roof. There was more equipment up here, machines which again looked like they had been taken from amusement arcades. I recognised an old air hockey table, where a series of little black boxes had been wired in along the centre, each emitting a different coloured flashing light.

The telescope we had seen earlier from the ground looked even stranger close up, like a cross between something you might see on a pirate ship and a Victorian camera. There was a black cloth draped over the back of it and Erasmus bent down and lifted it up.

'I think you will find the view through this most interesting.'

'I don't … I don't see how this is helping.'

'Come and look.'

'I can see where it's pointing. Just towards those trees.'

Erasmus looked again at the telescope.

He laughed. 'Well, my dear, you are entirely correct. Just give me a second.'

He tilted the telescope up until it was aiming directly at the sky. I noticed he was wearing a ring on every finger. In the middle was a silver one that doubled as a small watch and on his thumb was a yellow plastic owl. I was sure I had seen the same one in the amusement arcades in Bridlington.

He stepped aside and held up the cloth. 'Now you can take a look.'

I couldn't imagine what I would see apart from a passing seagull maybe.

'Please,' he said, when he saw me hesitate. 'Please trust me.'

'Why should I?'

'I do indeed understand your reserve. It is natural. But I do think this might answer some of your questions.'

I stepped forward.

It was horribly warm and claustrophobic underneath the black cloth. I groped for the telescope and tried to look through. 'I don't think it's working,' I said. 'Everything's just black.'

'Splendid.'

'I just said I can't see anything.'

'Good. Perfect. I suspected as much ... this really is too marvellous.'

'I don't ...'

'The viewer does take a little getting used to I'm afraid. You have to try to ... to look beyond the darkness. Feel your way through it as it were. You have to try to see things differently.'

It was no use. I just seemed to be staring into nothing.

I was about to give up when there was a small flicker of red light in the distance. I looked harder and started to see flecks of yellow and maybe purple darting across in front of me.

'There's … there might be something there. Lights.'

'Wonderful. Try to concentrate. You need to look more … what you are trying to see is beyond the surface. Take your time.'

My eye was watering. I blinked and looked again. Now I could see more clearly. The coloured flecks were swirling wildly now and I felt mesmerised by them. I tried to focus on one colour but it was difficult. I found myself suddenly thinking about places I had been to recently and years before. An image of Dad sitting in the garden reading a book seemed to float in front of me and then I saw Will coming into the classroom at school, the first day I met him. I was freaked out but I couldn't move away from what was playing out in front of me. Wyndrift House came into view and Mirabel, but before anything else appeared, I felt a hand on my shoulder. I seemed to come back to my senses and stepped out from beneath the black cloth.

'Are you alright?' asked Erasmus.

'Yeah, I think so,' I said, blinking at the intensity of the daylight. 'What just happened?'

'Isn't it remarkable? The technology behind this type of lens is well in advance of anything you will have come across before,' he said, ignoring my question. 'And it enables you to see … well not just see but experience. You can sense something can't you? The energy from within that darkness is immense. More than you can ever imagine. It is … a living thing. It has quite a profound effect on one.'

I nodded.

For the first time I understood exactly what he was saying.

'You are very gifted, Meg. The only other human I know of who … well, no matter. It is certainly remarkable.'

'I don't even know what I'm looking at.'

'Not yet perhaps, but it takes time to be able to control forces like those you have just seen. Training, like with anything else.'

'But how is this helping?'

'Because if I am to assist you, then you will have to realise that what we are dealing with here requires more understanding than you will get from any police officer or even from your family. By all means, go and get outside help. But they will fail as you have failed so far.'

'Then what can I do?'

He paused. The black cloth from the telescope had detached itself somehow and it slid to the floor. He bent down to pick it up.

'Firstly,' he said, 'do you accept, Meg, that there may be things about the universe that we do not yet understand?'

'Of course I do.'

'And one of those things is that there could be other universes, other worlds, other planets that we do not yet know of?'

I nodded. 'Yes, but …'

'Meg, what you have seen through the telescope is real and tremendously exciting. It is … well for the want of a better term a pathway … or a bridge. A link from one universe to another. What do you say to that?'

'It's impossible … it …'

'And yet you have seen it. If your mind is limited to only believing what you already know then how can I convince you that there may be other truths? Other amazing things out there, waiting for us to find them.'

I realised that my heart was beating really fast and I tried to calm down.

I took a deep breath. 'OK,' I said. 'So if you are saying that what I saw was some sort of bridge, then why was I seeing things … people from my life?'

'The Bridge is an amazing creation. It is as though it is alive in some way. It has an energy I have never come across before. If you can see it, it tries to connect to you and it asks that you connect with it. It really is the most incredible thing.'

'But who made it? If it's a Bridge, who's on the other side?'

'Good questions. I have been working so hard with Diggleby but there have been no positive conclusions as of yet.'

'You mean you don't know.'

'Correct.'

'And you don't know why it's there.'

'Correct.'

'Or whether we're in danger?'

'Correct.'

'Do you know anything?'

He paused. 'Diggleby cannot come to any satisfactory explanation as to why it works in the way it does. Or how someone could possibly pass anything through it or cross it. Not with such an energy field.'

'So no one could actually use it?'

There was a loud whirring sound and one of the black boxes suddenly exploded. Sparks leapt out and Erasmus rushed over.

He reached for a fire extinguisher and tried to aim it at the small fire but he couldn't get it to work. By the time he did, the box had melted into black sludge and there was a foul smell of burning plastic wafting through the air.

'Sorry about that,' he said. 'These monitors are rather temperamental. That's the third one I've lost this week.'

'This is fascinating but I don't see we're getting anywhere,' I said.

'Wait. There's more. I haven't finished.'

'I want to believe you,' I said. 'I really do. But there is no way that any of this can be true. You live on a cliff in a caravan filled with junk from arcades and you're telling me that Mr Ward is some sort of alien and that you have found another universe out there? There's obviously something weird going on but I can't deal with it right now. I have to go.'

'Not yet. Please.' He put down the extinguisher. 'The reasons that I have been forced into such unsatisfactory accommodation for my work … well that would take too long to tell. But you can imagine that when I was working for an official department it was difficult for some people to take me seriously. Few can see what you and I can see through that telescope.'

'But … but I don't understand what I was looking at.'

'Maybe not yet. But you know it was there. And intelligent though you obviously are, you can't explain away some of the things that have been happening to you.'

'I need to find Mum,' I repeated.

'Agreed. But to do that you have to realise who Mirabel is.'

'She's just a girl,' I said. 'She came to us …'

'Yes. And that is significant I think.'

'She came to us and … and …' I stopped. For some reason I had started to shiver uncontrollably.

'Oh my dear,' said Erasmus. 'I am so sorry. I forgot … well the ordeal obviously and the Bridge can be quite an experience the first time you encounter it … here. You must have this.'

He picked up a blanket that was folded next to the telescope. It was the palest green colour and when he wrapped it around me I felt warm immediately and also tremendously calm. It was as though the material was absorbing all of my anxieties and worries. I closed my eyes for a moment.

'Sensational, isn't it?' he asked. 'A Carper blanket from the planet Dalenium. Fabulous creatures the Carpers. If you listen carefully you can hear them.'

Sure enough, somewhere in the distance was a faint humming sound. It was incredibly soothing. Despite everything, I could feel myself falling asleep. I forced my eyes open and dropped the blanket down off my shoulders quickly. I couldn't afford to lose concentration now.

'Please, Erasmus. Just tell me what's happening.'

He nodded.

'First of all I have to say that the general fear of alien lifeforms is entirely unfounded. So many are here already, living amongst us. There are several established routes to earth at the moment and of course there are always passing ships and so forth. We have met many visitors through the years. Diggleby and I are friends with … we *used* to be friends with two Esks in Scarborough but then I'm afraid there was a very unfortunate incident. I had to insist that they return home on an Ansel transporter vessel. But perhaps that is not a good example.'

'This is mad. Someone would have noticed if millions of aliens were wandering about.'

'You may be wildly overestimating numbers, Meg. This

earth's atmosphere does not suit everyone and some civilisations do not have the ability to adapt. Of course, the vast majority of them who do come here are harmless. Wonderful creatures in fact. Most of them just want to move around unnoticed. It helps that your people are very unobservant. No one has even found my research site. I mean, of course there's Mr Howard, the site manager.'

'You're saying he's an alien as well?'

'I believe he hails from the Banonian region of Buke. There has been some tension there of late and it is doubtful that he will be able to return anytime soon. He lets us stay here rent free. Such a generous soul.'

He turned away from me and pulled another black box out of a cardboard container. Reaching down to a small toolbox, he brought out a very ordinary looking screwdriver. When he gave it a sharp tap, it glowed orange. He started to attach the new box to the air hockey table.

'Who are you, really?' I asked again, realising that he had been avoiding this question for some time. 'Are you one of these Kelve things? Like Mr Ward. Is that why you can use that cane and why you know so much about him?'

'Oh my word, no,' said Erasmus, looking up. 'Not at all. Not at all. I shudder at the very idea. The truth of the matter is that my origins are a little ... well uncertain. But not Kelve. No. Perish the thought.'

'But how do you know you're not like him if you don't know who you are?'

'Diggleby has assured me ... Tests and so forth. Know who I'm not, if you see what I mean. I was found in Whitby, actually. As a baby. In a boat. Diggleby says ... well perhaps another time, Meg. When we have less pressing matters to discuss.'

'It's hard to believe all of this is happening,' I said, rubbing my eyes.

'I understand but may I just ask *you* something now?'

I nodded. 'Have you noticed anything else significant that has happened in the last few days since Mirabel arrived.'

I hesitated. 'There's been so much. I don't know where to start.'

'Very well. I'll begin,' he said. 'On Friday Diggleby reported that there had been some changes in our recordings of the Bridge's energy. Very significant ones.'

'Friday was the day Mirabel arrived,' I said.

'No coincidence, I think.'

'But how? I mean she couldn't have had anything to do with that.'

'He also noted that there had been small, almost imperceptible slips in time. The data he was receiving was most intriguing.'

'I did … I did notice that there were some weird things happening,' I said. I remembered Will's repeated texts and conversations that seemed to happen twice. 'I thought it was just déjà vu.'

'I don't think it was. And there's something else.'

'What?'

'The energy you experienced when you looked through the telescope. There are traces of it on Mirabel. I sensed it almost immediately and I am confident that Diggleby will confirm that for us later.'

'That's ridiculous. She couldn't have …'

'Crossed the Bridge?'

'I don't believe it.'

'And yet you know that there is something different about Mirabel. You know it!' His voice had risen now and his eyes were bright with excitement.

'You're mad,' I said, trying to stand.

'Meg, things that you thought "ridiculous" a few days ago are now happening. And you have to believe it if I am to help you any further!'

My legs were still really shaky but I managed to get to my feet and I leant on the table again. This couldn't be happening and yet it was. Erasmus was talking rubbish but things had been happening which were impossible to explain away.

'I can't believe that Mirabel's from another world,' I said. 'I just can't.'

'Then can you explain why the Kelve has such an interest in her?' he asked.

I shook my head.

'I know the memories might be painful but when you met Mr Ward did he say anything else about Mirabel that might be useful to us?'

'No,' I snapped.

'Are you sure?'

'I can't … maybe there was something … he did say something about a reward for finding her?'

'Ah. The Kelve thinks there may be a reward. That is interesting.'

'But that doesn't prove anything.'

'Anything else?'

'No. Honestly. I don't think he was there to discuss things. Just to get what he wanted. If you hadn't arrived …'

'And might I ask you what led you to ask me for help in the first place?'

'There was a message. On Will's computer. But I didn't know what it meant. Then Mirabel said she had heard of you … she said her aunt told her about you.' I hesitated. I was thinking about the newspaper articles. I wasn't sure what I believed any more. 'I think she's confused sometimes. It's stupid, all of this. She can't be …'

'Not stupid at all. We will rely on Diggleby to assess the situation and try to make it clearer for us. At the moment we are just speculating and that is not helpful. Indeed it is just making you more anxious and I am sorry for that. Let's go downstairs and join the others. I have asked Diggleby to formulate a plan for us and I am sure that he must have thought of something by now.'

Erasmus turned away from me and headed for the ladder.

'Can I ask you something else first?' I called to him.

He stopped and turned towards me. 'Of course.'

'How come I could see the Bridge? There's nothing special about me.'

'Oh no,' said Erasmus. 'That's where you are wrong. There is something very special about you indeed.'

Chapter 27

I climbed down the ladder but by the time I had got to the bottom, Erasmus had disappeared. There was no sign of Diggleby either.

Will and Mirabel were sitting on the floor and in between them was a tray loaded with tea cups, a jug, and a large teapot. There was also a chocolate cake crazily decorated with pink marshmallows, jelly babies and what looked like spaghetti.

Nothing seemed right any more.

Will looked up at me and smiled but I could tell that he wasn't really himself. There was a bruise on the side of his face and I saw that there was still some blood matted in his hair.

'You OK?' I managed.

'Yeah. Fine. You?'

I nodded but I was anything but fine. We were no nearer finding Mum and the things Erasmus had told me were whirling around inside my head.

I stared down at Mirabel. She started picking at some of the sweets on the cake and lining them up on her plate like I used to do when I was a kid.

'You know you definitely don't look right,' said Will. 'You should try to drink something at least.'

Mirabel leaned towards Will. 'She was horrible to us today,' she said. 'She shouldn't sit with us.'

'I don't want anything anyway,' I said. 'I have to talk to Diggleby and Erasmus.'

'They went outside,' said Will. 'Diggleby's been telling us all this stuff about other planets and … well some of the people he's met that have come here … that can't be right, can it?'

'Erasmus has been telling me the same things,' I said, looking at Mirabel. 'It's hard to know what to believe.'

'Look, sit down with us, for a minute at least. Just wait for them to come back in. They said they were going to decide what was best to do next.'

'I think I should go and find them.'

Will frowned. 'Please, don't go yet,' he said. 'Not until I'm sure everything's cool between us.'

'You're not the one to blame. Mirabel's right. It was me who made a mess of things.'

'I think we should forget what happened before,' said Will.

'I remember it,' said Mirabel. 'I remember what she did.'

'Meg was under a lot of pressure,' said Will. 'None of it was her fault. If what Erasmus said about Mr Ward is right then … Well, we have to stick together now. That's the most important thing.'

Mirabel stared at him for a moment as though she was really thinking about what he had said. She reached for another of the jelly babies from the cake and when she spoke she looked at the sweet rather than turning to me.

'I think what you did was terrible,' she said. 'But I am

aware of why you acted in that way. My conclusion is that Will is right. You should sit with us and tell us more of what Erasmus said because you are not very good when you are acting on your own.'

'Thanks,' I said sarcastically. 'I could do with a confidence boost right now.'

'Why would you make sweets baby shaped?' she asked. 'I've never seen these before. The whole thing is macabre.'

I stared at her. She was very different to other kids I had met but she couldn't have travelled from another world, could she? It *was* ridiculous. All of this was ridiculous.

'I will tell you,' I said. 'But not now. Mr Ward still has Mum and I need to find out what Erasmus plans to do about it.'

'Wait,' said Mirabel. 'I remembered something else. The pendant. The one you took from me. Where is it?'

I had almost forgotten all about that. I reached into my pocket and pulled it out.

'I didn't take it,' I said, trying not to rise to her accusation. 'You gave it to me. I … anyway it's safe, look.'

I held it out on my hand. The crystal caught the light from one of the windows and glinted a little.

Will peered over to take a look. 'Wow,' he said. 'If that stone's real, it must be worth a fortune. No wonder he wants it.'

'Are you sure you can't remember where you got this, Mirabel?' I asked.

She shook her head. 'I just wanted to make sure you still had it,' she said. 'And if it helps to get your mother back you can keep it. I don't want it anyway.'

Just then my phone vibrated in my pocket. I pulled it

out but the screen was blank. It made a small whirring sound again.

'Someone's trying to get through,' I said. 'This stupid phone's on the blink. I'll see if I can get it to work outside. There might be a better signal.'

I didn't wait to hear Will's objections. I stuffed the pendant back into my pocket, opened the door and stepped outside.

Erasmus and Diggleby were nowhere to be seen.

At the bottom of the steps I looked at my phone again. Nothing.

There was a scuffling noise from under the caravan and then Diggleby emerged, wriggling like a worm. He stood up and dusted himself down. He stopped when he saw me.

'Are you alright, Miss Meg?' he asked. 'Do you need any help?'

'Where's Erasmus? I thought you two were together, making plans?'

'Indeed we were but in order to proceed he needed some further information. There seemed to be a problem with some of our wiring. I believe I may have …'

'Where is he then?'

'Erasmus? He has gone to see the site manager.'

'I'd better go and find him.'

'No, Miss. I would strongly advise against moving beyond the safety of the caravan at this precise moment. I will go and hurry Erasmus along.'

'And then we'll go and find Mr Ward, yes?'

He picked up another wire that was trailing over the floor and looked at it intently.

'Mr Howard may have some equipment that would help us,' he said, ignoring my question. 'And I did tell him that

I would run the bingo this afternoon but in the circumstances …'

'Bingo?'

'Yes. It's a game of chance.'

'I know what it is.'

'Do not worry, Meg. While I am gone you will all be safe. I have been able to improve the defences around the caravan. Nothing can pass through, now. You can be assured of that.'

'Then how will you get out?'

He smiled. 'We are not in a prison,' he said. 'It is only designed to stop people coming in.'

'Right,' I said. 'I wasn't thinking.'

The robot turned and walked away before I could ask him any more.

My phone sounded again.

This time a photograph of Mum flicked into view. The same shot of her that had been left with my shoes last night.

'What the …?'

And now a tune started playing.

'*Oh I do like to be beside the seaside*
Oh I do like to be beside the sea …'

I hit my phone hard and the noise stopped.

A message flicked up.

You have 5 minutes
The bungalow
Come alone

So much for Diggleby protecting us.

Chapter 28

There was a slight movement, just ahead of me in the woods. Through the branches of the trees, long white fingers of mist were approaching. The sea fret. Of course. Mr Ward would want to make this experience as horrible as possible.

I stopped and took a step back but the fog reached me quickly, swirling around, dampening my clothes and clinging to the back of my throat. It was difficult to breathe. Already it was impossible to see ahead or behind me. I had no choice but to edge forward slowly, trying to feel my way through the white blanket of cloud. I reached my arms out, trying to find a tree to grab but there seemed to be nothing around me. I couldn't be that far away from the cliff edge by now. Maybe Mr Ward hadn't planned to meet me here after all. He was just going to get rid of me. But I couldn't do anything about that now and I had to carry on.

The ground was wet and slippery and with the next step my feet went from under me and I landed heavily on my backside. As I tried to get up, I slipped again and my hands, my jeans, everything was caked in mud.

I'd had enough of this.

'I KNOW YOU CAN SEE ME!' I shouted. 'LET'S JUST GET THIS OVER WITH, SHALL WE?'

There was no reply but just when I was beginning to think he hadn't heard me, the fog cleared like a curtain being drawn open. No wonder I couldn't find the trees. There were none.

The temperature was dropping by the second and now I could see my breath, the vapour rising and turning into the shapes of butterflies. I knew he was trying to remind me of the trick he had performed in the bungalow, when he had used it to scare me.

I tried to sound defiant.

'MR.WARD! I KNOW YOU'RE THERE. JUST …'

I don't know how I hadn't noticed before but a few metres away was a white wooden gate. It led to a redbrick cottage.

I got to my feet and walked towards it. I could see it clearly now and it wasn't Mr Ward's bungalow. I realised that it was the house on the photograph that Mum and I had argued about the other morning.

The place where I was born.

I had learnt that Mr Ward could steal memories and recreate them. But this house wasn't somewhere I remembered, not in this detail and it didn't mean anything to me. Not really.

The gate swung open, inviting me to walk up the path to the front door.

I glanced around but none of the landscape behind me was familiar. Anyway, I couldn't go back. Mum was in this mess because of me. And Erasmus, whoever he was, didn't seem to have any ideas about what I could do to save her.

I pushed open the door and walked in.

The hallway was dark and I flicked a light switch to try and see more clearly but it wasn't working.

'HELLO?' I called.

No answer.

The first room I entered was completely empty and the noise of my feet echoed across the wooden floorboards. There were no curtains on the window and in the garden I could see a black Labrador lounging in the sun on a bright green lawn. I didn't remember any of this. I certainly never knew we had a dog.

'Mr … Mr Ward?' I called.

No reply.

I went back into the hall. A bare light bulb on the ceiling had started to flicker and it was making an irritating buzzing noise.

'STOP PLAYING GAMES!' I shouted. 'WHERE ARE YOU?'

A small movement caught my eye from the room at the end of the passage.

Someone was in there.

'MUM!' I screamed.

She was in the kitchen, standing in front of the washing machine.

'MUM!'

I ran forwards but just as I got there the door slammed in my face. It was locked and however hard I tried, I couldn't budge it. I hammered on it with all my strength. Something was happening. Wherever my hands landed, the wood became transparent. Soon I could see Mum again, through the clear spaces, unloading some washing from the machine.

'MUM! IT'S ME,' I yelled at the top of my voice.

She didn't even turn around.

She opened the back door and went outside.

I was about to bang on the door again, smash it down if I had to, when there was a flash of light and almost immediately Mum was back in the kitchen, unloading the machine again.

'What's happening? MUM! WHAT'S HAPPENING?'

There were tears rolling down my face now. I just wanted to break through this door, go to her and tell her I was sorry. About everything.

A yowling noise came from behind me. Then a spitting hiss.

I swung round.

The bald cat was staring at me, its bright yellow eyes glowing in the darkened hallway.

When I turned back to the door it was wooden again and Mum was out of sight.

'WHERE'S MR WARD?'

It didn't answer of course and it didn't move.

'I KNOW YOU CAN HEAR ME!'

It blinked and the hall was filled with a soft yellow light. The cat started to wash its paw nonchalantly, as though nothing terrible was happening at all.

'YOU STUPID CAT … I …'

It stopped, glared at me and then ran up the stairs. At least I knew where Mr Ward was now. I took a deep breath and set off after it.

Chapter 29

Although they looked wooden, the stairs felt soft and my feet kept sinking in, slowing me down.

When I finally reached the top, I hesitated. There were three doors but only one of them was open. There was no sign of the cat but there was a faint scratching sound from somewhere in the distance.

'You'd best come in,' a voice called.

Mr Ward.

I headed towards the open door, taking a deep breath.

He was in the centre of the room, sitting in an old arm chair, the same one Will and I had helped him into when we had taken him back to his bungalow. He looked even more dishevelled than when I had last seen him and the smell of whisky and cigarettes was stronger than I remembered. Some of the loose skin on his face had torn and had obviously been bleeding. If I didn't know what he was like, I might have even felt sorry for him.

'How do you like it?' he said, grinning at me.

I looked at him blankly.

'The house,' he said. 'Your house. This was your room.'

I looked around.

The walls were painted pale yellow with a border of teddy bears running around the centre, each one carrying a different letter of the alphabet. To my left was a white chest of drawers with red roses and exotic birds stencilled on the front. A lamp on top of it shone on to a fluffy pink rabbit and a small stack of books. Behind Mr Ward was a child's bed, wooden with pink bedding. A patterned quilt was draped over one end.

'I don't remember it,' I said, finding my voice at last. 'I was only little when we lived here.'

I was trying to sound confident but I could feel my legs trembling.

'Shame,' said Mr Ward. 'I thought it would be a treat for you to see your old house. This is one of your mother's memories. I was going to use one of yours but …'

He stopped and bent down to pick up his old shopping bag.

'But I couldn't get a clear reading,' he went on. 'In fact, I couldn't read you at all. You puzzle me, Meg. I thought I'd got the measure of you but I'm not so sure now.'

'What do you mean?'

He didn't answer. He reached into the bag and brought out a bottle of whisky. A small table with a glass on it appeared from nowhere.

'I … Please just let my mum go,' I managed.

My throat was dry and I felt sick.

'You look cold,' he said. 'That mist can be a bugger. Do you want a swig of this?'

I shook my head.

'No, I forgot. You don't like it.'

He poured some whisky into the glass and took a long

drink. He made disgusting slurping noises and some of the whisky dribbled down his chin.

'You've seen your mum. Downstairs. Yes?'

I nodded.

'So you know she's alright. She's probably outside by now.'

He signalled towards the window and I raced over. Down below, Mum was pegging out children's clothes on the line. I banged on the glass but she didn't even look up.

'She can't hear you,' said Mr Ward. 'But keep watching.'

Mum picked up the washing basket, turned and disappeared. There was the flicker of light I had seen earlier and suddenly she was back out in the garden again. I noticed the clothes she was putting out were exactly the same as last time.

'What's happening to her? What have you done?'

'A time pocket. Very clever, if I say so myself. I shoved her into one of her own memories.'

'I don't understand.'

'She's on a kind of loop. I needed a strong memory and this is what came up. Washday. Bit odd but never mind. Look. Round and round she goes. She could keep doing that for … well forever. She seems happy enough.'

'Just let her go!' I said angrily. 'She's nothing to do with all this.'

He sighed. 'You know, it's a pity. We don't seem to be on the same wavelength, do we? This could be sorted so easily.'

'What do you want?'

He didn't answer my question. Instead, he drained the rest of the whisky from the glass in one gulp and poured himself another.

'Look, you can't win,' I said. 'We've got someone looking out for us now. He …'

'Who? Professor know-it-all and that tin can he walks around with? I've seen 'em. In that little science lab they've got going there. The site manager, that Mr Howard, keeps me well informed of their shenanigans. If that's the best you've got then you're in bother.'

I was quite sure that Erasmus and Diggleby hadn't even considered that Mr Howard could be betraying them.

'Erasmus beat you at the diner,' I said.

'Lucky fluke. Caught me a bit off guard.'

'And he knows all about you … He knows you're a Kelve.'

Mr Ward laughed. 'So he'll know he doesn't stand a chance against me.'

He started coughing uncontrollably and he reached for his glass. 'What else did he say?' he spluttered. 'About me.'

'Nothing much. He said … he just said he didn't understand why you're here. Why you've stayed on earth so long. Why you don't just go and leave us alone.'

Mr Ward snorted. 'I'm not here out of choice, I can tell you that. Years and years I've been stuck here.' He pointed to the damaged skin on his face. 'Just look at me. Look what's happening to me. I won't last much longer unless I get out and that's a fact.' He took another drink. 'Look, Meg. I'm going to level with you.'

I didn't say anything. I glanced out of the window again and saw Mum pegging out the washing.

'Sit down, will you? There's no reason why we can't be civilised about this. Reach a compromise.'

Now a wooden dining chair, like the one I had sat on in the bungalow, appeared opposite him.

'No,' I said. 'I …'

I felt myself shooting through the air and I landed with a thud on to the chair. I tried to get up but I was completely stuck. My arms were pinned down and only my head could move. I struggled for a few seconds, trying to pull myself free but it was no use.

'That's better. Now we can have a proper chat.'

'Let me go!'

'Not until we've sorted this.'

He put down the glass and reached into his pocket, taking out a packet of cigarettes.

'You know,' he said. 'In all of the planets I've been to, I've never seen these anywhere else. Might take a few packets with me when I move on.'

He lit his cigarette but as soon as he put it in his mouth he started coughing.

'They're bad for you,' I said.

'Nice of you to care,' he wheezed. He was about to take another drag but he thought better of it and stubbed out the cigarette on the floor, crushing it with his feet.

'Now where were we? Oh yeah. The thing is, Meg, I can tell you don't much like me. You want me out of your hair, right? Gone.'

'Then go.'

'I can't. I need that girl.'

'I'm not going to let you harm Mirabel …'

He laughed. 'Why would I want to hurt her? She's no good to me dead.' He paused. 'I have to get out of here, Meg,' he went on. 'And I've found a way at last.'

He pulled an old dirty handkerchief out of his pocket and wiped his face with it. He was clearly in pain and blood was seeping out of his broken skin.

'That nutty Professor you seem so keen on. He's told you about me so I guess he must have told you about the Bridge. The one just up there.'

He pointed vaguely in the direction of the sky.

'That's what he's been looking at with that stupid telescope of his, isn't it? Thinks I don't know. Did you see it?'

He narrowed his eyes and stared at me, as though daring me to lie to him. He had said he was finding it difficult to read me and it was the only advantage I seemed to have over him so far.

I didn't answer.

'Well if I'm going to tell you the rest of my tale you're going to have to trust me,' he continued. 'Whether you like it or not. The daft bugger's right. There's been rumours flying about for months about that Bridge and where it leads to.'

He paused and dabbed his face again.

'Anyway I knew your pals on the top of the cliff were up to something so I got Mr Howard to investigate. He told me they'd found where it was. And by all accounts the world on the other side is way better than here.'

He leaned back in his chair.

'If the rumours are true,' he went on. 'They're miles ahead of you clowns down here. And all I have to do to get there is cross that Bridge.'

'Then why can't you go?'

'Not as easy as that. No one seemed to know if it was even possible to get across but now …'

'Now what?'

'Now I know it is. Shall I tell you how?'

'I don't want to listen to anything you have to say.' I tried to move but it was no use.

'Oh, you'll like this. It's a good story. You sitting comfortably?'

I didn't answer.

'Then I'll begin. Thursday night. You remember the storm? You must have heard it. Wind at around eighty miles an hour, sand whipping up, lightning, waves crashing, the works.'

I did remember of course. It had woken me up but I was determined not to engage with him any more than I had to.

'So Friday morning, when it died down and it got light I went down to the beach to have a look if anything'd been washed up. You'd be amazed what I've found down there in the past.'

He stared at me as if expecting some kind of response. I stared back.

'Anyway, I was right,' he went on. 'There was something. A young girl. Thought she were dead. Can you guess who it was?'

I didn't speak but he was clearly not going to move on until I answered him.

'Mirabel,' I said, at last.

'Well done. Top marks. Well, before I can get down to her, two coastguards beat me to it, fussing all over her. They whisked her away.'

He took another swig of his whisky.

'I stayed around for a bit. Had a feeling that something was up, though I couldn't put my finger on what. Then …' He leaned forward, his eyes gleaming. 'Then something else did happen. Another girl appears. Walks right out of the sea and heads up the beach towards me, bold as brass.'

'Fascinating,' I said sarcastically. 'Is there a point to all of this?'

'Not someone out for a swim. Fully dressed,' he said, leaning back again. 'She looked a bit like you if I'm honest.'

'It wasn't me.'

'No. I know that now. I need my eyes testing. You're nothing special. That girl on the other hand …'

He stopped and chuckled to himself.

It was hard to hide my surprise. I hadn't bargained for there being someone else involved in Mirabel's story.

He carried on.

'She was wearing a pendant, a crystal. I knew right off that it wasn't like anything you can get around here. Anyway, when she reached me I tried to say summat, be friendly like, but she blanked me and headed off towards the cliffs.'

'Is that it? Can we talk about Mum now?'

He ignored my question.

'I kept a sharp eye out all day but nothing. Saturday I did the same and lo and behold just as it was getting dark, I saw her again. This time she wasn't looking too clever. She was just sat on the sand, back against the pillbox with her hood pulled up over her face. Breathing was worse than mine. All rattly.'

He was looking at me intently and I turned my head to avoid eye contact with him. He wanted some reaction from me, and it was difficult to keep a straight face because the image he had drawn of the girl was reminding me of the figure I had seen in my dreams.

'Just had this feeling that there was something here that could be to my advantage,' he went on at last. 'You've seen that crystal yourself. Even you knew there was summat special about it, didn't you? That's why you stole Mirabel's.'

'I didn't …'

'Anyway, she wouldn't talk to me at first. Bloody rude. I tried to get in her mind. But no go. Closed book. So I had to use a different tack.'

'You threatened her?'

'No. I can be very charming when I want to be. I got round them police officers, didn't I? And your mam?'

That was it. I pulled and pulled at my hands but I was fastened tight.

Mr Ward watched me struggle. He took another drink and then sank back into his chair. He wiped his mouth with his sleeve.

'If you've finished squirming about, I'll carry on.'

I stopped. I was annoyed with myself for letting him rattle me.

'Had to let her know that I wasn't just some old bloke who'd turned up on the beach. Told her a few stories about me. Selected carefully of course. Then I showed her the butterfly trick. She wasn't as impressed as your boyfriend but I think it broke the ice. She knew I wasn't from round here and that I was being straight when I said I could help her.'

'You? Straight? A Kelve?'

For the first time he looked angry. He picked up the glass and for a moment I thought he was going to hurl it at me. Instead he drained what was left and placed it back on the table.

'Anyway. I'll cut to the chase because I can see your attention is wandering. The trick worked and it got her talking. After that she never stopped. Told me all about herself:

blah blah blah. I was only interested in the bit about how she got here. "You wouldn't understand," she says. "You have to use your mind to connect to this pendant first. It takes a lot of training." Training? Pah! I've been doing stuff like that since I was a nipper.'

I had known all along that there was something extraordinary about the pendant but I couldn't possibly have guessed why it was so special.

'Power of the mind,' he said. 'That's something I'm good at, isn't it? You know that first hand.'

'Is this going to go on much longer?' I asked.

'You'll like the next bit. Turns out this mission she was on about was to find a girl. The very girl I'd seen being carted off earlier.'

'Mirabel?'

'Got it in one. Only she's lost all trace of her. And while she's blabbering on about how she'll have to go back empty handed, my mind's racing. I'm making plans. See I was pretty sure I could get the girl no problem but what do I do then? Just hand her over? For nothing?'

'Doesn't sound like you.'

'No one does something for nothing if they've got brains in their head. You see, I was starting to realise that someone had gone to a lot of trouble here to find some scrawny kid. She had to be worth a lot. What if I stepped up to the plate and took the girl back myself? Crossed that Bridge! And I'm thinking, it would be easier for me when I get over there if I'd got something to bargain with.'

'You mean people on the other side of the Bridge might not like Kelves either?'

'People have been jealous of our powers for centuries.

They've chased us down to near extinction but, you see, Meg, I'm not a bad person. All I want is another chance. A future.'

'But this girl saw through you?' I asked. 'Maybe she wasn't as stupid as you thought.'

'Full of herself,' he rasped, pouring himself some more whisky. 'Kept going on about it being *her* mission. She was quite happy to let me find the girl, she tells me. But she's the one going to take her back.'

He laughed and touched his walking cane.

'The daft thing is,' he went on. 'That I wasn't going to hurt her. I was being more than reasonable. She wasn't well, Meg, and I said I'd get her some help as soon as I crossed the Bridge.'

'Funny she didn't believe you.'

'She was in no fit state to go anywhere. She knew that as well as me. I was genuinely doing her a favour but she couldn't see it. Got proper stroppy and said she didn't need my help. Started walking away. I couldn't have that. She went down like a sack of spuds as you lot say here.'

'You … killed her?'

'I'd call it more of an accident. I'll explain what happened when I get over that Bridge if I have to. I'm not in a court of law here.'

I looked away from him and stared at the teddy bears on the wall instead.

'No. Don't you worry your pretty little head about her. She's had a decent burial. That Mr Howard sorted it. Dumped her out at sea. *Sea-swallowed*, as they say – do you get it?'

I didn't respond.

'*Sea-swallowed*, that daft play your boyfriend's reading. He's got loads of it in his head.'

'The Tempest? What's that got to do with anything?'

He laughed. 'That's where all of this started, didn't it? The storm.' He leaned forward and smiled at me. 'But you know what I did next. I found Mirabel.'

'By pretending to be the caring granddad,' I sneered.

'That was the easy bit. Tried to make her feel at home by taking a few memories.'

'You're so caring,' I said sarcastically.

'She wasn't grateful. I managed to get a shot of her room and nicked that but I couldn't get a clear picture of the rest of it. I got all the other stuff from that boyfriend of yours. Now he's no bother. Good as gold.'

I thought about how Will had said he recognised the rooms downstairs in Wyndrift House and how I hadn't believed him.

'Everything was going well but … the one snag I came across was you,' Mr Ward continued.

'Me?'

'Yes, you. You're the one to blame for this mess if you want anyone to point a finger at. You took that pendant. And then you took Mirabel. That's why we're in a bit of a situation here.'

He reached into the bag and brought out some screwed up newspaper. He shook it and a pendant, identical to the one in my pocket tumbled out on to the table. 'So what you're thinking is, that if I've got this from little Miss Important Mission then why don't I leave here right now? Am I correct?'

'Yeah. Go. You won't be missed,' I said, without taking my eyes off the crystal.

'I would. But … you see I wanted to take the girl as insurance and I don't like having to change my plans for anyone. Especially not for a slip of a girl who thinks she can get the better of someone like me!'

His voice had risen now and he started to get up from the chair.

I took a deep breath.

'But now … now I think we can settle this once and for all,' he said.

'I just want my mum back,' I said, trying to sound calm. 'Why don't you let us go back to normal and you go across the Bridge yourself. Leave Mirabel out of this.'

'I told you. I've made my mind up and I don't appreciate being crossed. All you have to do is to bring me what I've asked for. Mirabel doesn't mean anything to you, does she? And as soon as all that happens your mum will be set free. There's not even a choice to make is there?'

I hated to admit that he was right.

He steadied himself and started to walk towards me. He was so near that I could smell his rancid breath, a mixture of cigarettes, whisky and dead things.

I tried to pull away.

'As soon as I get Mirabel and her pendant, then we'll be out of here and you can go back to doing whatever it is you do as though none of this had ever happened.'

'I can't let you hurt Mirabel,' I said.

'Haven't you been listening? She's no good to me dead, is she?'

He paused and when he spoke again I saw that there were actual tears in his eyes. 'I used to travel across universes, Meg,' he said in a pathetic voice. 'One mistake, a misunderstanding and I'm exiled here. Might as well have been a death sentence. You have to see that?'

I looked away from him.

'I'm not meant to live in just one place, Meg. It … it eats me up … it …'

I wasn't going to be drawn into his poor old man act.

He stopped snivelling and glared at me. 'You know, some people tried to beat me before. Years back now. Thought they were sharper than me. It didn't end well for them. I got the bungalow out of it. You know who I mean, don't you?'

'The magician? I said.

'Exactly. The not so great Mancello and his wife. Had a bit of an accident walking too near the cliffs. You have to be careful around here. They thought they were cleverer than me, Meg, and look what happened there.'

There were tears brimming in my eyes too now. My mind had been racing but I couldn't think of anything else to say or do that would save both Mum and Mirabel.

'So what do you think?' he asked. 'Do we have a deal?'

The thought of giving into him was unbearable but what choice did I have?

'Alright,' I said at last. 'Alright. I'll do what you ask.'

He laughed. 'This is good. We understand each other. You have what I want and I … well let's say I have the upper hand.' His smile dropped and he leaned forward. 'Now I'm going to tell you what's going to happen. Tomorrow morning, 5 a.m. the tide will be well out. You and Mirabel are going to meet me on the beach, just in front of Wyndrift House. She'll be wearing her pendant. None of the others are to come with you. You understand?'

'They know all about you. They are involved. They're not …'

'They're not going to be able to stop me, Meg. Neither are you. You can blab the plans to the Prof but he can't do anything. Who would he tell? Who'd believe him anyway? Have you thought about why he's hiding away in that caravan? I bet he hasn't told you, has he?'

'What do you mean?'

He laughed. 'It doesn't matter. But you'll crack up when you hear it. What I'm saying to you is that you won't be able to get help, Meg. Haven't you wondered about your phone calls? Why you can't get through to anyone? Why the police didn't arrive the other day?'

'How do you know about that?'

'Because I know everything. There isn't anything I can't do. Stuff like that is a breeze for someone like me. I control you, Meg. You have to know that.'

I thought about the message that had just appeared on my screen before I came down here. The way that I could never get a signal and the strange policeman I had eventually got to talk to about Mirabel. That hadn't been real.

He was right. I was out of my depth.

'So that's it. Just you and me. It'll be quiet on the beach that early in the morning. No one about. I'll bring your mum and we'll do a swap.'

'How do I know you're not just going to kill us all?'

'Meg, Meg. I just want to get this over as quickly and quietly as I can. No one needs to know I've even been here. If I'd wanted to kill you I could have done it already. You're just going to have to trust me.'

'Why should I?'

'Because you have no choice.'

I didn't reply.

'You see, Meg. I've been straight with you. I think we can get along now, can't we?'

I felt lighter all of a sudden and I realised I could move again. I got to my feet. As I did so I put my hands into my pockets. My phone was still there but the pendant had gone.

I glanced around on the floor but there was nothing there. I couldn't have lost it. I couldn't have. Had he taken it from me without me realising?

When I looked up again, Mr Ward had disappeared.

'You know I'm right, Meg,' came a voice from somewhere up above me. 'Your mum seems happy enough. If anything were to happen to me … see there's only me as knows how to release her so you'd better be sure I make it through until tomorrow. Bring me Mirabel and that pendant.'

'Please … just …'

'It's all in your hands, Meg.'

I looked around quickly. Where was the pendant? He couldn't have taken it. He was still asking for it.

I got down on to the floor to try to get a better look, to see if it could have rolled off somewhere. I was suddenly aware of how sticky the floor felt. I started sinking into it. The walls and doors were starting to blur.

I tried to get up but the floor was moving now. I managed to crawl out of the door but I could barely drag myself along. When I reached the top the staircase, it was already bending and twisting. I tried to grab one of the spindles but my hand went right through it. The illusion was disappearing fast and suddenly I felt myself falling and falling and I tensed myself, ready for the crunch as I hit the ground.

It never came.

Chapter 30

'You said you would help me,' came a voice from behind. 'You promised.'

I opened my eyes.

It was Mirabel. She was wearing a pink and white striped dress and someone had tidied her hair. It had been combed back into the sleek blonde plait and tied with a large pink bow. Her face was deathly pale.

Around her neck I saw the pendant.

'Can we go now?' she asked.

I tried to speak, to ask where Will was, but when I opened my mouth no sound came out. My head felt like it was splitting in two. Somehow I'd ended up on the beach, leaning against one of the pillboxes, facing the sea.

How had I got down here?

I tried to move but I seemed completely stuck to the concrete. However I struggled I couldn't pull myself free. Mirabel didn't seem to notice.

She reached into her bag and brought out a camera. I heard a click.

'Good shot,' she giggled 'Now take that hood off. I can't see your face properly.'

Hood? What hood?

She shrugged. 'Never mind. This one will be better,' she said.

There was a tremendous crack from overhead and a flash of purple streaked past me. Darkness was falling across the beach like a gigantic shadow. Above me, I saw the clouds in the sky pulling apart, revealing the lights I had seen and felt through the telescope. A kaleidoscope of reds and greens and purples danced in mesmerising patterns towards the horizon.

'Let's go down to the sea!' said Mirabel. 'We can take some more pictures down there.' I realised that she wasn't talking to me. A dark figure emerged from the pillbox behind me, a hood pulled over its face.

Another crack from the angry sky. A bolt of purple lightning flashed so near it stung like a whiplash. It sent me spinning away from the pillbox. The sand felt too soft and my feet started sinking straight away.

Mirabel and her new friend were walking down to the water's edge. The sea was changing colour. First an intense blue and then green and then red. It began to bubble and boil but neither of them seemed to notice.

'MIRABEL! WATCH OUT!'

My voice was back, loud and clear. It echoed right across the beach and Mirabel turned to me and smiled. The next second, a gigantic wave reared up behind them both and they were plucked into the sea.

I made one last gigantic effort to reach them but now I was sinking deeper and deeper into the sand. Something was clawing at my legs from the depths.

'You can't win against me. You must know that.' Mr Ward

had appeared from nowhere and was standing in front of me, grinning, watching me struggle, watching me suffo-cate.

He was right.

There was nothing I could do.

I let the sand swallow me up.

Chapter 31

I woke with a jolt and scrambled to my feet, not sure whether I was still dreaming or not. I saw at once that the wood was behind me and my old house had disappeared. No sign of Mr Ward's bungalow either. I could see right to the end of the cliff now, where a makeshift fence of old posts and barbed wire formed a flimsy barrier from the steep drop to the beach.

It all seemed real enough.

The blinding headache was real too. It suddenly felt so cold, even though the sun was shining and I began to tremble. My hands, my clothes, everything was covered in a thin grey dust.

My phone vibrated in my pocket.

I pulled it out and saw a string of texts from Will.

My hands were shaking as I tried his number but it was no use. I couldn't get through. Of course not. Mr Ward was controlling everything, who I spoke to and who I could message. I wouldn't be able to get help from anyone now.

Stepping nearer to the cliff edge, I hurled the phone over, as far as I could. At least he wouldn't be able to track me through that any more.

I had no strength left and I had absolutely no idea what to do next. I sank to the floor, put my head on my knees and sobbed. It seemed the only thing I was capable of doing. I had failed everyone and now … well now things had got out of control. How could I have been so stupid as to lose the pendant? Without that …

SHHHHHH

I swung round. No one. Maybe just the wind in the trees. I wiped my eyes with the back of my hand.

SHHHHHH

I had definitely heard something and it wasn't for the first time.

The ground beneath me seemed to shake and then I felt a definite jolt. I sprang to my feet. What was happening? The cliffs in this area were always collapsing and perhaps I was about to be launched on to the beach. The rumbling underground got louder and louder, sand and mud started flying into the air.

Just as suddenly everything stopped. In front of me, bright blue lines began to criss cross in the air. They danced about in a random pattern for a few seconds and then they began to form into definite shapes: circles, squares, rectangles.

'Is this it?' came a woman's voice.

I spun round but there was no one behind me. There was nothing except the cliffs, the trees and the fence. The weird lights flashed and twisted and the lines became thicker and a deeper blue. I thought I saw the shape of a head, maybe a hand. Something or someone was emerging from these lights and I didn't like it. I was all set to run when another voice cried out.

'No. No. Meg!'

'Don't go.'

'Not yet.'

'We need to …'

'We need to speak to you.'

'Who … Who are you?' I managed. 'How do you know my name?'

There was no response but the blue lights were fading now and I was certain that two women were starting to appear, their heads first and then the rest of them. Their bodies were moving and twitching as though they were trying to force themselves into shape.

'That's better.'

'Much better.'

'We're here now.'

'Yes. Here.'

'We're very pleased to meet you, Meg,'

'So pleased.'

The two women now standing in front of me were not like anyone I had ever seen before. The taller one had short brown curly hair streaked with white. She was staring at me and smiling. Her eyes were purple and her skin was the brightest pink I had ever seen on anyone. The other woman was much thinner and paler in the face. Her hair was cropped short and had been dyed pale blue. They wore identical outfits: blouse, cardigan, tweed skirt and flat shoes except the tall one was completely in red while the other was in yellow. They were both carrying handbags in the same colour as their outfits.

I must be still dreaming, I thought. This can't be happening.

Then the tall one spoke. 'I think we're in the right place.'

'Too far to the left?'

'A little.'

'Like in Scarborough ...'

'The hotel was fine before you ...'

'That's better.'

The woman in yellow had fished a pair of large spectacles out of her handbag and after she had put them on she peered at me. 'Hello,' she said. 'You *are* Meg, aren't you?'

I nodded slowly. I had been right all along. I was still asleep.

'Thank goodness.'

'You're alright ...'

'I thought,' interrupted the other woman, 'that ... wait ...' She tilted her head slightly to one side. 'Is this straight?'

Her head did seem to be on at a bit of an odd angle but she was fussing so much it was hard to be sure.

'Who are you?' I asked again, taking a step back. They looked harmless enough but there was no way of telling if that was true.

'I'm Agnes,' said the woman in red.

'And I'm Edna, of course.'

I looked at them blankly.

'We're the Esks,' Edna said.

'From the Shandian Delta.'

'Did Erasmus tell you about us?'

The name seemed familiar somehow. 'I ... think ... I'm not sure,' I said.

'A dear friend.'

'A very dear friend.'

'Such a dear chap.'

'I knew he wouldn't have forgotten us.'

'The Essskkks,' stressed Agnes, leaning towards me and raising her voice a little.

'I think she hears you, dear.'

'From Scaaaarborough.'

'Yes, dear, enough I think.'

They went silent and stared at me for a minute. I tried to think back to the conversation with Erasmus and I did remember something about the aliens he had mentioned, ones he had met. Maybe he did say something about the Esks?

'Were you friends once?' I asked. 'But then … didn't you have to leave?'

My voice sounded remarkably calm considering the situation, but I was aware that my legs were still shaking.

Edna's face seemed to be turning blue. 'That is correct,' she said quietly.

'We did.'

'We did.'

'Misunderstanding.'

'Totally.'

'We don't want to bore her, dear.'

'With the details?'

'Precisely.'

'Live here now.'

'Filey. Much quieter.

'Fewer people …'

'Fewer hotels.'

'Less trouble.'

'Look,' I said. 'I … I haven't got time for this. I …'

'But you can't go.'

'Not yet.'

'We came to help you.'

They both took a deep breath at the same time.

'I feel odd,' said Edna.

'You're going blue dear,' Agnes whispered.

'Sorry, dear.'

'Human colours are so tricky.'

'This isn't happening,' I said. 'I have to go.'

'She's in a rush.'

'We didn't think.'

'So sorry, my dear, but …'

'You see we've been watching you.'

'You and your friends.'

'And Mr Ward.'

'The Kelve.'

'Up to no good.'

'We tried to help.'

'Followed you.'

'Tracked you.'

'Tried to send messages.'

'But you have a strong mind, my dear.'

'Not easy to get in.'

'Sent a message to a little girl.'

'Alice, dear.'

'Of course.'

'The girl in the room.'

'Found the key.'

'And a machine.'

'My idea.'

'I think you'll find that …'

'Find Erasmus. Find Erasmus. That was the message.'

'All that was you?' I said. 'That girl and … the key and … that was you on the computer?'

'Agnes did it.'

'Not entirely alone, dear.'

'Of course. But you …'

'Come with me then,' I said. 'Erasmus is just up there. We can go to him and explain …'

To my surprise, the women's bodies seemed to shudder and then twitch. The blue lines appeared over their heads again, criss crossing and flickering.

'Oh no, my dear.'

'Oh no.'

'That won't do at all.'

'He can't see us like this.'

'Not like this.'

'What's the matter? You seem to be fading. I can't …'

'Erasmus was a friend.'

'Indeed he was.'

'But now …'

'Now …'

'He's cross with us.'

'Angry even.'

'Livid.'

'Exactly.'

'I doubt it,' I said. 'I haven't known him long but …'

'The hotel, you see.'

'The hotel.'

'The one that fell into the sea.'

'From the cliff.'

'It tumbled right in.'

'He thought that was us.'

'He said that was us.'

'But not entirely to blame.'

'Not at all.'

'A misunderstanding.'

'But he was mad.'

'He warned us.'

'Told us to leave.'

'Insisted.'

'"Or the ghost ships for you," he said.'

'The ghost ships.'

'Terrible places.'

'Terrible.'

'They would come for us.'

The small blue lines were becoming more frantic, flashing all around them now and their bodies were less distinct.

'What's a ghost ship?' I asked.

'For undesirables.'

'Criminals.'

'Pirates.'

'They would definitely come.'

'And we would be …'

'Don't upset yourself, dear.'

'Tortured.'

'Starved.'

'Vaporised … vaporised …'

'We would be no more.'

'Terrible places.'

'Terrible.'

As though we had been overheard there was suddenly the sound of a helicopter circling overhead. We all gazed up at the sky. The two women looked terrified for a moment but when they saw what was making the noise they both sighed at the same time and held hands. Presumably they had thought that a ghost ship had been passing. Whatever that was, it sounded horrendous.

Agnes and Edna looked towards me again. Their feet had disappeared altogether and their legs were becoming blurry.

'We want to help.'

'We can help.'

'But you …'

Edna held out her hand towards me. Her skin felt re-markably solid and very soft.

'You have to promise,' she said.

'Promise.'

'Promise what?' I asked.

'Not to tell.'

'Not to tell anyone.'

'Where we are.'

'That we are here.'

'They must not find us.'

They glanced up at the sky again. 'Promise?'

'Promise?'

'I promise,' I said. 'Look, I have to go.'

Edna dropped my hand quickly.

I had more important things to do than to worry about these creatures. I had to get back to Erasmus and the others.

I stepped forward but the women blocked my path.

'Didn't want to be involved in all this,' Agnes continued.

'No involvement, absolutely.'

'Keep a low profile.'

'But then we saw the goings on.'

'Couldn't avoid it.'

'And now we've found her.'

'Sorry?' I asked.

The women's quick-fire chatter was making me dizzy and I had had enough.

Edna raised her eyebrows. 'The girl.'

'We've seen the girl.'

'What girl? What are you on about?' I asked, but they ignored me and carried on.

'We didn't know what to do.'

'A mess.'

'No one else must find her.'

'Could be awkward.'

'What are you talking about?' I asked. 'What girl?'

'THE GIRL!'

'THE ONE THAT FELL FROM THE SKY!'

SHHHHHH

I realised what they meant. 'Look, if you mean Mirabel, then she's safe with me. We …'

'No, not her. The other one.'

'The one like you.'

'The girl with the hood.'

'There's nothing we can do for her,' I said, looking away from them. 'Mr Ward saw to that.'

Agnes took a deep breath and her face was clearer again and more flesh-coloured although a lot paler than before.

'You must rescue her,' she said.

'From the pillbox.'

'Rescue.'

SHHHHHH

'I just told you, Mr Ward … he attacked her. He … he put her body in the sea. She's dead.'

'No no, my dear.'

'Not dead.'

'Must have washed up.'

'On the beach.'

'She's in the pillbox.'

'Very sick.'

'Not moving.'

'Not moving at all.'

'But breathing.'

'Yes. In and out.'

'Rattly. Not right.'

'She's still alive? She can't be.' I said. 'Even if she's down there then the sea must have been in several times by now and …'

'We've been holding the tide back.'

'Just a little.'

'Just away from the box.'

'Not strictly allowed.'

'Promised Erasmus there would be no more of that sort of thing.'

'No more interfering in nature.'

'Spoiling the "status quo" he said.'

'Like in Scarborough.'

'And yet.'

'We did it again.'

'But that's the last.'

'Too tired for any more.'

'Tide in ten minutes.'

'Thing will drown, now.'

'Can't help this time.'

'You have to get her out.'

The bottom half of their bodies were now a swirling blue cloud. I glanced over in the direction of the beach and I could see that the tide was definitely coming in. What these women were saying was ridiculous. No one could hold back the sea, could they?

'Is this some sort of trick?' I said.

Edna was just about visible now.

'Doesn't trust us.'

'Why should she?'

'No reason.'

'I mean … if she heard about Scar …'

SHHHHHH

'Not again.'

'What to do though.'

'Show her.'

'Show me what?' I asked. 'Look …'

Agnes held out her hand and there was the pendant.

'That's mine! Where did you get it?'

'You dropped it, dear,' she said … although her mouth started to twist in a rather alarming way.

'We took it.'

'The Kelve.'

'He wants it.'

'We took it.'

'But only to save it.'

'To help you.'

'We want to help.'

Both of their heads were jumping about now, various rectangles and triangles dancing in the air.

'What is happening … to you? I can't see …'

'Take it.'

She held out the pendant to me and I grabbed it, stuffing it into my pocket.

'Find her …'

They were disappearing fast now and their voices were a lot fainter.

'Wait'

'Don't tell Erasmus'

'Don't tell ANYONE!'

Their voices trailed off into the distance and now all I could see was faint blue smoke in the air.

'Hello!' I called. 'Are you still there?'

SHHHHHH

The ground under my feet rumbled a little.

But there was no reply.

Chapter 32

I waited a few more seconds but the women didn't reappear and I couldn't hear the strange noises from underground any more. From where I was standing I could see down to the beach. There was a pillbox just below me, the exact one I had seen in my dreams. Hardly anyone came up on to this stretch of sand and today there was no one around.

I wasn't sure about the Esks, or whatever they called themselves, but they were right about one thing. The tide was coming in. It was already almost reaching the pillbox. Had the Esks really been stopping the water? Could the girl Mr Ward talked about still be alive?

There was no time to run all the way round to the path to get help and even if I had not chucked my phone away it would be no use. I wouldn't want Mr Ward to know what I was about to do. I had to scramble down the cliff.

The sharp teeth of the barbed wire stabbed me as I climbed over. The cliff up at Wyndrift House had been child's play compared to this and climbing down was always more difficult than going up. The boulder clay had large cracks in it and it didn't look safe to stand on.

I hesitated for a second and then moved forward. I slid

almost immediately. I decided the safest way down was to turn around and lower myself with my hands. I had just moved again when I slipped and I felt myself flying through the air. I landed on my back with a thud but my fall had been cushioned by a bank of soft grass that was growing near the bottom. I inched my way down on to the beach.

The pillboxes were grey and ugly and this one was leaning at an odd angle where it had slumped into the sand. There were dark slits in the side for windows and one large entrance door. It was pitch black inside and I couldn't make anything out from where I was standing.

'Hello?' I called.

No reply.

Ribbons of sea water were already snaking up to the entrance.

I picked up a pebble and threw it into the opening. It clattered noisily on to the stones on the other side and I waited.

Nothing.

Maybe there was no one inside.

Or I was too late.

I walked forward cautiously. I could see straight away that there wasn't anyone in the first chamber. I winced at the smell; a combination of seaweed and public toilets. Light was streaming through the window slits, illuminating the pebbles on the floor. There were a few small pools of water but no sign of anyone.

'Hey!' I called. 'Anyone there?'

There was a second room just ahead, through a doorway. It had no window slits and it was much darker in there.

I hesitated.

I touched the walls with my fingers to reassure myself

that this place was real before I went any further. It had been very difficult recently to believe in anything.

My foot struck against something.

A rucksack.

Some of its contents had spilled out on to the pebbles.

A can of coke

A bar of chocolate.

A pink flip flop with a yellow flower.

The same that Abbie had given Mirabel at the cafe?

There was no time to think about that now.

I stuffed them into the bag, closed it and slung it on to my back.

'Hello' I said, very tentatively. 'Are you there?'

I took a deep breath and walked forwards, into the second chamber. Through the darkness I could just make out something, a figure maybe, slumped against the wall.

Someone wearing a hoodie.

The girl from my dreams.

'Hey … are you alright?'

She didn't move.

I edged forward but then I heard someone crunching across the pebbles just outside the hut.

There was nowhere to hide. I cowered behind the wall and held my breath. The best I could hope for was that whoever it was would decide that the place was empty and go away.

'Hello,' came a voice. 'Anyone in here?'

I recognised it immediately. 'WILL!' I yelled, coming out from behind the wall.

He ran up and threw his arms around me. 'Thank God,' he said. 'Are you OK?'

'Of course,' I said. 'How did you find me?'

'Diggleby,' he said. 'He managed to trace you. Why the hell did you leave without saying anything?'

I pulled away from him. 'I'm sorry but I had to.'

'You went to meet Mr Ward didn't you? I thought we agreed we're in this together.'

'I can't explain now. Look, there's a girl in here. Well a sort of girl.'

'Sorry?'

'Let's just say she's not from round here.'

'What do you mean?'

'She's … I know it sounds mad but I think she's … well she's from another world.'

'OK,' said Will, not responding in the way I had expected him to. 'Did she come across that Bridge thing as well?'

'How do you know about that?'

'Erasmus has been telling us. About all the creatures and people and that who come to earth. He thinks Mirabel travelled across a Bridge to get here. How cool is that?'

'And you're OK with it? With all this talk of aliens?'

He hesitated before answering. 'No … but I mean … it sounds crazy but some pretty mad stuff has been happening. And Mirabel … she's definitely different. To be honest, talking to Erasmus has … well it's all making kinda more sense now than before.'

'I know.'

There was the sound of water slapping against the side of the pillbox.

'Look we can talk later,' I said. 'We need to see if we can help this girl.'

He stepped forward and gazed down at her. 'She's very still,' he said.

'I know. I'm hoping that we're not too late.'

'Bloody hell. Shall I go and get Erasmus?'

'There isn't time. We need to take a closer look.'

Will nodded.

I went over to her and bent down. I touched her hand. It was ice cold.

'What do you think?' asked Will.

I leant over her. 'I don't … wait. Hand me your phone.'

He held it out and I grabbed it. I clicked on the torch icon and shone the light over her quickly. As I did so, her eyes flickered slightly just for a second.

The Esks were right. She was alive. But only just.

I turned off the light and handed the phone back to Will. Another wave splashed itself against the side of the pillbox.

'We have to get her out of here right now,' I said.

'Sure.'

'Do you think we can carry her?'

'Yeah, but I'm not sure you're supposed to move people when they're ill, are you? Or is that accidents? I mean …'

'I think she'll be worse off if we leave her to drown, don't you? And asking for help might be tricky. She's not just anyone is she? I wonder …'

I knelt down properly and carefully pulled back her hood. If I could wake her then she could tell us if she was in pain or if she thought anything was broken.

Will flicked the light on again and shone it on the girl.

'Can you see … oh my God, that can't be right,' Will exclaimed dropping his phone. It clattered over the pebbles.

'What the hell's the matter?' I picked up the phone and shone the light around the chamber. 'Did you hear something?'

249

'No. Look at the girl,' he said.

'I have.'

'Really look at her.'

I directed the light towards the girl and held it steady.

'That's … that's not possible,' I said, realising at once what he was looking at. 'There's no way … I mean …'

'Bloody hell,' said Will, leaning over to stare into the girl's face. 'Meg. What the hell is going on?'

The girl in the pillbox was me.

‣

Chapter 33

'You haven't got a twin sister you haven't told me about, have you?'

'Don't be stupid, Will. Of course not.'

'Then who the hell is this?'

He shone the light in the girl's face again and her eyes opened for a moment. I bent down nearer to her and touched her arm. 'Hello!' I said. 'Hello! Can you hear me?'

She raised her hands to her face.

'Move the light, Will! You're blinding her.'

'Yeah. Sorry,' he said. 'Is that better?'

She lowered her arms and closed her eyes.

There was a loud rumble above our heads. 'Thunder,' said Will. 'Erasmus said there would be a storm. And my feet are already getting wet. The water's really coming in fast.'

'We haven't got time to ask her anything now. We need to get going before we all drown. Come on. Let's see if we can get her to stand.'

'Hello,' said Will, leaning down and shaking the girl gently. 'Are you alright? You don't think you might have broken something? Are you in pain?'

To my surprise the girl shook her head. She opened her eyes and then she moved slightly, as though she was trying to get up.

'No, no. Don't do anything,' said Will. 'We'll help you.'

The girl had crammed herself into a corner and there wasn't much room to move. It seemed to take ages to raise her up and by the time we managed to shift her a little, water was already sloshing into the back of the chamber. It began to swirl and foam around our feet. When we reached the entrance I looked out and saw black angry clouds hanging in the sky. The moment we stepped outside, wet spray slapped me in the face, stinging my skin.

I wondered where the Esks were and whether they could hold the water back, just until we reached the path, but I had no idea how to call for their help.

Will tried to pull his jacket around the girl to protect her. We could only inch along. We were getting soaked, not only from the rain that was pounding down now but also from the incoming waves which were breaking over our legs.

It seemed an age before we reached the path and as we stepped out of the water and on to the tarmac, I glanced up. The road looked really steep and I wasn't sure we were going to be able to drag her up with us.

Losing my concentration I almost let the girl slip. Her hoodie was wet through.

'IF YOU WAIT HERE. I'LL GO AND GET ERASMUS!' Will yelled.

'NOT IN THIS STORM! COME ON. KEEP MOVING!'

'WHERE ARE WE GOING NOW?'

'OVER THERE.'

There was a huge flash followed by an enormous crack of thunder and Will nodded. Wyndrift House was already in sight and at least we could shelter. The thought of Mr Ward being there made me shudder but I was convinced that he had only used the house to trap Mirabel. He was hiding somewhere with my mum until tomorrow. I tried not to think about that.

By the time we reached the front door my arms and legs felt like they were about to drop off. I pushed the door but it was locked.

'Damn,' I said. 'Damn, damn, damn.'

'What now?'

The girl raised her head a little.

The door in front of us shimmered for a moment and then vanished. Nothing was surprising me any more. We stumbled into the house and laid the girl down against the wall. When I looked up again the door was back and firmly shut.

We were both too exhausted to be able to speak and all I could hear was the sound of our heavy breathing in the silence of the room.

'She ... the door just disappeared,' said Will at last. 'How ... how did that happen?'

I shook my head, showering droplets of water everywhere. 'I have absolutely no idea,' I said. 'I can't ...'

'Where's everything gone?' interrupted Will. 'What's going on ?'

I looked up. The place was a wreck. There was no sign of furniture, or anything. It was hard to believe it was the same house. Now, old boxes and bits of broken furniture were piled up in one corner and the floor was covered in dust and bits of rubble. It didn't look like anyone had lived here for years. This mess was what I thought I had seen when I looked through the window, the day I rescued Mirabel.

'It wasn't real, Will,' I said. 'The first time we came, Mr Ward stole one of your memories.'

'Bloody hell. You're kidding me? Like at the diner?'

'You said you recognised it and I didn't believe you.'

'How is he doing it though? And why pick on me all the time? I mean …'

The girl let out a sort of groan.

'We could do with something to make her more comfortable. Dry her off at least,' I said. 'See if you can find anything.'

'I'll try the kitchen. Although that's going to look different now, isn't it? That Kelve needs to stay out of my head!'

When he had gone I tried moving some of the junk to see if I could find anything of use but there wasn't anything. I was shivering now and the damp air in the house wasn't helping me to feel better. I glanced back at the girl. Her eyes were still shut but she was moving a little. I hurried over to her and crouched down.

'Are you alright? We're trying to find something to make you more comfortable only …'

'Meg …' she said. 'Meg.'

'Yeah. That's me. How do you know my name?'

She didn't answer.

Chapter 34

Will had come back with blankets, and also said that he'd got a signal in the kitchen. He'd been in touch with Erasmus. They were on their way down to the house.

'How long are they going to be?' I asked.

Mr Ward was probably tracking his phone as well but there was nothing I could do about that. I had to have Mirabel with me by the morning.

'He just said he's on his way.'

'You're going to have to go and get them yourself,' I said.

'In that rain? Look, there's no need to panic. I told Erasmus about finding the girl and he said to try and keep her warm but not to give her anything until we know for definite who she is.'

'Alright. But I still think you should …'

'And I sent a message to Dad.'

'What about?' I asked nervously. 'Will, we can't get him involved in this.'

'I know but he'll be wondering where I am. It's getting late.'

'You didn't tell him …?'

'No. I didn't say anything about what was really going

on. How could I? I told him I was staying over at Tom's tonight to practise with the band. I couldn't tell him the truth. I mean I don't understand anything that's going on. Where would I start?'

I didn't like the thought of Will lying to his Dad but it was likely that any message he had sent was being monitored by Mr Ward anyway. At least Mr Clarke would not be worrying about where Will had got to.

The girl stirred a little and let out another groan.

I knelt down on to the floor beside her but she fell silent again. She was breathing erratically and she looked really ill. 'She's shivering, Will,' I said.

'There's more covers here.'

He picked up another of the blankets he had found and shook it. It wasn't very clean and it was full of holes. Clouds of dust bloomed into the air as he moved it.

'That's weird,' said Will as he tried to wrap it around the girl's shoulders. 'She's dry. I mean, she was sopping wet a moment ago.'

I touched her hoodie. He was right. Bone dry.

'She still feels cold though,' I said, touching her hand for a second. 'I wish we had some better blankets.'

'Do you think I should try and find some water for her or something? I mean … Erasmus said not to but that couldn't do any harm, could it? I don't know anything about … well about people from other worlds.'

'Right. And I'm an expert,' I said sarcastically.

'The weird thing is that … well she doesn't look alienish does she … she looks …'

'Like me. I know.'

'How come?'

'I don't know.'

'Unless she's just made herself look like you. She's one of those things that can change shape? Is that possible, do you think?'

'Nothing seems impossible any more, Will.'

'Perhaps she just saw you or something. Chose someone at random to copy. Made herself look more human.'

'Maybe. Although that's even more freaky. Mr Ward said she looked like me. That must be why he … why he …'

For some reason I had started really shivering now.

'Bloody hell, Meg. Are you alright? Here. Take that wet jacket off. There's one blanket left. It's the worst one but it might be alright.'

I did as he said. I wrapped the blanket around my shoulders. It smelt old and fusty and not a patch on the Carper one that Erasmus had lent me before.

I looked over at the girl and without warning tears sprang into my eyes. I didn't want to cry in front of Will but I suddenly felt really weak and helpless and I wished I could just make all this chaos go away.

'Come on, Meg,' said Will. 'We'll find a way out of this. I promise. Either that or I'm going to wake up in a minute and everything will be back to normal.'

I couldn't speak. Tears were running down my cheeks now whether I wanted them to or not.

'Don't cry. Look, I'm as freaked out as you, but we're in this together. No more trying to do this on your own.' Will came and sat himself beside me. 'I wish you hadn't gone to see Mr Ward by yourself.'

'I had to,' I managed. 'He sent me another message. I couldn't risk him hurting Mum.'

'What did he say to you?'

'Mirabel,' I said, wiping my eyes. 'Just the same. I have to swap Mirabel for Mum. There's no other way.'

Will put his arm on my shoulder.

'I'm not surprised that he wouldn't change his mind,' he said. 'I just wish … I feel like I keep letting you down.'

'You don't. There's nothing anyone can do. He said I had to keep you all out of it.'

'Of course he did. But we're involved now. Did you … I mean do you know if your mum's still ok?'

'I think so. He's trapped her in something called a time pocket. It's like she's been caught in a memory and she just keeps reliving the same thing over and over again.'

'Bloody hell.'

'He's not going to let Mum go until he's got Mirabel.'

'Where is he now? Still at the bungalow?'

'No. That wasn't real either. Those people … the magicians. It was their house but he … he killed them, Will, and took everything they had.'

'He made out he was best mates with them,' said Will, rubbing his hands through his hair. 'I can't believe I was so taken in by him.'

'We've all been fooled by him. This girl was as well. He managed to get her to tell him everything. It seems that Erasmus was right. Mirabel did cross the Bridge and my double was sent over here to take her back.'

'But why? Why did Mirabel come here in the first place?'

'No idea. Neither has Mr Ward but he's convinced that Mirabel is someone important.'

'I don't get it. Any of it. I mean Mirabel just seems like an ordinary kid.'

'She's not though, is she? And even we've seen that she's … well she's different. And that thing in her neck; hiding her memories. There's plenty we don't know about her.'

'That's true. But you haven't told me the rest. How come this girl ended up in the pillbox?'

'Mr Ward said he wanted to take Mirabel back across the Bridge himself. When she wouldn't have that, he attacked her. He thought he'd killed her.'

'It looks as though he almost did. She looks terrible. How did you know where she was?'

The question caught me by surprise. I looked away and started wiping my eyes with my sleeve while I thought about what I could say. I hadn't had a chance to think about how I would explain knowing about the pillbox. I had promised not to say anything about the Esks and I certainly didn't want to be responsible for them ending up on a ghost ship. I seemed to be good at getting things wrong at the moment and I didn't want to break my word.

'Can you … can you find me something to blow my nose on?' I asked.

'Yeah, sure. Sorry.'

He reached into his pocket and pulled out a tissue that was all screwed up and covered in fluff.

'Best I can do, I'm afraid,' he said. 'I'm wondering if I saw a kettle in that kitchen. Maybe I can find some tea as well and …'

'Wait! Don't go. I've just remembered something.'

I got up and walked over to the door to retrieve the rucksack that I had dumped there when we came in. 'Perhaps there's something in here that might tell us who she is.'

'Is that hers?'

'Well I think so. I found it on the floor of the pillbox. Look. Still got its price tag on. *Hunmanby cafe. £3.99.*'

'That's where we were the other day. When we rescued Mirabel.'

'What's that got to do with it?'

'Remember when we met Abbie? She said someone had broken in,' Will said.

I had forgotten that and it was strange to hear the name Abbie again. The real world seemed so far away now. 'I think we've found the thief,' I said, opening the rucksack.

I pulled out the chocolate, the coke and the pink flip flops that I'd stuffed back into her bag. Will picked up the shoes.

'The same colour as the ones Abbie gave Mirabel,' he said. 'Do you remember?'

'No one could forget a pair of flip flops as beautiful as those.'

I delved a bit further into the bag. There were some sticks of rock, a tea towel with 'Recipes from Yorkshire' on it and a box which contained a 'Grow your own Alien' kit.

'These are well cool,' said Will taking it from me. 'They feel gross when you open this little pod thing.'

'Yeah. Odd stuff to nick though. There's a bit more chocolate … wait … there must be about a hundred quid here!'

'Blimey. Anything else?'

'There's another section … let's see what else she's got.'

I unzipped it. And was shocked at what was inside.

My silver bracelet.

My watch.

My diary.

There was another smaller pocket on the inside and in there, wrapped in a soggy tissue was a blue rock from my stone collection. It was one of my favourites. I had collected it years ago on the beach with Dad and we used to joke together about it, pretending it was worth millions. We even planned how we would spend the money.

Looking at it now, in this light, it just looked like any old bit of rock that you would find on any stretch of sand.

'What's all that?' asked Will.

'My stuff. These are all mine!'

'Are you sure?'

'I thought I'd lost the jewellery. And look. It's my writing in the diary if you don't believe me.'

'And that bit of rock?'

'Definitely mine. I know my own stuff. She must have … well she must have been up to the house … into my room and taken all of these things.'

I picked off some of the bits of tissue that had clung to the stone and put it into my pocket, then started to collect the other items that were mine.

'What are you doing?' Will asked.

'Getting my things back.'

'You can't do that.'

'Why on earth not?'

'She'll know we've been in her bag.'

'So?'

'So it's not right. Look, just put them back and we'll ask her when she's awake.'

'That's ridiculous,' I said. 'They're mine.'

'I know. But you'll get them back. Isn't it better to know why she took them? Maybe she had a good reason.'

'Like what?'

The girl must have heard us arguing. She stirred slightly, although her eyes stayed firmly shut.

'Meg, please. She's exhausted. We can talk to her when she's stronger.'

I stuffed the jewellery back into the bag reluctantly. I took the stone out of my pocket but instead of putting that in, I picked up a piece of rubble from the floor that was about the same size.

'What are you doing?'

'She'll never know,' I said. 'And this one is my favourite. Can I at least keep my diary?'

'I think you should put it back, for now.'

'Well, she'd better not have read it.'

'Why? What's in it?'

'Nothing.' I felt myself blushing. 'At least not anything I want anyone else to read.'

Chapter 35

I could hear Will moving around in the kitchen. He'd said he was going to try to find us something to eat and drink, even though it was obvious there wouldn't be anything in there. The girl was still sleeping and actually I was glad he had gone. I felt that I just needed to be completely by myself for a bit.

I headed towards the stairs and found myself climbing up to what had been Mirabel's room. It was empty, of course. There was a suffocating damp smell and I walked over to the large glass doors. It would have been nice to stand on the balcony but they were locked. It was horrible in here but I didn't want to go downstairs again. Not yet.

I sank to the floor and stared out at the beach.

I had forgotten how far you can see along the coastline from Happy Valley. The storm had passed and the sky was clear. There was no one at all now on the wide expanse of sand and I think I had never felt so lonely in the whole of my life. Dad, Mum, the life I used to lead seemed so far away and I longed to be back at home, where I felt safe and where everything made sense.

I took the pendant out of my pocket and laid it on the

floor in front of me. The crystal in the centre was still for a moment but the more I stared at it, the more it lost its solid appearance and I could see small flickers of lights blinking beneath the surface.

'You alright?'

Will's appearance made me jump.

'Not really,' I said, instinctively picking up the pendant.

'Can I get a proper look at that? I didn't really see it up close before.'

'It's more than a pendant,' I said. 'Mr Ward told me it's what Mirabel used to get over the Bridge. The girl downstairs had one too.'

'Bloody hell. How does it work then?' he asked leaning in to take a closer look.

'No idea.'

'I don't see how something as small as that can actually do anything. Can I hold it?'

I nodded and handed it to him. I felt reluctant to let it go and I was uneasy as Will turned the pendant over in his hands.

'I don't get it,' he said at last. 'It just looks like a stone in a cage. Are you sure you're right?'

'I think you have to connect to it in some way,' I said, remembering snatches of what Mr Ward had told me. 'It does kind of make you feel connected to it when you hold it, doesn't it? Like it's waiting for you to tell it to do things. Does that make sense?'

'Not really,' said Will. 'I'll take your word for it. It's a nice looking thing though.'

Much to my relief, he handed it back to me.

I stared at the crystal in the centre for a moment, wanting something to happen, to prove I was right.

Nothing.

I held it up to the window and I noticed again that there was something odd about the way it was reflecting the light.

'I wish I knew how to use it,' I said.

I thought I could see more colours now, swirling around in the crystal. The shapes were stronger and more definite. It reminded me of looking through the telescope at the Bridge, and I remembered how Erasmus said that you sometimes had to look at things differently.

Retina recognition complete

Identified user is Megan Rowlands.

A female voice sounded from somewhere in the depths of the crystal and I dropped it on to the floor.

'What's the matter?' asked Will.

'Someone … spoke to me.'

'I didn't hear anything.'

'Not out loud … I mean …'

'Try it again.'

I picked it up again tentatively.

Welcome Megan Rowlands

Please select an option.

Option? What options were there? There was nothing to select.

How can I help you today?

Where do I start, I thought?

The usual place to start is the beginning.

'It's answering me, Will. It's actually answering my questions without me saying anything out loud.'

'You're kidding. How is it doing that?'

'I don't know. But it knows who I am. I swear I'm not making it up.'

'No, I believe you. Try asking it something again.'

'What?'

'I dunno. The weather or the news or …'

'Maybe I should ask something about Mr Ward,' I said. 'If the people over the Bridge know about Kelves then maybe I can find out something more about him. Something that might help us.'

'It's worth a go,' said Will.

I concentrated hard.

Nothing.

'It's not working now,' I said.

'You were really staring at it before.'

'OK.' I focused and tried to find the lights again. It took a bit longer this time.

'Mr Ward,' I said aloud. 'What do you know about Alfred Ward?'

'NEGATIVE. NO MATCH AVAILABLE FOR ALFRED WARD.'

The voice was so loud we both jumped.

'Well that worked,' said Will. 'I think you may need to lower the volume though.'

'I would if I knew how.'

'Never mind. Ask it something else.'

'Mirabel,' I said. 'Who is Mirabel Kendrick?'

There was a long pause and I was just about to repeat the question when the voice sounded out again.

'THE PRESIDENT REQUIRES AN UPDATE OF YOUR SITUATION.

PLEASE ENTER AUTHORISATION CODE IMMEDI-ATELY.'

Chapter 36

'What is this place?'

The girl was standing in the doorway with her rucksack slung over her shoulder. Neither of us had heard her come up the stairs.

I slipped the pendant into my pocket.

'Sorry?' Will said, turning around. 'We … we thought you were still asleep.'

She didn't answer.

Her hood was down now and I could see her clearly. Her skin was a pale grey colour and under her eyes were dark circles, almost like bruises. Despite that, and the fact that her hair lacked the bright orange streak, there was no doubt about it. She did look like me. Exactly like me.

She held on to the door frame for support but she didn't speak.

'I'm Meg,' I said, getting up and moving towards her. 'And this is Will.'

'Hi,' said Will. 'You look like you need to sit down.'

Again there was no response.

We both moved over to her and helped her to lower

herself on to the floor. She put the rucksack by her side and slumped back against the wall.

'We rescued you from the pillbox,' said Will. 'Do you know how you got in there?'

'The Kelve's … the Kelve's not here, is he?' she asked, looking agitated.

'No way,' said Will. 'No. Relax. Honest. I promise you're safe with us.'

'I feel dizzy,' she said, closing her eyes.

'You shouldn't have tried to move so soon,' said Will. 'And we should have come downstairs to check on you.'

There was silence between us for a moment.

'Would you like us to get you anything?' asked Will.

Her eyes flicked open. 'What is this place?' she muttered.

She looked like me but I didn't think she sounded like me. Mind you, on the few occasions I'd heard myself, I didn't think I sounded like me, either.

'This is Wyndrift House,' Will said. 'We dived in here to get out of the rain. Don't you remember?'

But the girl didn't answer. She seemed to drift off to sleep again.

'Do you think she's alright?' whispered Will at last.

'I don't know,' I said.

'It's freaking me out that she looks so much like you. Do you think she's some sort of shape shifter or something?'

The girl's eyes opened again. 'A shape shifter …?' she asked. 'Is that something native to this region?'

'No,' said Will. 'No. We just … well we don't get why you look so much like Meg.'

She gazed at both of us with an air of disbelief. 'Isn't it obvious?' she said.

'Well, no,' I said. 'Not at all.'

She didn't say anything else but she looked around the room as though she was taking it in for the first time.

'You came from over the Bridge, didn't you?' I asked.

Again she didn't answer but continued to stare at her surroundings. 'Everything is so … primitive in this world,' she said at last. 'I don't know how you live like this.'

'This is not a proper house,' said Will. 'Not like we have here. On earth, I mean. Well it's proper but no one actually lives here.'

'We just brought you to the nearest place we could find,' I explained.

'It isn't very nice,' she said. 'I'm not very comfortable.'

'Like Will said, no one actually lives here. It was the best we could do.'

I hadn't wanted thanks for rescuing her, but I hadn't expected her to complain about her accommodation.

'I can't stay long,' she said, trying to push herself up. 'I have to go and find someone.'

'Yeah. We know,' I said. 'But you can relax. She's safe with us.'

'What do you mean?'

She was clearly still very weak and she slid back to the floor.

'We've been looking after Mirabel.'

'I don't believe you,' she said, her face suddenly very alert.

'She came to us on Friday.'

'That can't be true. Why would she come to you?'

'I meant she was brought to us, well to my house.'

'Then where is she now?'

'I'll tell you when you explain to us what this is all about. We know you came here to find her but we don't know why. And we know you met with Mr Ward …'

'I should have killed the Kelve when I had the chance,' she said angrily, interrupting me. 'He caught me off guard. I should never have trusted him but I didn't realise he was a Kelve until it was too late.'

I thought about how there were moments when I had been dragged into Mr Ward's poor old man act. That was before I realised he would stop at nothing to get what he wanted.

'How did I get here?' she asked. 'How did you find me?'

'You were in a pillbox on the beach,' Will said. 'A few more minutes and the tide would have been in. You were lucky Meg was around. We carried you here and …'

'I have had some unfortunate experiences, it is true,' she said, not looking at either of us. 'But I have learned my lesson now. I trusted someone who meant me harm. I won't make that mistake again.'

'You can trust us,' said Will.

'I hardly think so. I don't need your help. The fact is that I would have found a way out myself,' she said. 'I'm extremely resourceful. That's why I was chosen specifically for this mission and I won't let a simple Kelve or any inferior life forms get in my way from now on.'

'By that you mean us?' I asked.

'If you like.'

'Then maybe we should have left you in the pillbox to fend for yourself,' I said. I was getting really annoyed now.

'I don't need you,' she said. 'I don't need anyone.'

She tried to get to her feet again but there was no way

she had the strength to stand. I was certainly not going to help her.

Will moved towards her but she waved him away. 'I can do this myself,' she insisted.

'It looks like you are managing just fine,' I said sarcastically, watching her struggle.

She slipped back on to the floor.

'I think you should maybe try to stop talking for a while,' said Will sitting down again.

'You said you know where Mirabel is,' the girl went on, ignoring him.

I wasn't going to tell her anything but Will jumped in before I could stop him. 'We've met a professor called Erasmus and he has a robot called Diggleby with him,' he said. 'They're taking care of her. They know all about the Bridge. They'll be here any minute.'

'And the pendant? Mirabel had a pendant with her. Does she still have it?'

Will looked across at me. He couldn't expect me just to hand it over.

'No, I have it,' I said. 'But it's staying with me. I'm not convinced that Mirabel is any safer with you than with Mr Ward. He's ...' I was about to tell her about Mum but I stopped. We had said too much already. 'Look, we don't know anything about you. You say you don't trust us but why should we trust you when you won't even tell us who you are?'

She didn't say anything for a while. Then she nodded.

'Very well,' she said.

She reached into her pocket and brought out a small disc, the same size as a two pound coin but with a slightly domed top, rose gold in colour. Its surface was completely smooth apart from a small crystal set into the very top. It reminded me of the one in the pendant and it glinted a little as she placed it on the palm of her hand.

'Now if you are too … too unintelligent to work this out for yourself then I will have to show you.'

The disc started to spin slowly and glimmering lights flowed upwards, swirling and spiralling into the air. Now they were forming into distinct shapes, fitting together like the pieces of a 3D jigsaw. At last a large black and grey rectangular building with huge glass windows came into view.

'The Science Institute,' she said. 'The greatest place in the universe.'

'We've heard that name before,' said Will. 'Do you remember, Meg? Mirabel told us her aunt works there. We even tried to find where it was but …'

'Of course her aunt is there,' snapped the girl. 'Be quiet and watch.'

The building turned slowly and more shapes started to emerge. A tall glass tower appeared in the centre. There was something about the place that was familiar, glimpses of other buildings in the background that I felt I had seen before.

'You could never have anywhere exactly like this,' the girl continued, as though she was reading my thoughts. 'We have made so much more of our talents and resources. Our universe may be parallel to yours but our advancements outweigh yours considerably.'

'What did you just say?' I asked.

Suddenly the building started to collapse in front of my

eyes and the light streamed back into the disc she was holding.

'A parallel universe!' exclaimed Will. 'Of course. That's it! You come from a parallel universe! That's why you look like Meg, isn't it?'

'Oh my God,' I said. 'That's why I recognised some of the buildings. Your world, the world over the Bridge. It's is the same as this one and … you … you're me.'

'That is an oversimplification. But if it helps you to understand, then fine.'

I stared over at her. 'Bloody hell,' I said. 'You're kidding! That's incredible!'

'There are two Megs!' shouted Will. 'You're meeting yourself! How amazing is all this?'

'So you're exactly the same as me,' I said excitedly. 'You have the same family and you like the same things and …'

I stopped. My eyes caught sight of her rucksack lying by her side.

The jewellery and diary.

Did she own the same things as me?

I was about to say something when I realised I couldn't admit I'd been snooping around.

'Meg … Meg,' she said. 'Please. I really don't feel well and your hysteria is overwhelming. And you are mistaken. Things don't work exactly like that. Parallel yes … but I am not the same as you. Not exactly.'

'No, I can see that,' I said, suddenly feeling deflated.

The girl was so much ruder than me, even on my worst days.

'None of us are the same now,' she went on.

'What do you mean?'

'It's to do with choice. Someone may have chosen to go left when you turned right. And since we discovered …' She stopped. 'Well, let's just say that we have been able to make advancements that you could not even imagine. Our world is superior to yours in every way.'

To my amazement we both pushed a hand through our fringes at the same time.

'This is so … well it's totally awesome!' said Will. 'Do you know me, then? I mean over there. Me as in another Will. Like me but someone else …'

She shook her head.

'You must know him,' I said. 'He should be your best friend. If the worlds are parallel …'

'It doesn't work like that,' she said. 'I told you. We have emerged from our primitive state and we have made progress in science and technology that you could not even begin to think of down here.'

'So what kind of things have you got?' asked Will. 'Flying cars and that? Maybe …'

The girl raised her hand. 'I have no interest in discussing this with you and there is no time. I have to complete my mission and I … I seem to have got myself … things haven't worked out as planned,' she said. 'Ridiculous as it may seem, you are perhaps correct. I do need some help from you.'

'Sure, Meg. Anything,' said Will.

'And my name is Megan,' she said. 'At least you could get that right. Now …' She started to cough and for a few seconds she was unable to say anything else.

'Are you alright?' asked Will.

'Could you … could you get me something to drink?'

Megan stuttered. 'I think that would help to strengthen me. I can usually help myself much more than this but without the pendant ...'

Will looked over at me but I shook my head. Some things were making more sense now but there was no way I was handing it over. Not yet.

She reached into her pocket and brought out a small clear bag. Inside were some blue capsules.

'What are they?' asked Will.

'Drop one of these in my water. It ensures it's ... it's clean,' she managed. 'Don't touch them. I don't want to catch any infection from you.' She held out the bag for him. 'They contain crushed Pamphilion flowers,' she went on. 'You must have heard of them, surely?'

'No,' said Will. 'But ...'

'Well go and do as I say,' she snapped. 'Surely you are able to follow simple instructions?'

'I'll do my best.'

'Why is everyone in this universe so ridiculously slow?' she asked, after Will had gone.

I was seriously hoping that I was not as annoying as my double.

Chapter 37

'You didn't explain how you found me,' Megan said, after Will had gone. 'How did you know I was on the beach?'

'Maybe I'm cleverer than you think,' I said.

She was staring at me intently. It was beyond incredible that I was meeting an alternative version of myself and there was so much I wanted to ask her. But Megan was obnoxious and difficult to talk to. More importantly, Mum was still with Mr Ward and we were no nearer to coming up with a plan to get her back.

'We have to decide what to do next,' I said.

'I don't understand. Will told me that Mirabel was on her way. And you have her pendant. As soon as she comes, I will go and find the Kelve and make him return mine. I will be better prepared this time.'

'How?'

She didn't answer.

I needed to tell her what had happened to Mum but even the thought of it brought that tight knot back into my stomach.

'You can't take Mirabel,' I said. 'We have rescued her from Mr Ward but ... but ... he's taken my mum. He's put her in a time loop. Unless I go down to the beach tomorrow with Mirabel and the pendant then … I can't see that I have a choice.'

'There's always a choice,' Megan said. 'How could you have got into this mess?'

'I don't think you can blame me,' I snapped. 'I wasn't the one who started this. If you hadn't come here or even if you'd not been so easily conned by Mr Ward then …'

'The information you have given me certainly complicates things.'

'So? What do you think?'

'You are raising your voice and your face is flushed with red. I really don't see that getting so emotional is helping. I have always felt that it is better to solve a problem logically.'

'THEN THINK OF SOMETHING!'

My voice echoed around the room and I was annoyed with myself for losing it. I turned away from her and stared out of the window for a moment, even though it was getting dark now and there was nothing to see.

I needed to calm down.

Megan took a deep breath. I turned to look at her and saw that her eyes were brighter and she seemed a little stronger.

'You're right,' I said at last, trying to hold it together. 'I know I am being emotional. But this is my mum we're talking about. And I honestly don't know what to do. You must understand something of the way I'm feeling, surely? You can't be all that different to me.'

'The Science Institute has taught me to be able to control my feelings,' she said, her voice much clearer now. 'To work things out carefully and precisely before committing to any decision.'

Like with Mr Ward, I thought, but I didn't want to get into another argument.

'It's an honour to be part of such a remarkable place,' she went on. 'And I have to make the most of my opportunities. You cannot imagine how much we are learning. The next stage is time travel. I have to be a part of that.'

'Very exciting. And it would be amazing to talk to you about all of this stuff. But …'

'We probably were similar once,' she said. 'Perhaps when we were children. I have obviously taken a different path since then. I have concentrated on my studies and I have tried to better myself.'

'Yeah. Well I work hard too but that's … look you must still have parents. And if it was your mum that Mr Ward had got, then you'd be trying to do something, right?'

'You don't understand. Things are different for me.'

'How? They've managed to suck all the feelings out of your body?'

'Don't be absurd. But I am clearly much better at controlling myself than you are. I see a clearer picture. I don't know what your mother is like, but mine was always too sentimental. She was against me going to the Institute, even though it was obvious that I was very gifted. We haven't spoken in years.'

'Why not? Isn't it allowed?'

'Only if you put in a request. But why would I do that? She's a very dull, ordinary person. She didn't realise how important it was that I fulfilled my potential.'

Megan was so full of herself and it was hard listening to

her. She looked like me but that was where the similarity ended. My relationship with my mum might be rocky at times but I couldn't imagine what life would be like without her.

'The law stated that children with special gifts should be reported to the Institute,' Megan went on. 'Even my father refused to support me. I walked all the way there by myself and told them I was ready to be accepted into the training program.'

'How old were you?'

'Eight.'

'And your mum and dad didn't come and find you? Bring you back?'

'They knew where I was and by then it was too late. I was already registered. I couldn't let them prevent me from following my dreams. Working for the President is the biggest honour anyone can have.'

'Is that who runs the Institute?'

'Of course. Only he controls everything now. He has to.'

'What do you mean?'

'The system changed when I was little. The President realised how slow things can be relying on governments and systems and all of that. When he took over completely, our whole world was transformed. I can't expect you to understand how advanced we are now. How advanced I am in comparison to you.'

'No I can't. Look, I don't get most of what you're telling me to be honest. Our lives are so different and maybe I'm a bit thick, like you keep saying. But if you are so much more intelligent than me then surely you'll be able to help? Think of a way out of all this?'

She stared at me for a moment as if she was contemplating her answer carefully. 'Your domestic situation is of no interest to me.'

'I don't care what you're interested in!' My voice rose to a shout again. 'This is *your* fault and whether you like it or not you are going nowhere until we can find a solution. You don't care about my mum. I don't care about your mission!'

'Here we are,' Will said cheerfully as he came back into the room, his mood wildly at odds with what was going on between Megan and me. 'I hope I've done it right.'

He handed her the water and she drank in big gulps.

I got to my feet. 'I'm going to find Erasmus,' I said. 'Will, you need to stand guard over Megan while I talk to him.'

'Stand guard? What are you on about? What's going on?'

'You're being ridiculous,' said Megan. 'You can't keep me prisoner. I don't have to do anything you say.'

'You have no choice. Let me spell it out for you. Mirabel is staying with me, the pendant is staying with me and you are staying in this room until *I* decide what to do.'

'These outbursts are not helpful.'

'Maybe not. But I'm not the same as you. I have feelings. I came to find you because I thought you were going to die,' I said, unable to contain my frustration any longer. 'When you told me how brilliant you were I stupidly thought that you were going to be able to help us. If I'd known what an arrogant, selfish brat you were I'd have left you to rot in the pillbox.'

'Give me that pendant! If I have to take it by force then I will!'

She tried to raise herself up but she wasn't strong enough.

Before I had the chance to say any more, the front door slammed.

'They're here,' Will said.

'Don't let Megan out of this room,' I said. 'I have to talk to Erasmus.'

Chapter 38

Diggleby was standing in the front room with his head bowed. He had obviously been caught in the storm earlier and he was dripping all over the floor. He didn't move or acknowledge me and I wondered if his circuits had been damaged by the water or something.

'Where have you been?' I asked. 'We really need you.'

He didn't say anything but he raised his head.

'Where's Erasmus?' I asked. 'And Mirabel? Why aren't they with you?'

'They are on their way. I was sent on ahead,' he said at last.

He was staring at me but there were odd glimmers of lights in his eyes that I hadn't noticed before.

'How long will they be?' I asked. 'I need to talk to them.'

His mouth opened slowly but no sound came out.

'I said … how long will they be?'

He didn't seem to understand me.

'Are you … are you alright?' I asked, approaching him cautiously.

He attempted a smile.

'Perfectly … I … if you will excuse me … I am … there seems to be a problem.'

His eyes snapped shut and he didn't move at all for a few seconds. I thought he had stopped breathing until I realised that he had never started breathing because he was a robot.

He did look incredibly lifelike. I reached out to touch the surface of the skin on his face. It was ice cold. Without warning his eyes opened and I sprang back.

'Ah, Meg. There you are. Problem solved. I understand there is an emergency.'

'Yes but you've been ages … never mind. There's someone upstairs you need to meet. She says she crossed the Bridge looking for Mirabel. She told us she's from a parallel universe.'

'I understand.'

'She's me. Me from another dimension.'

'Yes.'

His lack of any surprise made me wonder if he had any idea what I was talking about.

'She calls herself Megan.'

'Yes.'

'So you already knew?'

'Not about the girl. But the likelihood of an alternative dimension has been …'

'Then why did Erasmus say you didn't know what was over the Bridge?'

'He would have been correct in stating that we did not *know*. Only that we *suspected*.' He stared at me blankly and although I knew that he was just a robot, I was sure I'd seen much more expression in his face previously.

'I have brought some tea and milk with me and a rather nice Victoria sponge,' he went on. 'Rhubarb and …'

'Diggleby,' I said. 'FOCUS!'

He blinked frantically and his head twitched. 'My apologies. You were saying something about someone travelling across the Bridge?'

'Yes. But ...'

Suddenly the voice sounded out from the depths of the pendant.

STATUS UPDATE REQUIRED.

'What is that?' asked Diggleby staring around in alarm. 'I do not believe it was from my systems ...'

'No. No. Don't panic. It's from this.' I pulled the pendant out of my pocket and held it out to him. 'Mirabel used this to travel across the Bridge. I seem to have activated it somehow. Have you seen one before?'

Diggleby's expression changed completely. A broad grin spread over his face and to my surprise he clapped his hands. 'Marvellous! Wonderful! May I hold it?'

I nodded and passed it to him. He turned it over carefully in his hands but he didn't say anything.

'It ... it seems to know what I'm thinking,' I said.

'You are able to respond telepathically? You must be very gifted, Meg. It usually takes years of practice to be able to do that.'

'I've only asked it basic questions.'

'Even so. That is impressive. These devices are designed to help you access a vast store of information,' he said 'But even when you are into the system, negotiating its many levels can be tricky. It takes great skill and this one is different to the ones I have encountered before. The crystal in the centre is not something I can identify.'

'I know it seems crazy but it's a bit like when I looked

into the Bridge. There are lights and … maybe I should try again,' I said, holding out my hand so that he could return the pendant.

He didn't move.

'You may have been able to get the device to recognise you and link you to the system but I would advise caution. It will be protected by numerous security features and if you try to access the restricted areas of the device, you might be detected.'

'You mean you have to have passwords or codes or something?'

'Sometimes. But some ask for memories that you have to feed in telepathically. If you get anything wrong at that stage, the communicator might lock you out permanently. It would most certainly trigger an alarm to whoever is in charge.'

'I just feel that it can help us in some way.'

'Even if we do access the data there is no guarantee it will be of any use.' He stopped. 'I once …'

'You know how to get into this, don't you? I knew you would. Please. I need any information you can find.'

Diggleby looked at me. 'Erasmus … he … I have already said too much to you and he would not approve of … I am under strict orders not to … If I interfere with this technology without express permission, I am breaching all sorts of laws. Agreements that stretch way beyond this universe. If I am caught they could decommission me.'

'Please,' I begged. 'Erasmus isn't even here yet and I won't say anything. It'll be our secret.'

I seemed to be keeping a lot of those lately.

'Secrets are a human attribute,' he said. 'I don't …'

'I see.' I held out my hand for the pendant again. Diggleby looked confused. 'Sorry. I just didn't realise,' I said.

'What?' said Diggleby.

'That this is too difficult for you. You are right. It is a very advanced piece of technology and I shouldn't expect you to be able to access it.'

I wasn't sure if it was possible for a robot to look peeved but Diggleby did. He was furious at the insinuation that he wasn't clever enough to help me.

'Give me a second,' he said. 'I could try something.'

He was actually grinning now. He moved his hand carefully over the gold cage. There was a faint click. 'Of course, we have to keep this strictly between ourselves ...' he said.

'Won't say a word.'

'A secret, you say?'

'Absolutely.'

'Now,' he said. 'Let's have a proper look. Hold out your hand. Palm flat.'

He put the pendant on the counter and he placed the crystal right in the centre of my hand. I was shaking so much it was difficult to keep steady.

'Now hold out your other hand,' he said.

He unscrewed the tip of his forefinger and placed it on my other palm.

The finger was soft and cold and it was all I could do not to gag. I tried to focus on what Diggleby was doing instead. In the place where his finger had been there were now what looked like three tiny screwdrivers, the ends of which glowed alternately green and blue.

'I was once owned by some very unsavoury characters on Lutra 43,' he whispered. 'They taught me ... well a few tricks of their trade … I have never mentioned it to Erasmus, you understand?'

I nodded. I couldn't speak and I couldn't move. I was afraid to look into the crystal in case it communicated with me again and I was trying not to think of the soft finger on my other hand.

He leaned towards me and one of the mini screwdrivers touched the crystal. The stone turned blue for a second and then a bright orange spark flew out. I almost dropped the thing.

'Careful!' he said. 'You must keep absolutely still. This may take several attempts.'

'Can't we just put it on the worktop?'

'I may need to use your connection with it to get us started. You have to hold steady.'

He touched the crystal again and this time it turned bright green. 'That's better,' he said. 'Won't be long now.'

He didn't move for what seemed like an age but eventually he lifted the screwdriver away from the stone and it returned to normal.

'There now. You may put it back into its cage. I have downloaded as much as I dare,' he said. 'Some of the information is too heavily encrypted for me to access safely and it is not reacting like anything I have seen before. The energy being transmitted is very powerful for such a small object. Hopefully, no one should know we have been inside.'

I was glad to put his finger down at last. I retrieved the pendant and opened the cage. I carefully let the crystal drop back into its resting place.

The robot was unscrewing his left hand. He pulled it off

and laid it on the counter beside his finger. 'Almost ready now,' he said.

A white light shot out from his wrist and on to the wall. Immediately a series of yellow numbers on a blue background scrolled round and round in a dizzying sequence.

'What's that?' I asked.

'Nothing to worry about. I'll just …' He stopped and banged his right hand down on the table. 'This is the part, I think … yes … here we are.'

An image came into view. It was definitely the beach at Scarborough, I recognised the promenade but all the shops were boarded. There were several large digging machines lined up on the sands and sections had been divided by barbed wire fences. There was a row of cone-shaped lights leading down to the sea.

'That's … that's what I saw in my dream,' I said. 'The sand was horrible, like that. Kind of black and sludgy. I didn't see those lights though.'

'They are for security. No one is allowed on this beach, now.'

'This isn't … I mean this isn't the Scarborough I know, is it? Are we actually seeing what's over the Bridge?'

'I believe so. There is a sign with information … wait … yes … it says that the only people allowed into the town are those authorised by the Science Institute. I think we should be able to see it in a moment.' He flicked on to a different image. 'Ah, yes. Here it is.'

The building that Megan had showed us, the one with the huge glass windows came into view.

'That's it,' I said. 'That's where she comes from.'

'The rest is more of the same,' Diggleby said. 'Many excavations and tests are taking place throughout the whole area. My conclusion would be that they are looking for something.'

'What?'

'I cannot tell. But Filey seems to be next on the list for something called "Evacuation and Reassignment".'

'What the hell does that mean?'

'I'm afraid that there are several planets I could name who have advanced technology beyond the bounds of expectation but at terrible cost. I can name at least ten planets which are completely uninhabitable now and one where the only remaining creatures are living entirely below ground. Indeed in Calvi ...'

'Diggleby,' I interrupted. 'This is fascinating but we don't have time.'

'Yes. Of course. My apologies.'

'What else can you tell me about Megan's world?'

'The next images are of an area you call "The North York Moors," I believe. There are a few researchers in the area but other than that ... no one. I believe the people have been rehoused further north and their properties have been destroyed. It would seem that most of the scientists sent from the Institute have not found whatever it is they are looking for and have moved on.'

Mum and Dad had taken me on several walks on the Moors and although I had moaned that there was nothing there, I do remember it being very green with trees and huge patches of bright purple heather everywhere. In Megan's world, the hills were brown and scarred with deep lines. Blackened stumps seemed all that was left of the forests; grey clouds of smoke were still rising from the ground into the murky sky.

Megan had boasted about their advancements but she had not mentioned any of this.

'What the hell happened?' I asked.

'There are more views of the same devastation all the way up to Whitby if you would care to take a look.'

'No. Let's move on. I want to look at the Science Institute again.'

'I think I can … I can zoom in, if that helps.'

Diggleby adjusted his hand. The picture was grainy and it wasn't as clear as the image Megan had conjured up, but it was definitely the place she had shown me.

'Can we look inside that tower?'

'I have not been able to gain access,' he said. 'And I dare not go back into the crystal.'

'Well … can you find out anything … anything at all about Mirabel or her aunt? About what happened to them? Her name's Rhiannon. Rhiannon Kendrick.'

Diggleby nodded. 'There's something …'

'What?'

His voice became mechanical now, as though he was reading a school report or something. 'Rhiannon Kendrick. Human. Theoretical Physicist Level 1. Gifted. Status: Powers of time travel and telepathy removed. Prisoner for treason. Awaiting execution.'

'What? That can't be right.'

'Mirabel Kendrick. Human. Student. Gifted. Status: Missing. Sightings to be reported directly to the President.'

'Is there any more?'

Diggleby shook his head. 'I dared not go any further in,'

he said. 'I did not access the material for long but apparently there has been an amount of unrest. Some objections to the President's ideas which have not gone well. A series of protests have ensued and been dealt with most violently, I'm afraid.'

'And Rhiannon is in the centre of it?'

'I cannot confirm the details, but it is possible. The facts tell us that Mirabel's aunt is a gifted scientist and she is clearly in trouble.'

'It mentioned time travel. The girl upstairs talked about that, too.'

'Indeed. It would appear that the society over the Bridge is way ahead of us in terms of scientific discovery although why, I cannot say. Nor do I know why they are arresting some of their most eminent scientists.'

'What if … what if Rhiannon Kendrick knew she was about to be arrested and she sent Mirabel across the Bridge to keep her safe?'

'I cannot confirm that theory. But I can tell you that Ms Kendrick is certainly responsible for the invention of the pendants. She has been given many awards, it seems.'

'So she gave a pendant to Mirabel to help her to escape?'

'There is nothing here to suggest that. But your theory might help to explain something else we have forgotten about.'

'What?'

'The device in Mirabel's neck. The one designed to suppress her memory. Her aunt could certainly have provided her with such a thing and if she wanted her to start a new life, it would be expedient to have done so.'

We fell silent for a moment. If this was Mirabel's story, it was an incredible one and it bore no resemblance to the newspaper report that Will and I had found on the laptop. In Megan's world, although Rhiannon and Mirabel had obviously not been lost in some freak accident, they were definitely in trouble now.

'We'd better not say anything to Mirabel about any of this when she arrives,' I said. 'Not about her aunt. Like you said. She can't remember most of it, which is for the best.'

'More secrets?'

''Fraid so.'

There was a loud blip, more numbers scrolled across the wall and then suddenly Mum was on the screen in front of me.

'What the hell's this?'

'I don't know,' said Diggleby. 'I seem to have accessed another file unintentionally.'

Mum was wearing that stupid flowery jacket she'd bought recently and the skirt that doesn't go with it.

'My apologies. I shall try to get back to where we were.'

'No … wait. I want to see.'

This time, I was watching a video of me in my school uniform, standing in the garden. I was holding an ice lolly. It was melting all down me and I could hear us both laughing. 'These are all from Mum's phone,' I said. 'How did that get there? What's going on?'

The light snapped off. Diggleby picked up his hand from the counter. 'I am sorry. That's all I could do …'

He stopped and his hand fell to the floor. I saw a bright white light flicker in his eyes a couple of times and then his mouth dropped open. 'Diggleby!' I said, touching his arm cautiously. 'Diggleby! Are you alright?'

The robot remained motionless for a few more seconds

until his mouth snapped shut and his head spun around a couple of times.

I stepped back from him quickly.

Someone must have found out we what we were doing.

'Diggleby!' I shouted. 'Diggleby! Speak to me! What's happening?'

'I am … I am … I am …' His head turned to the front and his eyes flashed around the room, as though he was looking for something. 'I am … I am … perfectly fine.'

'You don't look it.'

His head stopped moving and his eyes dulled again. 'No need for concern,' he said, his voice back to normal. 'Just a slight problem with some of my programs today. Absolutely nothing to worry about.'

'Are you sure? You didn't seem to be able to hear me or anything for a minute there and your eyes …'

'A temporary malfunction only,' he said.

'Maybe it was because of the pendant. If someone knows what we've been doing …'

'There is no possibility of that, I assure you,' said Diggleby, sounding really annoyed. He bent down and retrieved his hand from the floor and put it on the worktop. 'And I would thank you to have a little more faith in my abilities. I have done this sort of thing many times before, as I told you and …'

He didn't finish what he was saying. An ear piercing whine came out of his mouth.

'Diggleby!' I shouted. 'What's happening now?'

He didn't answer. The sound was so high pitched that I had to cover my ears. 'DIGGLEBY!' I yelled. 'Can you turn that off? It's deafening and …'

The noise stopped instantly and the room fell silent.

'I'm going to find Erasmus,' I said. 'Something's happening to you and …'

'I am 95% operational at this moment,' he snapped. 'But I think agreeing to help you was a mistake. When Erasmus arrives I have to insist that you say nothing about what happened here.'

'Of course not,' I said.

I wouldn't mention the pendant but I was going to explain that there was something very wrong with the way Diggleby was behaving. Stuffing the pendant back into my pocket, I headed towards the door but it slammed shut. The lock clicked.

'What's going on?' I said furiously. I swung round to face the robot. 'Did you do that?'

'I'm afraid it was necessary,'

'Open this door!'

Diggleby was walking towards me. The bright light had returned to his eyes and it was blinding me.

'What … what's going on? What are you doing?

Suddenly he stopped walking. He smiled.

I turned and pulled at the door but it was fastened tight. I tried kicking at it but it was no use.

'I thought you might like to know I've not forgotten you.'

I swung round. That was not Diggleby. He was speaking but it was Mr Ward's voice that was coming out of his mouth.

'Diggleby!' I cried. 'DIGGLEBY! Wake up! Come back! You need to stop him! Mr Ward …'

I didn't finish because the whining noise had started

again and I was forced to cover my ears. I slipped down against the door and huddled against it, willing the sound to stop.

When it did, my ears were still ringing and I didn't move. Diggleby was standing over me, his brightly lit eyes boring down. I raised my arms.

'Are you listening to me now?' he asked, in Mr Ward's familiar tones.

I nodded.

'Good. I just thought I'd send you this little message before you start thinking that you can get the mad professor or anyone else involved with our little agreement. I know where you are and whatever you are up to won't be of any use. This is between you and me and Mirabel. So I'll see you tomorrow. Five o'clock sharp. None of the others. And then we can all get back to the way things were.'

Chapter 39

Diggleby was mortified at how easily Mr Ward had by-passed his security systems. He wouldn't stop ranting about what he was going to do to the Kelve if he got hold of him. I couldn't calm him down for ages. Eventually he said he was going to close some of his systems for a while to try and make sure that Mr Ward had completely gone. Before he stopped communicating altogether, he received a message from Erasmus to say he was definitely on his way. There was nothing to do now but wait.

I went upstairs to find Will who was still watching over Megan. She had fallen asleep again and didn't wake even while I was telling Will about what I had just seen. I could see that Will was trying to take it all in but he was exhausted and his eyes started to close too.

I crept out of the room.

I was tired as well but I couldn't afford to sleep. I needed to be by myself for a while, to think, so I went downstairs and into the front room. I sat down near the window, turning the pendant over in my hands. It was quiet now and I didn't dare risk talking to it again in case someone had discovered we had been trying to get into the security systems. I wasn't sure what would happen if they did. I undid the clasp and hung it around my neck.

My eyelids felt so heavy and at one point I think I may actually have dozed off. I stood up and opened the window. It was dark and I couldn't see anything but the smell of the sea rushed into the room carried on a light breeze. It was good to feel the fresh air on my face. The tide would be going out now and the deadline for meeting Mr Ward was getting closer. No one was going to be able to stop that. Not my genius double or Erasmus or Diggleby. Mirabel was going to have to come with me tomorrow and I would just have to hope that she would be alright on the other side of the Bridge. Her aunt might be in trouble but Mirabel was only a kid. Surely that would count for something.

I heard someone come into the room behind me and a torch shone around the room. Without turning round I knew it was Megan. 'I thought I told Will to keep you upstairs,' I said.

She ignored that and came over to the window. I watched her lower herself down to the floor carefully, putting the light and her bag in front of her.

'I'm going to get Will,' I said. 'Diggleby arrived while you were upstairs.'

'The robot? Yes, I saw him. He gave me the torch. He's rigging up some sort of lighting system now so that at least we can see what we are doing.'

'Is he alright?'

'I used to own something similar to him at the Institute,' she went on without answering my question. 'But of course we are way beyond needing that sort of equipment now. Where are the others?'

'On their way. In fact I need to …'

'Don't go. I have to talk to you,' said Megan. 'Please. Sit down.'

'I don't have to do anything you say.'

'I think, on reflection, that I may be able to resolve our problems.'

'You said you couldn't help us.'

'Yes. Well, I am not doing it for sentimental reasons. At the moment I don't have access to either of the pendants and I am unable to proceed until that situation changes.'

'I'm not handing this one over. I told you.'

'You made that very clear.'

'And Mr Ward has the other.'

'At least listen to what I have to say.'

I hesitated and glanced towards the door, willing it to open and for Erasmus to appear. The house was still and silent and it was ridiculous of me to think any knight in shining armour was suddenly going to appear and save us.

'You've got five minutes,' I said. 'And then I'm going to find the others.'

'Very well. But close the window first. It's very cold in here.'

I did as she said, pulling it shut with a firm bang. There was a blanket on the floor under the sill and I picked it up.

'Wrap this around you,' I said, handing it to her.

'Thanks.'

It was the first time I had heard her be grateful about anything. Was she softening a little or was she just trying to find another way to get round me? I sat down beside her but I was still on my guard.

'Will's very good looking, isn't he?' she said.

That wasn't what I was expecting her to say. 'Maybe you should look out for him on your planet,' I said, sarcastically. 'You could start dating.'

She shook her head. 'I have no desire to make a marriage contract. I am much too important to be distracted by … I was just being factual. Will is a good looking human.'

'If you say so.'

There was silence between us.

'Is that all?' I asked. 'I thought you had a plan or something.'

She didn't reply at once.

'What's it like living here?' she asked eventually. Her tone was definitely friendlier now. She seemed almost human.

'What do you mean?'

'It's not a difficult question. I want you to tell me what your life is like.'

I thought about images of Mum and me that Diggleby had downloaded. How much did she know about me already?

'I … I don't really … why are you bothered about what my life's like? You've done nothing but say how primitive it is here.'

She shrugged. 'I'm just curious. You're not … you're not like me at all.' She paused as though she was expecting me to answer her back. 'And I noticed that your surroundings are very different too.'

'What do you mean?'

'The colours. And the smell. My mother used to read a poem about the sea to me, before I went to the Institute. Something about the way it sang, almost as though it were human. I couldn't see the point of it.'

'Poets use images,' I said. 'They help to describe exactly what something is like. The way it makes you feel. You wouldn't understand.'

'I fully comprehend the concept,' she said. 'But why would you feel anything about the sea? Is that what you waste your time reading? No wonder you are in this fix.'

She reached for her bag and pulled it on to her lap.

'Look,' I said. 'If this is all you've come to say then ...'

'No. No. I need to explain something to you. If I am going to persuade you to listen to my ideas, then you have to trust me.'

'I think I'd rather wait to see what Erasmus says.'

'That's because we have started badly. But I think we should spend this time getting to know each other.'

'No thanks. Look ...'

'I saw your mum,' she said, interrupting me.

'What? Where?'

'At your house. The other day. I couldn't find any trace of Mirabel when I arrived and I didn't know what to do.'

She hesitated. She looked away from me. I had the feeling that she was genuinely feeling embarrassed about what she was telling me.

'I knew ... I knew that my equivalent must live here and I tried to use the pendant to trace you,' she went on. 'I thought that if you were like me then you might provide me with ... with some help so I went to your house.'

'You came looking for me?'

'I just said.'

She certainly had my attention now. 'But you were taking a massive risk, weren't you? What if someone had seen you?'

'Your mother was talking to some official looking people on the doorstep and I thought that … well it seemed impossible but I wondered if they were looking for me. I almost left but the back door was open and I went in to see if you were inside. You weren't, obviously.'

'And what if we'd met ? I mean I had no idea about any of this then. I'd have freaked out.'

'No doubt. You are very highly strung and you seem rather hysterical in a crisis.'

'Look, I never asked for any of this. I didn't know about Bridges or doubles or aliens until a few days ago and …'

'I took a few things,' she said. 'When I went into your room. I should not have done that. It is unlike me to be so impulsive.'

'What … what did you take?' I asked, trying to sound casual.

She unzipped the main section of her rucksack and brought out my jewellery and my diary. She held them out towards me. 'It was totally against protocol. I should have been focusing purely on my mission. I have never done anything like that before, I can assure you.'

'It doesn't matter.'

'It does. It matters a great deal. I want to return them to show that I can be trusted.'

I looked at my things. They seemed so ordinary. A few days ago I was writing in my diary about Abbie and school and how my mum didn't understand me. It made me feel emotional again and I turned my head away.

'Do you trust me now?' she insisted. 'You have been very open and honest with me and I respect that.'

Suddenly I thought about the stone I had swapped in

the smaller compartment. I seemed to have the upper hand at the moment. I didn't want her to know that I had been in her bag.

'Keep them,' I said. 'I've got more important things to worry about.'

We were silent for a moment. She put my stuff back into the bag and placed it carefully beside her.

'Your problem,' she said at last, 'is that you are limited by your environment.' The uncertainty in her voice had gone and she had raised her head to look at me directly. 'Your education is patchy at best,' she went on. 'I mean it isn't your fault. If you had the equivalent of the Institute here you might stand some chance of bettering yourself.'

'You may have nosed around my house and taken things from me but you don't know anything about me,' I snapped. 'Not about who I really am. Or what's important to me.'

'But everything here is so ... small. So insignificant,' she said. 'You have achieved so little.'

'Maybe.' I shrugged. 'But to be honest I'm not sure that all this advancement has done you much good.'

'What do you mean?'

I panicked. I couldn't let her know what Diggleby had done. I turned away from her and pretended to look out of the window.

Then I remembered something. 'I ... I've been having these dreams,' I said without looking at her. 'I keep seeing the beach that I know out there, but it's all black and sludgy. There's never anyone on it. Were you getting into my head? To show me things?'

Megan shook her head. 'Your mind is completely locked

to me which is strange given our connection and the training I have had at the Institute. I have certainly not communicated to you through your dreams.'

'Is it true though? Is your world like that?'

She hesitated. 'I would have to admit that in daylight the views here are much more attractive than the ones at home,' she said. 'But what use is that? Look at how we have progressed compared to you. The President has led us all to great enlightenment and important discoveries.'

'But when you say "us" do you just mean the people in the Institute?'

'I don't understand what you are asking.'

'I mean, what happens outside of the Institute? Do you even know?'

'It is of no consequence.'

'And what about you? The real you. You must talk to someone over there and not always about work.'

'What else is there?'

'Friends. Family.'

'I told you. I don't need them.'

'Do you even have any idea if your mum is OK?'

'I don't …' She paused and I could tell that for once I had hit a nerve. 'I don't have to concern myself with such things. Emotional involvement with anything is just a distraction.'

'So you've never asked yourself whether the things that are happening on your planet may be wrong.'

'The President knows everything,' she said, clearly agitated now. 'He's the most gifted of all of us and he sees the future … he …'

'No one knows everything, especially about what is going

to happen in the future. You should talk to him more. Ask him some questions.'

'The whole reason that I have taken on this mission is that I get a chance to meet him and to talk to him. I want to learn everything there is to know. It would be such an honour.'

'So you haven't actually ever met him?'

'I will one day. Only the most senior of scientists and engineers are actually allowed to even see him.'

'Like Rhiannon Kendrick.'

I knew I was taking a risk mentioning Mirabel's aunt but I wanted to know if Megan was aware of her situation.

'Definitely not like her.'

'What do you mean?' I asked, trying to sound as casual as I could.

'She's lost her mind, I think. She's opposed the President and he's having to make an example of her. He found out she was planning a rebellion. He sent his people to arrest her and he intended to take Mirabel as well. They arrived too late. Rhiannon had managed to send Mirabel over the Bridge.'

It was exactly as I had thought. Rhiannon had been trying to save her niece.

'It was totally reckless,' Megan went on, as though she had guessed what I was thinking. 'The girl might have died. She hadn't had enough training and her gifts are considerably inferior to mine.'

'But despite that she made it.'

'Yes. She was lucky,' she admitted.

'And you intend to take her back? Across the Bridge again where even if she survives that, she's going to be in danger?'

She paused and closed her eyes. 'Will says I have to help you, which is not correct because I don't have to do anything.'

I didn't answer so she continued. 'But as I cannot proceed with my mission without you, it would seem that the most logical way forward is to help each other.'

'Like I said, I'd rather talk to Erasmus.'

'I have the solution to our problems.'

'Brilliant,' I said. 'And there I was worrying that we were in trouble.'

She didn't seem to hear the irony in my voice.

'Firstly, you need to understand something. I am sure that Mr Ward will be able to find a way into some part of the pendant; Kelves are adept at using the power of the mind to control their world. But he hasn't got the skills to take himself over the Bridge. He no doubt thinks that Mirabel will be able to help him.'

'What do you mean?'

'It would not seem unreasonable to surmise that he plans to use Mirabel's gifts to enhance his own. The pendant by itself is difficult to control but if he links himself to Mirabel then he might just be able to manage the forces he will encounter.'

'You're wrong. He told me he needed Mirabel to bargain with on the other side.'

'He might still do that if they survive. But that is extremely unlikely. I found the journey challenging and I am aware that going back will not be easy. This is what I need to explain to him. The facts are indisputable. If he attempts to cross the Bridge in such a way, both he and Mirabel will die.'

I felt that knot tighten in my stomach again. I had always known that handing Mirabel over to Mr Ward was a terrible thing to do and now Megan was confirming it.

'Even if … even if that's true, how are you going to explain that to him?' I asked, trying to keep my voice steady. 'He'll just blast you into pieces before you get past the first sentence.'

'No, he won't. You're forgetting something.'

'What? The Institute? Can they really help?'

Just for a moment I thought that Megan was handing me a lifeline. Surely even Mr Ward would not be able to take them on?

But Megan was already shaking her head.

'I would really like to resolve this before I enter into communication with them.'

'You mean you don't want to tell them what a mess you've made of this.'

'It hasn't gone as smoothly as I planned,' she admitted. 'But in truth, I think the Institute will be reluctant to send me any aid at this point. They do not want to draw attention to themselves over here after all and there is something else we have at our disposal.'

'What?'

'Diggleby. You have an A4025 automaton at your disposal. Of course it is not the very advanced model but still …'

'I can't see him being much good against Mr Ward. What's he going to do? Throw a Victoria sponge at him?'

'You and Will seem to be under the misguided impression that the machine in there is only fit for domestic duties. Even though he is an inferior model he still has several defence mechanisms he can use. And he can attack if given the correct command. I am fully qualified to up-grade a few of his systems before we set out. He will be able to protect us, at least long enough for me to talk to the Kelve.'

'To tell him he's stupid? You talked to Mr Ward before, didn't you? That didn't go so well.'

'Yes, but he failed to defeat me and now he will see how strong I am.'

She started coughing again and I could see that her hands were shaking. She pulled the blanket tighter around her body.

It was my turn to sigh. The situation was hopeless. All that Megan had done was to confirm my worst fears. To get Mum back I was going have to betray Mirabel.

'You're not even well,' I said. 'And Mr Ward's never going to listen to you.'

She ignored me and tried again. 'I will explain to Mr Ward that I will not report his conduct to the President and in fact I will say that he was the one who helped us. The President might agree that he should be rewarded in some way.'

'I don't think "might" will be enough.'

'Well, there are no guarantees. But in the meantime I will give him this.'

She reached into her pocket and pulled out the small disc she had used earlier.

'I can't see how showing him a few snaps of your world will get you anywhere.'

'This does much more than that. It was designed by Rhi-annon Kendrick. It's a prototype of the pendants and I was given it a few years ago to practise with. You have to connect to it in the same way but it isn't as good, obviously. You can't travel far with it, certainly not over the Bridge, but you can use it to communicate across huge distances if you know how to do it.'

'Let me see.'

She handed me the disc and I held it on the palm of my hand. Again as I looked into the crystal I began to feel some sort of connection with it. Swirling shapes in vivid colours appeared on the smooth surface. Then it started to spin, very slowly at first, but then gathering speed. I saw faces I recognised from school, places I had visited as a child, and Mirabel. She was standing on the beach holding the bin bag.

It made me lose my concentration and the disc rolled off my hand and on to the floor.

'That's not bad,' conceded Megan. 'Considering you've had no training. It is clearly much easier to operate than the pendant and the security on it is child's play to bypass. Mr Ward could use it to make contact with someone or he could secure a place in a passing ship. He would never find an object like this here. He has to accept.'

'I don't think he has to do anything,' I said. 'This is just a ridiculous plan. It's never going to work.'

'I think you are wrong and I am sure that when the others arrive they will see my point of view.'

'Even Mirabel?'

'I don't think that you giving into Mr Ward secures her such a bright future.'

There was silence between us for a few moments. Megan was beyond annoying but she was right about Mirabel. Mr Ward did not care about her. And now I knew that handing her over would be a death sentence.

'Say by some miracle this works and Mr Ward agrees to accept what you say,' I said. 'What happens to Mirabel then?'

'She comes with me, as planned.'

'But she's still going to be in danger?'

'Not at all. I will help her across the Bridge.'

'But you said it isn't easy crossing it.'

'No. But we'll manage.'

'And on the other side?'

'Mirabel wasn't complicit in her aunt's plans. I was told that the Institute intends to take care of her in the absence of … her guardian. Anyway how can she stay here? What if questions are asked about who she is?'

'We'll look after her.'

'She cannot stay here long term. You must see that.'

Megan slowly raised herself to her feet. 'Mirabel will be safe with me, I give you my word,' she went on. 'And I also promise to do my best to ensure that your mother is returned to you and you can resume your life without any more involvement in matters that are obviously way beyond your understanding. Do you agree?'

I didn't answer. I couldn't think straight.

'In this case, you have to examine the facts and they will tell you that I am now your only chance of a reasonable outcome. I doubt you can come up with a better idea.'

'I still think …'

The room was suddenly flooded with light and a door slammed in another part of the house. I heard voices.

'Diggleby has done his work,' said Megan.

'And Erasmus is here,' I said, getting to my feet.

'Then let us go and tell him what we have decided,' said Megan.

310

Chapter 40

Erasmus was standing next to the worktops in the kitchen and he didn't look up when we entered. He had changed his clothes and was now dressed like someone about to go to the Goth weekend in Whitby to hang out with Dracula. He wore a pair of black trousers tucked into knee-length leather boots. I noticed the silver chain of a pocket watch hanging from his waistcoat. The large sleeves of his white shirt kept getting in the way of what he was doing and he obviously wasn't happy with the position of the goggles he was wearing because he kept fussing with them. He had removed one of Diggleby's arms and was busy with what looked like a blowtorch. Sparks were flying and there was a horrible smell of burning plastic in the air. A top hat sat on the worktop beside him, its brim singed and still smoking a little.

Diggleby was standing near to him but not moving at all and his eyes were completely vacant. I thought about how easily Mr Ward had breached his security systems and shuddered. It was impossible that Megan's plan to placate Mr Ward with a trinket was going to work. Everyone was going to have to accept that in a few hours I would have to meet with him and do as he said. Whatever the consequences.

'Ah, Meg,' said Erasmus, without looking up. 'Will has told me a little of your adventures since we last met. I trust you are well?'

'I'm fine,' I said. 'I ...'

'Where's Mirabel?' asked Megan, anxiously.

'Your friend Will was kind enough to say he would try to talk to her. She has become very agitated I am afraid.'

There was a loud bang and Diggleby's arm lifted into the air a little. The smell of burning became stronger. Erasmus wafted the air a little and then leaned over the arm, peering into the smoke.

'For some reason he seems to be stuck in sleep mode,' said Erasmus 'It is most infuriating because ...'

'You clearly have no idea what you are doing,' said Megan. 'I have worked in Robotic Engineering as part of my training and I insist that you let me see what the problem is.'

Erasmus stopped.

He turned towards us and raised his goggles. 'Oh ... my ... word!' he exclaimed. 'Oh my word! Will told me of course but I have been too absorbed in ... but ... forgive me. Forgive me my dear. This is ... this is wonderful!'

He looked over at me and then at Megan and ran his hands through his straggly hair.

'I never thought that I would live to see this day,' he said. 'Welcome! Welcome!'

He raced over with his hand outstretched but Megan turned away from him.

Erasmus lowered his arm.

'Is this the professor?' she asked, staring at me. 'Is this Erasmus? I thought you said he was a brilliant man.'

'He is,' I said, embarrassed at her reaction.

'Then why isn't he moving out of the way to let me get on with my work?'

'Yes, yes indeed,' said Erasmus, still attempting to smile. 'Of course. Most exciting. But I fear I would be reluctant to put my dear friend into the care of someone he doesn't know.'

'He's a machine,' snapped Megan. 'I know what I'm doing.'

She pushed past Erasmus and picked up Diggleby's arm from the worktop. She reattached it to the robot in seconds and lifted a small panel on the side of Diggleby's neck.

'I don't think that is the right course of action, my dear,' said Erasmus. 'You see …'

To my surprise, Diggleby's eyes blinked and his whole body gave a shudder.

'He's back online,' said Megan. 'But there is still a lot of work to do. You've damaged the mechanisms in his arm but if you have the right equipment with you I can probably make a temporary repair that will be enough for our purpose.'

'Our purpose?' asked Erasmus.

'Yes. I have no wish to waste any more time. I need full access to the robot without interference. My calculations show us that we only have a few hours left to prepare ourselves for my plan so if you can step out of the way I shall be able to perform my tasks much more easily.'

Erasmus looked completely dumbfounded.

'Megan has a plan,' I said. 'I need to explain it to you so that you can tell her how ridiculous it is.'

'Yes. Yes. Marvellous,' said Erasmus, not really listening to me. 'There is my toolkit my dear … Megan … and you are welcome to use anything. You … you need to take great care with Diggleby. He will not be used to a stranger and I fear that it will very much upset him if he feels I have abandoned him.'

'You will only get in my way. Now stop talking because I need to concentrate.'

'Let's go outside for a moment, Erasmus' I said, taking his arm. 'Please. We need to talk. I'll tell you everything.'

Erasmus glanced over at Diggleby and then nodded.

'You can ask Will to come and help me,' said Megan, without looking round. 'He can be my assistant.'

It was still dark but the sky was clear and the moon was so bright that it was sending a shaft of light over the sea towards us. I stared over to the patch of sky where I had first experienced the Bridge but of course I couldn't see anything. Not without the telescope.

I felt like I was going mad.

'I … I don't think I should leave Diggleby for long,' said Erasmus.

'This won't take a minute.'

'I seem to have upset your friend.'

'She's no friend of mine,' I said.

'Not as agreeable as you?'

'You have no idea.'

He sighed. 'No matter. I'm not sure that I should have let her loose on Diggleby but she seemed to be so certain and …'

'She reckons she's a genius.'

'Well, it is true that the civilisation over the Bridge must be more advanced than us in so many ways. The Bridge it-self, I mean. It is astonishing to meet someone who has made that journey. I would really appreciate the time to talk with her …'

'You're welcome to that. But there are more urgent things I need to talk to you about. Did Will tell you what Mr Ward said? About Mum?'

'Indeed. And I am truly sorry. Diggleby has assured me that your mother will not be feeling any ill effects from the time pocket. She will not be aware of what is happening.'

'But there's no way we can get her out?'

He shook his head. 'Not while Mr Ward has control,' he said.

Despite the fact that it was cold outside now, Erasmus seemed to be sweating. He pushed up his shirt sleeves. I could see that his hands were trembling.

'Then that's that,' I said. 'I have to hand Mirabel and the pendant over at five o'clock this morning. There's no choice. Megan's come up with a crazy plan but you have to go back in there and stop her. It's never going to work.'

'What … what does she propose?'

He sat himself down on the steps.

I started to explain what Megan had said but I wasn't sure he was listening. He kept glancing back at the house as though he was listening out for Diggleby crying for help or something.

The plan sounded even less convincing when I said it out loud and I couldn't believe for one moment that Mr Ward was even going to give us the chance to talk to him, let alone agree to do as we said.

When I had finished speaking, Erasmus didn't respond. He leant back against the steps.

'Well?' I asked impatiently. 'You see how crazy it is? Go in there and tell her she can't get involved in this. This is between me and Mr Ward now.'

Erasmus looked up at me but he still didn't say anything.

I was furious. 'Fine! I'll tell her myself! There's no way she's putting Mum in danger.'

I turned to go.

'Wait,' said Erasmus. 'Wait. Please.'

I stopped.

'You must realise,' he went on. 'That even if you go alone, and take Mirabel, exactly as Mr Ward insists, there are no guarantees that he will keep his word. When he has what he wants he may simply … well let's just say he is under no obligation to let you or your mother go.'

'I know.'

'He is a ruthless being. Kelves are arrogant and selfish. You should never have gone to see him alone. Megan is right about one thing at least.'

'What?'

'You need our help.'

'Gah! I wish … I wish I could just think straight for a minute,' I said. 'I don't know what to do!'

Erasmus got to his feet and came over to me. He put his hand on my shoulder. 'I wish I had brought the Carper blanket for you.'

'It wouldn't do any good. This is such a mess.'

'Please, sit down. Let's talk this through. There may yet be some light amongst this darkness.'

He reached into his waistcoat pocket and brought out what looked like a fountain pen. He blew on it and sparks of light flew into the air. They danced around for a moment before joining together and forming a spotlight over the steps.

'That's better, isn't it?' he said. 'If we need to find our way, we need to be able to see clearly.'

'How did you …?'

'Diggleby was able to acquire a small quantity of Whynstone. It's only found in the caves on the north side of Brax. Marvellous properties. Did you know …?'

'I don't want to hear about it.'

'Of course. But please sit. There may yet be an answer to our problems.'

I sank down on to the steps and put my head in my hands. It was impossible to think. Images from the last few days were whirling around in a chaotic jumble. Mr Ward, the dark beach in my dreams, Mirabel screaming for my help. I couldn't make it stop or even somehow straighten any of this out into something sensible. There was a pain deep in the pit of my stomach that wouldn't go away.

I was aware of Erasmus sitting down beside me.

'I think Megan is right,' he said at last. 'Maybe in his determination to get what he wants, Mr Ward has not considered the risks of the task he undertakes. Maybe he would be open to an alternative solution to the situation.'

'He's not going to listen.'

'You say Megan is offering him a prototype of the pendant?'

I nodded.

'Then that may give him what he wants. His freedom. It has to be more powerful than anything he can find here.'

'Maybe. But I don't think he's going to agree.'

'If we can convince him to take the disc in return for your mother it has to be worth a try. Everything could work out splendidly in fact.'

'Not quite.'

'I don't understand. Have I forgotten something?'

'Mirabel.'

'Ah. Yes'

'Even if he does agree, which is more than unlikely, what does that mean for her?' I asked. 'She's in danger whatever we do. Megan still wants to take her back. She's not going to be safe there.'

'How so?'

'Megan told me that her aunt is in real trouble at the Science Institute and ...'

'Ah, the Science Institute,' he said, a smile flickering across his face. 'Of course. How remarkable. I worked there once.'

I looked at him in astonishment.

'What? Over the Bridge? But you said ...'

'No. No. You misunderstand me. I meant the Science Institute here. Over in Scarborough. It might still exist in some form. It was set up years ago as part of the Science Department in the University to look for other dimensions, other lifeforms etc.'

'My Dad worked there for a while and he never mentioned anything about an Institute.'

'It was all top secret, of course. Hush hush.'

To be honest, I never listened properly when Dad was going on about work. I couldn't say that I knew exactly what he did but I was pretty sure that I would have remembered if he had been looking for aliens.

'What is your father's name?' he asked.

'Michael. Michael Rowlands.'

Erasmus shook his head. 'No. No, I never had the good fortune to meet anyone of that name although there were several departments of course. Also my time there was cut short. The Institute was not deemed a great success by the powers that be, I am afraid. Our findings were inconclusive and I … well even though I had discovered the Bridge, no one else could see it. You are one of the first people I have met who could.'

'But the lens you have? They must have seen something through that.'

He shook his head. 'It was Diggleby who designed it but as I explained, it takes the power of the mind to engage with what you can see, even feel. It was he who introduced me to the variety of life forms who have found their way here, although no one believed me about that either. He is an invaluable assistant. A friend, if that is possible.' He looked back towards the house. 'I really hope that the girl does know what she is doing. I couldn't bear to lose him.'

'She seems to have worked with robots over the Bridge. The two Institutes must use the same things, which makes sense I suppose.'

'Diggleby wasn't from the Institute. I found him. On the beach just over there. He was in the most appalling state but I managed to revive him and … well he had a wealth of knowledge that I could never have discovered by conventional methods. I merely improved him, although he would not thank me for saying that.'

He smiled.

I thought about Diggleby hinting at being owned by

criminals on another planet. I wasn't sure if Erasmus knew about that.

'He already knew about the Bridge, of course,' Erasmus went on.

'I wish I'd never seen it,' I said. 'I wish none of this had happened.'

I put my head back on my knees. I didn't want to listen any more. I was so exhausted and the mention of Dad earlier had made me feel terrible. I had made a big mistake. I had been so wrong not to contact him when I had the chance, to let him know what was happening. If he had heard of the Institute then perhaps he would have believed me if I had told him what was going on.

Maybe it wasn't too late.

I wiped my eyes quickly and pulled myself to my feet. 'That's it!' I said, excitedly. 'I need to get in touch with my dad. If he knows about the Institute then I can explain it all to him. He'll understand! Or maybe you could contact some people from the Institute here? Perhaps they would believe you now and …'

'Meg. Meg. The Institute barely exists any more. There were still some remnants a few years ago but they have probably ceased functioning. And as for your father. I am sure that he is a good man but you have to realise that in this situation, he can be of little help. Besides, I am certain that Mr Ward has ensured that our lines of communication have been cut.'

I had forgotten about that. We wouldn't be able to get through to anyone.

'Dammit!' I said, feeling deflated again. 'He seems to be in control of everything. He's been tracking me the whole time. Did you realise he was watching you too?'

'Me? Is that what he told you? Impossible!'

'He was using Mr Howard, the site manager.'

Erasmus looked at me in astonishment. 'Well that is a pity,' he said. 'I really liked him and so did Diggleby.'

I flopped back down on to the step. I watched the moon disappear behind a cloud and the light above us started to fade too.

Erasmus reached into his pocket but instead of the pen, he brought out something wrapped in foil. He started to open it. 'I believe I have some coconut and beetroot flapjack left if you would care to try it?' I shook my head. 'You know, it has been hard. No one believing in our research. At the Institute my funding was eroded year after year. Eventually it was impossible to function properly. And then I heard that I was soon to be "surplus to requirements". So, one night, Diggleby and I ... collected ... some things that we might need to continue our work and we never returned.'

'You mean all that stuff in the caravan is stolen?'

'Borrowed,' Erasmus said. 'We knew that our work was vital and eventually we would have to make people see how important our discoveries are.'

'But how? If no one can see the Bridge.'

'That is what we are working on. And more information about the universe itself, of course.'

'What I don't get is how the things in Megan's world are really different to here. Like the Institute. The place you worked at doesn't seem anything like the one she described.'

'Did she give any indication herself as to why that might be?'

'She said something about a moment when everything

changed but I don't get it. What could have happened to have made things go in such different directions?'

'I do not know, but maybe something that seemed quite insignificant at the time may have changed the destiny of the whole universe beyond the Bridge. Indeed, it seems that their advancements have led them to create the Bridge itself. We are centuries away from that kind of technology and as for where the energy itself comes from or how it is harnessed, then …'

He stopped.

'But there will be time for this later. What I wanted to say was that I understand how difficult it is being alone with this information. With no one to believe you or help you. You may have felt like that, Meg, but then so have I. And as for the future. Well, we have each other now. You're not alone any more and neither am I.'

We sat in silence for a moment. My head ached and I was fighting the tiredness I felt.

'Why did it take you so long to follow Diggleby down here?' I asked. 'You left us alone for ages and Will told you it was urgent.'

'And I am sorry for it. I … there were a few personal matters I had to attend to. Leave my house in order as it were.'

'Why?' I said, suddenly alarmed. 'You said everything was going to be OK.'

Erasmus put the last bit of flapjack into his mouth and got to his feet. 'Do not worry,' he said, turning away from me. 'Megan is right. We have to offer Mr Ward an alternative solution to this problem. You cannot go out there alone. Staying together is the best option. I am convinced of it.'

I was not convinced at all and what he had just said about 'personal matters' confirmed my worst fears. Erasmus was going to agree with Megan and her plan. But he didn't really think that it was going to work.

Chapter 41

As the light strengthened, I could see the huge white cliffs of Bempton to the right and the seaside town of Filey to my left. I desperately wanted to believe in the plan we had devised but talking about it seemed very different from actually being here. Once Mr Ward saw that I was not alone, that might be the end of it.

Everything centred on the upgrades to Diggleby and the fact that Megan was alive. The old man would not be expecting that and it might just put him off guard. It wasn't much to hope for but it was all we had.

'Are you alright my dear?' Erasmus asked me as we headed towards the beach.

'Not really,' I said. 'I'm still thinking I should have come on my own.'

'We have discussed everything at length,' he said, raising up his cane with the bird's head. 'I have this, as you see, and Diggleby is well prepared for any eventuality. Mr Ward has his weaknesses, Meg, and we must exploit them.'

I turned around to look at the others who were walking slightly behind us. Mirabel had linked arms with Will and she was leaning against him. She had not taken well at all to the fact that Megan was my double and even Will had struggled to calm her down at first. Megan's frosty tone towards her had not helped either. Now she was obviously exhausted and her hair was dirty and wild. There was hardly any sign of her blonde plait. The hoodie she had borrowed from Will made her look tiny and she seemed younger and more vulnerable than ever before. He hadn't told her the details of the plan, only that we were going to get my mum back and it had made me feel more guilty than ever when she had said sorry for her behaviour and that now she wanted to help. I had begged Erasmus to stop Megan from taking her back across the Bridge if we managed to get out of all of this, but he had simply told me that everything would 'work out'. It was too terrible to think that, even if we saved Mum, we were going to have to betray Mirabel in the end.

Megan was walking with Diggleby. She was deathly pale. She had been brighter for a time when working on the improvements to the robot but that seemed to have taken its toll on her. Even when we reached the beach, I could tell that walking on the flat sand was a struggle.

It was hard to feel positive about anything.

When we had walked about halfway to the sea we all stopped.

'He's not here,' said Will, breaking the silence. 'How long do you think we should wait?'

'He'll come,' I said.

'He won't be expecting all of us, will he?' said Will, as though he was reading my thoughts. 'I mean … it's good that we're all together isn't it?'

It really wasn't, but I kept quiet.

'Diggleby, you need to secure the area around us as far as you can,' said Megan.

'I am quite aware of my part in this task,' snapped Diggleby. 'If we have decided to stop here then I can get on with my work.'

'Then we just have to stick together. If everyone does exactly what I told them, then we can expect a good outcome,' said Megan.

For the first time, her voice wavered a little and I knew it wasn't just because she was exhausted. To my surprise, she moved herself to stand by Will and she linked arms with him as well. She might be trying to sound brave but I could sense that she was as scared as me.

I tried not to let it bother me that I was standing by myself and stared out across the sea. Gannets were flying down from Bempton cliffs and diving for fish. A couple of oyster catchers, Dad's favourite birds, were busy searching for food at the water's edge. It was hard to think that he was so far away and had no idea about what was going on.

It just looked like a normal summer's day but I knew that in Megan's world, sights like this had gone forever and I wondered if she was thinking the same thing.

I was wrong.

'Have you got the pendant, Meg?' she asked.

I nodded and pulled the neck of my t-shirt down a little so that she could see it.

'Perhaps you should give it to me now,' she said.

'I told you. No way.'

'You're shivering,' Will said. 'Would you like my jacket?'

'No, I'm fine. Thank you.'

I turned away from them and noticed the sand blowing

in thin ribbons across the surface of the beach. A fine mist rose from the ground and started rolling towards us.

'He's coming,' I said.

'How do you know?' asked Will.

'Look.'

The familiar figure of the old man emerged from the sea fret, shuffling slowly along the sand towards us.

I stepped forward.

'Wait! ' said Megan. 'Concentrate!'

I stopped. I couldn't believe I had nearly blown the plan apart in the first few seconds. The area Diggleby could secure was only small and I had nearly stepped out of it.

Mr Ward did not seem to be in a hurry. He was using his stick to help him and to anyone watching he would have just looked like a tired old man struggling to walk.

Suddenly the plan seemed even more pathetic and I glanced over at Megan for reassurance. She was staring straight ahead and refusing to catch my eye. There was no turning back now. I just had to hope that she was as good at negotiating as she seemed to think she was.

'Well, look who we have,' he said, pointing his cane towards us. 'What's the collective noun for a bunch of idiots? A clutch? A gaggle?'

'Meg has informed us of what you have done,' said Erasmus. 'And let me tell you that ...'

'Why did you bring him?' asked Mr Ward, pointing his cane towards me. 'The mad scientist. And all these. It's not a social event. I told you to come alone. If you think any of them are going to be of any use then ...'

He stopped and lowered his cane. He had obviously just spotted Megan and he looked confused for a second.

'What kind of stupid trick is this?' he asked. He stared at Megan and then back at me. 'If you think this is funny, then I've got news for you.'

'This is Megan,' I said, trying to keep my voice steady. 'The girl you tried to kill.'

'That was after lying to me and creating havoc in this world,' said Megan. 'You have made a mistake in taking on the power of the Institute.'

'The only mistake I made was not finishing you off myself,' he snarled. 'But maybe you've given me the chance now. I might have known that Mr Howard ... if a job needs doing ...'

He was still looking from one to the other of us, and I could see he was trying desperately to make sense of what was happening.

'You really have to listen to Megan,' I said. 'I think she may have thought of a way to help.'

'I don't need any help,' he said. 'I told you to come on your own and showing me that ghost of a girl isn't going to do you any good. I ...'

'I am from the world beyond the Bridge as I told you,' Megan interrupted him. 'I am a member of the Science Institute and I am also Meg's equivalent from a parallel universe. We are essentially the same person and any attack on either of us is an attack on both. Everything you have done will be reported to the highest authorities. You will never succeed against us.'

I could tell that her aggressive tone wasn't going down well with Mr Ward. He fidgeted with the cane.

'Did you hear what I said?' insisted Megan.

Mr Ward ignored her and looked directly at me. 'Your

twin sister kept telling me she was clever,' Mr Ward said. 'But she's a miracle worker. I thought the sea would have done for her, for sure.' He suddenly chuckled. 'Sea swallow'd though some cast again. Is that right Will? Isn't that what you're thinking right now?'

Will looked a bit rattled and he looked over at me.

'Stop it,' I said. 'This has gone far enough.'

'You should listen to us,' said Will. 'We're all here to support Meg and ...'

'I couldn't care less. Now just hand me Mirabel and all this will be over.'

'Now look here,' said Erasmus. 'We are not going to do anything of the kind. We have come to make a deal with you and I must say ...'

Mr Ward snorted. 'I don't do deals at the best of times,' he said. 'And I don't think you're in a position to bargain.'

'I think you'll find that we are in a strong position,' said Erasmus.

'You've got nothing. I'm the one in the driving seat.'

'You can't take Mirabel,' said Megan.

'Who says?'

'The facts say. It is perfectly obvious. You intend to take her across the Bridge but that's impossible. You have had no training. You may have had some success with the pendant but not enough. It's much more difficult to control than you imagine.'

'You don't know what I'm capable of,' said Mr Ward. 'I'm going across that Bridge and that girl is coming with me.

I looked over at Mirabel. Will had wrapped his arms around her and she was obviously very scared. We had promised her that we wouldn't let Mr Ward take her but maybe she was beginning to doubt we could keep our word. This was harder than I had ever imagined.

'I've heard a lot about that world over there,' Mr Ward went on. 'I've done my research. It sounds like I'd fit right in. I don't care how many Megs you bring out. I'll be leaving ...'

'You are not a fool,' interrupted Erasmus. 'I am sure that with your experience of travelling between worlds you think you are well equipped to take on such a journey. But I am urging you to give up this reckless plan. You will never have never encountered anything like that Bridge before. Do you have any idea of the forces you are dealing with?'

'My calculations would confirm that it is most inadvisable,' said Diggleby, his voice sounding surprisingly businesslike. 'I would give an average survival rate of 2%, taking into account your age and physical state.'

There was silence for a moment and to my surprise Mr Ward looked worried for the first time. He glanced up at the sky, as though assessing his chances. His hand moved up to his neck to touch the pendant.

'I ... I'll make it. Don't you worry about that,' he said. He certainly didn't sound as confident now and I wasn't convinced he totally believed what he was saying.

'You may have been able to manipulate some aspects of the transportation element of the device around your neck,' said Diggleby. 'But set against the energy within the Bridge you are unlikely to be able to control it without considerable training. Both Megan and Mirabel have been part of the Science Institute program. You have not.'

'What do you know?' asked Mr Ward. 'I've transported myself through more worlds than you can shake a stick at.'

'Then why are you still here?' asked Megan. 'You have the pendant. You could have left before now.'

Mr Ward glared at her and pointed his cane directly at her head. 'Don't you dare to tell me what I should and shouldn't do. I …'

'You haven't gone because you need Mirabel to help you negotiate the Bridge. You think she will get you across. That is not going to work. She isn't strong enough.'

Mirabel was still clinging fast to Will. Even Mr Ward would have to admit that she didn't look capable of helping anyone with anything at the moment.

'There is an alternative,' Megan went on. 'Firstly, you must agree to release Meg's mother.'

'Why should I?'

'I don't think the President will want to get involved with someone who has taken a hostage,' said Erasmus. 'And who has wreaked havoc in another world. There will be an investigation here obviously. So many questions. Release her. She is of no further use to you and she may prove an obstacle for you in your new life.'

'It's not much of a plan so far.'

'I have not said anything about your conduct to anyone yet and if you agree to our terms, I will give you my word that I'll say nothing about what you have done to the President on my return,' said Megan. 'In fact, the opposite. I will report that you helped me and that my recommendation is that as soon as a less hazardous way of crossing the Bridge has been developed, that you should be allowed to travel then.'

'You must think I was born yesterday,' Mr Ward sneered.

'I'll guarantee that I will press your case with the President and in the meantime I will give you something else. This.'

She stepped nearer to him, holding out the disc.

'Careful,' I warned, worried that she might get too far away from Diggleby's protection.

'I have to show him this,' she said. 'He will realise that this is a genuine offer.'

Mr Ward stepped forward too, his eyes narrowing. 'What the heck is that?' he asked.

'It's a prototype of the pendant,' she explained. 'It won't get you across the Bridge but I do believe that it will help you communicate with others who may be willing to assist you with anything you need. It can be used for travel, obviously, although that would require some further training and adjustments to the disc itself. Maybe in time ...'

'Stop talking,' said Mr Ward. 'This is a trick. I don't know why I'm even listening to you.'

'Let me show you what it does.'

She stared at the disc and it started to turn slowly on her hand. Images of the world beyond the Bridge started to emerge into the sky, spiralling upwards but this time they seemed more jumbled and confused. I guessed it was because she was feeling nervous.

Mr Ward stared at us all for a moment as though he was considering everything carefully.

Megan took a few steps back and I was relieved that she was now safe again in Diggleby's protection zone.

'So if I could work with that thing, it would help me get out of here?' asked Mr Ward.

'It's quite technical,' Erasmus said. 'You'd have to know what you were doing but it is possible. It is considerably easier to manipulate than the pendant and there is little security embedded in it. You should be able to use it as you wish.'

Eventually he nodded. 'Alright,' he said. 'I'll take that.'

I looked over at Megan in surprise. Surely it couldn't be that easy?

'But I'll need something else,' he went on.

'What?' I asked. 'If you have the disc then …'

'I haven't finished speaking,' he snapped. 'If I am to get that thing to do what I want then I'll need help.' He paused. 'I want the robot.'

'No,' said Erasmus. 'Absolutely not.'

Megan turned to look at Erasmus. 'You are letting your emotions triumph over reason,' she said. 'Diggleby is not human. He has no feelings. He is expendable.'

I looked over at Diggleby who, in contrast to what she had just said, had a look of horror on his face.

'We agree,' said Megan, without bothering to listen to Erasmus's protests. 'The robot may be of great help to you. He can make your life here much more comfortable while you are waiting to travel and he is, as you will be aware, something of a communications expert. I am quite sure that he could work with the disc and arrange transportation for you to wherever you need to go.'

'Quiet,' Mr Ward snarled. 'I need to think.'

He stared over at Diggleby as though contemplating his answer. Diggleby looked over at Erasmus but the professor turned away.

The robot lowered his head.

Mr Ward reached into his pocket, brought out his dirty handkerchief and dabbed his face with it.

'So do we have a deal?' asked Megan. 'Only ...'

'You must think I'm simple,' he said.

His hand shot up and he fired at Erasmus. A purple flash streaked through the air but before it could reach him, it hit the invisible defence shield Diggleby had created around us. It bounced back to where Mr Ward was standing and it almost struck him. Somehow he managed to keep on his feet.

'You ... you ...'

He fired again but this time the explosive power was a lot stronger. Maybe Diggleby, realising he was to be sacrificed, lost his concentration. Whatever happened, the defence seal must have been breached because the whole area around us started shuddering.

I saw Megan reach for Diggleby but before she could do anything there was another enormous crash. Sand whirled into the air creating a gigantic dust cloud and I was knocked off my feet. I tried to get up but the more I struggled the more I felt myself sinking back into the sand.

From somewhere in front of me, Mirabel screamed and then purple streaks crashed and banged all around me.

'DIGGLEBY!' I screamed. 'DO SOMETHING!'

I tried to look over to where Diggleby had been standing. As the dust cleared I saw that one of Mr Ward's shots must have caught him. He was half buried and Erasmus lay unconscious next to him.

'KEEP AS STILL AS YOU CAN, MEG!'

It was Will.

He wasn't far away from me but I could see that he too

was being swallowed up by the sand. I stretched out my hand but I couldn't reach him.

'NO!' he shouted. 'JUST DON'T MOVE. YOU'LL ONLY SINK QUICKER.'

He was right. I tried desperately to resist the temptation to move but it was hard, especially when in the next second there was another explosion and more sand blew into the air. The cane that Erasmus had been carrying flew past and landed in front of me but I was half buried now. There was no way I could get it.

I could see Megan to my right but she wasn't moving. She wouldn't be any help now.

Mr Ward had somehow managed to grab Mirabel and he stood in front of us, laughing.

'That's better,' he said. 'Now things are back on my terms which is as it should be.'

Mirabel looked terrified but I couldn't do anything to help her.

'Please …' I managed.

'You thought you could get the better of me, Meg. Bringing your little friends and your twin sister in on the act, trying to fob me off with a cheap trinket and a tin can. Well, bad news. I'm not thick and you can see what happens if you cross me. I've managed to finish off your double properly this time,' said Mr Ward. 'And you'll all be dead soon. Serves you right. You've always thought that you're a cut above me. Well, now you know how things are. I'm in charge and I always have been.'

Mirabel was not attempting to struggle but tears were streaming down her face.

'Now listen,' said Mr Ward. 'This is what is happening

next … I …' He was seized by a fit of coughing and he had to stop for a second. He certainly wasn't faking his illness although he had been lying about nearly everything else.

'Please,' said Mirabel, wiping her eyes. I saw her take a deep breath. 'I know what you want me to do and I will. Please. Just don't hurt my friends.'

I knew it had taken every bit of her strength to have said that. Maybe I had underestimated her. She was obviously much tougher than I imagined and it made me wish I had tried harder to understand her from the beginning.

Mr Ward stopped coughing and looked at her.

'If you try anything I'll finish them off right now. I'll start with that stupid lad you're all so fond of.'

'NO!' shouted Mirabel.

'Now go and get the pendant from Meg. One false move and I'll blow them all sky high.'

As she nodded, he let go of her arm.

She started walking slowly towards me. For some reason she wasn't sinking at all. When she reached me, she knelt down.

'I'm sorry, Meg. But I have to take the pendant.'

'No … no. I'm sorry … I … should have kept my promise.'

'It's alright. I understand.'

'But Mum …' I mumbled. 'My mum … please …'

'Of course.'

Mirabel turned around to Mr Ward. 'I don't want you to kill them,' she said, her voice wavering.

'Don't tell me …'

'You have what you want. And it'll be a lot easier for you if I come with you willingly. Megan was wrong about me.

And Meg. I'm stronger than anyone thinks. I can help you to navigate the Bridge and I will. If you promise to leave my friends alone.'

Mr Ward laughed. 'You kids and your deals. I told you before. I'm not simple.'

'I know,' said Mirabel. 'But Megan was right about the Bridge being hard to cross. You will need my help.' She paused and I could see that Mr Ward was listening to her. 'I want you to return her mother. It's only fair.'

Mr Ward laughed. 'I'm not bothered about fair. Now hurry up.'

'Please,' said Mirabel. 'You've won. It's over now and there's nothing to be gained by hurting more people than you already have. You should return Meg's mother.'

He hesitated but then he reached into his pocket and took out a small tin box. He tossed it over towards Mirabel.

'No use to me now, anyway. Come on. We need to get going.'

She picked it up cautiously and placed it by my side.

'What … what do I do?' I rasped. 'How do I …?'

'I don't know,' said Mirabel. 'But you have her back now and I have to go.' She leaned over me and reached for the pendant. I could feel her hands trembling as she unclasped it. 'Your mother took me in when I needed help. I will always be grateful to her,' she said.

'Mirabel. Don't … I …' I stopped.

Something, someone had grabbed one of my ankles. Then I felt hands close around the other one. It was just like in my dreams but they were not pulling me under. They were holding me steady. I felt a slight push and found that now there was a firm surface under my feet.

'This is taking too long!' Mr Ward shouted. 'Come on. We …'

There was a gigantic cracking sound and I heard Mirabel scream. She was knocked flat on to the sand. A bolt of purple light flared past me only a few centimetres from my head.

'Just a warning shot,' he said. 'Show you what I'm capable of if you try anything. Now come on. The next blast is aimed at your boyfriend.'

Mirabel slowly dragged herself to her feet. There was a small gash on the side of her face which was bleeding and she was shaking. She managed to walk over to Mr Ward.

'Right. We'd better get going. Put that thing on.'

'I'm not sure that I can remember exactly what I did last time,' she said as she tried to fasten her pendant. 'I mean …'

'Stop stalling. We need to get going.'

SHHHHHH

From deep within the sand I heard it.

SHHHHHH

I knew who was helping me now and I also knew that with a push I could probably heave myself on to the beach. But what use would that be? I couldn't be quick enough to reach Erasmus's cane without Mr Ward spotting me.

'This is your chance.'

'Your only chance.'

'She knows, dear. She …'

SHHHHHH

Before I had time to debate any more I was shoved up-wards and realised I was free. I tried to grab the cane but I was a fraction of a second too late. Mr Ward had seen me.

'What the …?'

He raised his arm and I flinched, throwing myself to the ground again, covering my head with my hands. I waited for the crack and the pain.

Nothing.

I glanced up. Mr Ward was standing with the cane raised in the air. He wasn't moving. Neither was Mirabel. Even the sand that had been blowing around was still, suspended in mid-air, glinting like jewels in the light from the sun.

SHHHHHH

Of course.

'Edna? Agnes? Where are you? What have you done?' I called.

SHHHHHH

From behind me there was a slight rustling noise and I turned around. Edna was coming into focus but Agnes was still a series of blue lines.

'Sorry, dear,' said Edna. 'Did we startle you?'

'Have to be quick.'

'Very quick.'

'Seconds.'

'No time to be human. No time.'

'Stopped time.'

'Only a few seconds.'

'Very hard.'

'Very tiring.'

'Not allowed.'

'Strictly not allowed.'

I could see an outline of Agnes's face now amongst the flashing lines. I pulled myself up on to my feet.

'Save the girl,' Agnes said,

'All of them, dear.'

'That's what I meant.'

'And you must promise.'

'Not to tell Erasmus.'

'Not to tell anyone.'

'Wouldn't do.'

'Not at all.'

'They wouldn't let us live.'

'No. They wouldn't.'

'The ghost ships …'

'But we have made up a little for our …'

'Indiscretions.'

'Just a little.'

'Hurry now … hurry now …'

'Pick up the cane!'

I bent down to get it but I had never even held it before. There was no way I would be able to control it. I glanced at the bird at the top but its eyes were blank. 'Agnes. Edna,' I managed, 'I can't … I …'

'Promise. You have to promise.'

'OK, I promise,' I said. 'I won't tell a soul but …'

Agnes's face was beginning to blur. Edna was already hardly visible at all.

'No buts …'

'You have to save them.'

'We can't help any more.'

'Too difficult.'

'Will have to let go …'

'Let go, Agnes …'

'We're letting go …'

I felt a slight breeze hit my cheek and the sand started to trickle to the ground.

I remembered what Erasmus had said about me being able to see the Bridge and I knew that something had changed inside me over the last few days.

The Esks believed in me, too.

I had to do this.

'You have to protect me,' I said to the bird. 'You can't let him win.'

The bird's eyes glowed for a moment. I knew I could connect to it now.

'What the …?'

Mr Ward came to life so quickly I had no time to think about what to do next. A purple shard shot towards me and there was an enormous cracking sound just behind.

'MIRABEL! GET DOWN.'

She looked over at me in horror and then threw herself on to the sand.

'Get him!' I shouted aloud at the bird. 'GET HIM!'

The bird's eyes smouldered a little and then it opened its mouth and let out an ear-splitting screech. Purple fire flew towards Mr Ward. He looked towards me with a startled look. The flame reached him but didn't consume him. Instead it twisted itself around him, taking him off his feet and into the air. His own cane dropped to the ground and he was swirled round and round in the purple light. Then there was a massive explosion and sand, stones, pebbles rushed through the air knocking me off my feet.

I landed with a thud on the sand.

I looked up quickly, but Mr Ward had gone. His cane lay smouldering on the ground beside Mirabel.

'We did it!' I said, scarcely believing it. 'We … we did it.'

I tried to scramble to my feet but my hand caught something metal, lying beside me.

The tin box. The lid was open. It was empty.

'No ...' I said frantically, grabbing hold of it. 'No. No. No. Not after all of this.'

I could hear some movement all around me but I didn't care about anything else now.

There was nothing in the box.

Nothing at all.

I closed my eyes and hoped that the sand really would swallow me up this time.

Chapter 42

When I opened my eyes I thought for a moment that I had just had another bad dream. I raised myself up a little and realised that I had not been asleep. I was still on the beach and the sand beneath me was definitely real.

Megan was lying quite a way off, but she wasn't moving. Erasmus and Will were leaning over her.

'Meg!' came a familiar voice.

Mirabel.

'MEG! You're OK! Thanks goodness. You saved us. You saved us all.'

I didn't say anything. Not everyone was safe but I couldn't bear to say that out loud.

'Diggleby says you have to drink this,' she continued, holding out a small beaker to me. A strange looking green liquid was inside.

I pushed it away.

'What's the matter? We've all had some. Diggleby said …'

'I don't care,' I managed. 'I don't care.'

'You don't need to worry any more. We're all OK. Diggleby's smashed his face and he's lost one of his fingers. But he's still able to help us. Erasmus and Will are fine and they're looking after Megan. She went under the sand but she's alright. Just a bit shaken. I'm … Thank you, Meg.'

She put her hand on my shoulder. I tried so hard to keep back the tears but they started flowing from my eyes and a gigantic sob began somewhere in the pit of my stomach. Suddenly I was crying so hard it actually hurt and I couldn't have stopped even if I had wanted to.

'Meg. Meg. It's OK.'

The next thing I knew, Will was next to me and he put his arms around me. I was aware that Erasmus too had come over to see what had happened. I couldn't speak I was sobbing so hard.

'Meg, my dear girl,' said Erasmus. 'Amazing. Truly amazing. To take on a Kelve at your age! How on earth did you get out of the sand?'

I couldn't speak and anyway I had nothing to say. I didn't want to lie to him. I had made a promise to the Esks not to mention them and for some reason that still seemed to matter.

'Please stop crying, Meg,' said Will. 'It's alright. We're all OK.'

He held on to me until eventually I calmed down a little. I felt my breathing becoming more steady.

'You really are remarkable,' said Erasmus. 'I knew from the first time I met you that you were someone special.'

I managed to look up. Erasmus had a large bruise on the side of his face and some of his hair looked very singed.

'And the good news is that we have the pendant Mr Ward was wearing,' he went on. 'It must have broken off in the explosion. It's a little damaged but only superficially. Diggleby is sure he can repair it.'

I turned my face away. I didn't want talk to anyone.

I saw Diggleby lumbering up towards us. 'We have succeeded in ridding ourselves of the Kelve,' he said triumphantly as he reached us. 'I have examined the cane. It is badly scorched and its power has gone. I am 95% certain that Mr Ward poses no threat to us any more.'

'I thought we'd seen him off completely,' said Will.

'I cannot locate him but that does not mean he is dead. Kelves have the ability to hide in their own memories when they are attacked. It is possible that he has done that but without the cane and given his age … well my calculations suggest we have nothing to worry about. Have you had some of the juice I prepared, Meg? It is good for shock.'

I shook my head. I still couldn't speak. I reached down by my side and picked up the tin box that Mr Ward had thrown to me.

'Is that …?' started Will. 'What happened to the time pocket?'

'Oh I see,' said Erasmus. 'That is the problem. Now, Meg, you must listen to me. You must calm yourself. You are all safe and this box is nothing. Another of Mr Ward's tricks I am afraid. A time pocket is not an actual *thing*. Your mother was caught in a memory controlled by him and now he has lost his hold over it.'

'What do you mean?' I asked anxiously.

'Diggleby, my friend,' said Erasmus. 'Am I right? Mr Ward must have let go of the time pocket?'

'Certainly such a device would require a lot of energy to maintain.'

'THEN WHERE IS SHE?' I yelled at him. 'Where the hell is she now?'

'She will be free,' said Erasmus. 'What Diggleby is telling you is that she may be back at home right now.'

'Really?' I asked, starting to get to my feet. 'I need to go and find her then.'

'That won't be possible,' said Diggleby shaking his head. He looked over at Erasmus and then back at me.

'But Erasmus said ...'

'I'm afraid his optimism may be misplaced,' interrupted Diggleby. 'If Mr Ward did not actively free her before he came here, then the fact is that she might still be caught up in the memory. My sensors have indeed failed to locate her.'

'So what now? Is that it?' I cried. 'DIGGLEBY! IS THAT IT?'

'Not necessarily,' he replied. 'There is a way but it requires calmness, and unless ...'

'OK. OK. I'll be calm. Tell me what to do.'

I felt my legs weaken beneath me and I sank back to the floor again.

Diggleby stepped nearer to me. 'My understanding of time pockets indicates that as Mr Ward has weakened his hold, there is a chance that someone else can get into the memory,' he said. 'They have to be someone closely involved in it of course and strong enough to find their way in.'

'Think, Meg,' said Will, crouching down beside me. 'If you're in that memory you can definitely do this.'

'I'm not!' I said, trying to keep the tears at bay. 'Mr Ward kept saying that I should remember the house and every-thing, but I had only ever seen a photograph. I don't re-member being there.'

'Please. Try to think hard,' said Erasmus. 'There might

be something. A trace of a thought buried deep within you. One you may have forgotten about yourself.' He picked up the box and stared into it. 'This might do very well,' he went on. 'You need something to help you to focus.'

He handed it to me.

'You said that was useless,' Will said.

'Yes. It is at the moment. But look again, Meg. Really concentrate.'

I stared into the dented silver lining of the box. All I could see was a faint, blurred reflection of the shape of my face. No details. I looked up at Erasmus.

'I can't ...'

'Remember the telescope. Remember how I told you to look. You have to see beyond what is obvious. Try as hard as you can to get into that memory yourself. It's the only way.'

I brushed away the tears from my face and rubbed my eyes. Grains of sand were still stinging me but I nodded.

'Start with what Mr Ward showed you. What he wanted you to see.'

I tried to picture Mum standing in the kitchen, the washing, her moving towards the door. Each time I thought about it I could only get as far as her pegging the washing on the line, the baby clothes and then the scene started again.

'It's hopeless,' I said. 'I wasn't there.'

'The memory used to create a time pocket has to be a particularly strong one,' said Diggleby. 'There has to be a reason why your mother has such a vivid remembrance of that time.'

'It's just Mum pegging kids' clothes on a washing line.'

'*Your* clothes,' said Will. 'You *must* have been there. There *must* be something.'

I tried again. I watched Mum bending down to the washing machine and I looked around the room, trying to think where I would be. Maybe at the table? Mum opened the back door and stepped outside. The next second she was back in the kitchen.

'It's no use,' I said, trying to keep my eyes focused. 'I can see her but she's stuck in the loop. I can't break it.'

'If you provide the next thing that happens, the time pocket will start to unravel,' said Diggleby.

'How can I? I don't know what …'

'Remember the Bridge,' interrupted Erasmus. 'You have to look at things in a different way.'

I looked again, trying to remember how Erasmus had told me to look beyond the darkness. To feel my way through the layers and to see what lay beneath. There was a flicker of light and this time the scene was a little different. I was seeing the same things but from a new angle. Mum was at the washing machine but this time I saw my yellow teddy bear on the table. I hadn't noticed him before. I blinked and Mum was back at the machine.

I started again. I saw more detail each time Mum appeared. Now there was paper and then pencils on the table. I was drawing. There was a beaker full of juice beside me. But each time the scene just began again.

'I can't do it …' I said. 'I …'

'There's something else … something important that you're missing. Remember. Not just what you see. Try to use all of your senses. Your mother must have kept that memory for a reason.'

When Mum came into the kitchen again I tried to think about the smells in the room. The washing itself perhaps with its flowery perfume or the aroma coming from the pots on the stove. None of those worked. There had to be something else.

'If you would allow me, I think I can help,' Megan said, her voice sounding softer than I had ever heard it.

She had somehow managed to walk over to where we all were and she flopped down on to the sand beside me. She looked all in.

'I don't see how,' I replied. 'This is my memory.'

'Megan's right,' said Diggleby. 'There is a strong chance that she experienced the same thing.'

'But you said things weren't exactly the same and ...'

'It's worth a try,' said Will.

I hesitated. 'OK. So what do I do?' I asked. 'Talk you through it?

'No. Play it to me. Play the episode on the inside of the lid.'

'I can't. I mean I don't know how.'

'You do,' said Megan calmly. 'Mirabel, give Meg your pendant for a moment.'

She unclasped it and handed it to me.

'This will help you. Hold it tight then close your eyes. Keep playing the scene you can see over and over. Don't think about anything else.'

I remembered the pictures that Diggleby had projected on to the wall. I had to be able to do this.

'OK,' I said. 'OK.'

I ran through the loop again in my head and then I stared at the lid of the box. My reflection was much clearer this time and I willed myself to be able to see what was happening to Mum. Each time she went through the loop the images in front of me got stronger and more detailed.

'That's it!' said Megan. 'I recognise it! Do it again.'

I played the scene once more but this time I heard something different.

A massive bang.

The back door slammed shut.

Now something else.

There was a distinctive smell, something burning on the stove.

Smoke pouring out of a pan.

I looked again. Mum had just gone out, closing the door behind her. There was something, something in the back of my memory that I had to bring forward.

The air in the kitchen seemed different each time. Now I could actually feel it stinging my eyes and the taste of it was streaming into my mouth, thick and bitter and choking. I started to splutter and I heard Mum shouting. This time she was outside the door, looking in through the glass window. She couldn't get in and I couldn't get out. There was a look of horror on her face.

'MEG!' she was screaming. 'MEG!'

The memory began again only this time I actually felt more of the panic. It was difficult to breathe. I heard Mum's voice screaming though the window. And then I saw her pounding on the glass, not from inside but from outside. I called to her and she swung round in amazement. I remembered sitting on the grass, looking over to the burning building.

I closed my eyes and everything started to spin. Lights

swirled around in my head and voices came from every direction although I couldn't hear anything of what was being said. Every so often I saw fleeting images of Mum, Dad, Will, Mirabel floating through the darkness. Someone, my dad I think, called my name and it all stopped.

In the lid of the box I could see Mum.

She was lying on the bed in Mirabel's room. There was a pot of yellow paint on the bedside cabinet and the radio was playing.

'She's out,' I managed to splutter. 'I think I got her out.'

Chapter 43

'I have located her,' said Diggleby. 'Meg. Your mother is back at home.'

'And she's alright?' I asked.

'She may be a little confused for a few days perhaps, but it is unlikely that she will remember her spell in the time pocket.' He paused. 'Although I once met a man from Selgad IV who had been in a time pocket for over a month. An interesting case and one ...'

'But he was OK?' asked Will.

'Absolutely fine. The drinks on his planet are notorious. He blamed it on the Zecon juice. I think you might find that here on earth, humans are similarly adept at explaining things away.'

'I don't think I'll be so quick to dismiss things again.' I paused. 'Thanks for your help, Diggleby. My mother wouldn't have been saved if it hadn't been for you.'

To my surprise I saw what looked like a smile flicker across Diggleby's face. 'I do believe it is Megan who deserves most of the credit,' he said. I swear he was blushing. 'After all, she was the one who convinced us to stand up to the Kelve, even if it did not go quite to plan. And she was able to be of invaluable assistance with the time pocket.'

'I know. I need to talk to her.'

Megan had walked away from us and was sitting by herself staring out at the sea. She was still covered in sand and debris from the beach. She attempted a smile when I reached her.

I sank down beside her and I noticed we were sitting in exactly the same position again. This time I didn't move. 'Thanks.' I said.

'What for?'

'For everything. Helping me out. You saved my mum's life.'

'Yes … well. I promised you I would get your mother back and I have. There is really no need for gratitude.

'Well, thanks anyway.'

'It wasn't that difficult,' she replied. 'We must have some of the same memories. My mother left something on the stove when I was little. The kitchen set alight very quickly and although she tried to rescue me, the door jammed. I was trapped. I … well, I obviously didn't know I was gifted then, but I found myself on the grass outside. Everyone was so busy breaking into the house they didn't realise I was there for several minutes.'

'Yes, but that couldn't have happened to me. Not like that. Mum would have said. And how did I get out through a solid door?'

'You must have travelled.'

I remembered the final scene from the time pocket when I was outside the house, calling to Mum.

'I … I can't do that. It's impossible.'

She shrugged. 'You're still here, aren't you? And today I saw you fight off a Kelve and release your mother from that time pocket. You must have some gifts after all, even if they are not as well developed as mine.'

I smiled.

Ridiculous though it seemed, somehow what she was saying did strike a chord. Ever since this adventure had started, I had felt different somehow. I had done things that I would never have thought possible.

Suddenly Megan started coughing uncontrollably.

'I'll get Diggleby,' I said, getting up.

'No ... no ... I'm fine.'

I ignored her and went to fetch the robot who was deep in conversation with the others. They all came over but Diggleby took a while to reach Megan and I realised that he was more damaged than I had first thought. It took him quite an effort to scan her but eventually he nodded knowingly. 'The young lady may benefit from some of the juice I prepared. Her main issue is exhaustion though.'

'There's plenty left in here,' said Will, holding out a beaker. 'Drink some of this, Megan.'

She drank some of the juice without an argument.

'Is that better?' asked Will.

She nodded. 'But you look pale,' she said. 'Are you alright?'

'I still have sand in my ears and it's really itchy. But I'm fine,' he said, smiling back at her. 'I can't believe what's just happened. I thought Mr Ward was going to finish me off.'

'Me too,' said Mirabel. 'I cannot believe that he pretended to be my grandfather and that I was taken in.'

I saw that she too was covered in dust. The cut on her

face looked very sore. 'Don't worry,' I said. 'We were all fooled by him one way or another.'

'Well, I deffo don't want to meet him ever again,' said Will.

'I concur,' said Erasmus. 'And now it is getting late and I think it is imperative that we make a move before people start to come on to the beach. Diggleby assures me that you are all as well as can be expected. Do you think you are ready to travel, Megan?'

She nodded but I was not convinced.

'It is time I … I took her back, I think,' he said.

'What are you talking about?' I said.

'Megan does have remarkable powers on her planet but she is more limited here, I am afraid. Her breathing is causing concern and I am worried about the possibility that she has …'

'I was talking about you. What do you mean about taking her back?' I interrupted. 'You can't cross the Bridge.'

Erasmus smiled. 'I think you may be underestimating my capabilities, young Meg. Diggleby and I have been studying this Bridge for a while now and I have a good idea of how it all operates. Megan will need help and I feel that I have sufficient knowledge to get us both across safely.'

'There is absolutely no possibility of that happening,' said Megan, her voice much stronger now.

'Erasmus. This is stupid,' said Will. 'I mean …'

'This is the most important mission of my life,' interrupted Megan. 'I cannot fail. I came to get Mirabel and she is coming with me. There is no room for you Erasmus, we only have two pendants.'

'You know perfectly well that it is impossible for you to take Mirabel back,' he said.

'I don't agree,' said Megan. 'I can do this.'

'You surely do not suffer from the same blind ignorance that afflicted Mr Ward? You are far too intelligent for that, I think. The facts are indisputable.'

Diggleby stepped forward. 'Mirabel would be in the gravest danger were she to return,' he said. 'Her aunt …'

'Diggleby!' I warned. 'Not now.'

Mirabel had been through quite enough. I didn't want her to know the truth about her aunt just yet.

'Indeed. Indeed. I am forgetting about human emotions. I …'

'What does he mean?' asked Mirabel.

'He means that your aunt would never forgive me were I to allow you to cross that Bridge at the present time,' said Erasmus, quickly. 'I know it may be difficult, but I think the best course of action would be for you to stay with Meg until … until your aunt and I can find you safe passage. Megan would not be able to help you, if you find the journey troublesome. The device in your neck is unpredictable. Diggleby has promised to keep researching until he has found a way to disconnect it.'

Mirabel didn't say anything. I saw tears starting up in her eyes.

'Erasmus is right,' I said. 'We'll look after you. Promise.'

'Alright,' she said. 'But only until my aunt comes.'

'Fair enough.'

'This is unacceptable,' said Megan sharply.

'I'm afraid that you have no choice. Your "mission", my dear, is over and your time here is at an end,' said Erasmus, firmly. 'Meg is more than capable of handling the situation down here until I return. I trust her implicitly. She saved our lives today, after all.'

He smiled over at me but I looked away embarrassed. I didn't want Erasmus to keep praising me for something I didn't do.

'Erasmus, you mustn't go. It's far too dangerous,' Will said.

'Your concerns about my welfare are gratifying, Will, but I have taken instruction from Diggleby and as you know I have had an affinity with the Bridge for some time.'

'But what about when you get there?' I said. 'The President …'

'He poses no threat to me,' said Erasmus. 'I know that.'

'How?' I asked. 'You can't know anything about him. Even Megan hasn't met him.'

'This is absurd,' said Megan, pulling herself up on to her feet. 'None of you have any idea what you're talking about.'

'That is where you are wrong, Megan,' said Erasmus. 'Diggleby came out with a very plausible theory just before we set off for the beach. He seems to be surprisingly well informed about the universe over the Bridge.'

I looked over at the robot but he was suddenly finding the wires hanging out of his wrist very interesting. I realised that Erasmus must have found out about him hacking into the pendant and I hoped he didn't think I had broken my promise not to say anything.

'But no matter,' he went on. 'I cannot say I approve of his methods, but what he told me was certainly interesting. He believes that the President is a recluse. Rather like myself. And obviously an eminent scientist, the one who created the Bridge and controls it, understands its strengths and weaknesses …'

'That's ridiculous,' I said, suddenly understanding what he was saying. 'You can't be …'

'Yes, Meg. Diggleby, like I said, presented me with a theory. You see it was actually Mirabel who found me, wasn't it? I believe she was told to "Find Erasmus". Doesn't that strike you as rather odd? Why me?'

'That doesn't mean …'

'I think someone knew I would be here,' he interrupted. 'You may not be the only person to have found a double from another world.'

'That can't be right,' said Megan. 'I don't believe it. You are not the President's double.'

'Let us try a little experiment,' he said. 'May I take that pendant back for a moment, Meg?'

I nodded and handed it to him. He hesitated for a moment and then stared into the crystal in the centre. Suddenly a voice sounded out.

Retina recognition complete.

'Bloody hell, said Will. 'That's how Meg got in. It recognised her. It knows you as well!'

'That thing may be faulty,' I said. 'Or …'

'I do not believe in coincidences, rather like you, Meg.' He paused. 'If what I think is true, then this pendant will take me over the Bridge. I need to do everything in my power to try to convince the President that his programme of destruction is wrong. If he is my equivalent then he will have the good sense to know that working together is the way forward.'

He fastened the pendant around his neck.

'I refuse to accept this!' said Megan. 'I can't believe …'

'Megan,' said Will. 'Erasmus is right. You're a really cool girl, and dead clever and all that. But you're wrong about this. You have to allow us take care of Mirabel now and you have to let Erasmus try to sort things out. It's the only way.'

'You can't take her to the President,' I said. 'She stays here with us.'

Megan didn't answer.

'I don't want to cross the Bridge with you,' said Mirabel. 'I think it is better if Meg and Will look after me.'

'I wasn't going to let anyone harm you,' said Megan, angrily. To my surprise, tears were forming in her eyes.

'Not on purpose,' said Mirabel. 'I want to wait for my aunt. She'll come and get me, won't she?'

'I am sure of it,' said Erasmus, although he didn't look at her when he said it. 'I am telling you now, Megan. You have no choice but to come with me.'

She didn't respond and she lowered her head. I think it was taking every gram of her concentration to even stay standing. I went over to her and put my hand on her shoulder but she shrugged me off.

'What about Diggleby?' asked Will.

'I am afraid I shall have no room for an extra passenger. Would you … would you take care of him for me? Just until I can make arrangements? I will return as soon as I am able.'

He turned away.

Despite sounding brave, his face was very red and he was sweating. He pulled a handkerchief out of his pocket.

'I can't do this!' said Megan, miserably. 'I am not prepared to tell the President I have failed.'

'Then don't say that,' I snapped. 'Just tell them that you couldn't find Mirabel. You've been gone ages. They don't expect Mirabel to be alive do they?

'And instead of Mirabel, you've brought me back,' said Erasmus. 'If Diggleby's theory is correct, I expect he will welcome me with open arms.'

Megan hesitated. 'I won't know what to say,' she said at last. 'I will have to lie.'

'Then let me do the talking,' said Erasmus.

'I don't want the President to know that a Kelve got the better of me.'

'I see no need to bring him into it. Indeed I have no desire to mention that Kelve's name ever again.'

'I still don't think … I don't think …' She suddenly seemed to be having trouble focusing and she started to sway. I just managed to catch her before she fell.

Will grabbed her other arm. 'Steady,' he said. 'Megan, you have to let Erasmus take you home, now. He's right about everything.'

'No. I can't do this …' she said.

'You can. Look, what you did today was amazing. We know that. But you've been through a lot and you're not well. Just let Erasmus help you now. Everyone needs help sometimes.'

She let go of me but she kept hold of Will.

'And it'll mean that you stay safe and Mirabel stays safe,' Will went on. 'It's win win, isn't it?'

She didn't answer.

'There are some people coming along the path to the beach, sir,' said Diggleby, urgently. 'They will be here in four and half minutes. We should not be seen.'

There were small lights flickering from the workings inside Diggleby's face that were now exposed. There was a sadness about him that I couldn't have believed possible in a machine.

'Thank you, my dear friend,' said Erasmus. 'And I am truly sorry. About before. We would not have let you go. It was merely a way of getting the Kelve to listen to us.'

Diggleby did not seem to respond to this. 'I corrected the faults in the pendant worn by Mr Ward and I have reattached the links where it had broken,' he said. 'I have also taken the liberty of reconfiguring the coordinates for travel across the Bridge, sir. The journey will not be comfortable but I estimate that you should arrive in … in approximately seven minutes.'

'Splendid. Megan, can you put it on, please?'

She took the pendant from the robot without saying anything.

'I will undertake to look after your walking cane, sir. It would not be wise to take it with you across the Bridge. To arrive with a weapon known to belong to a Kelve might not be the most suitable introduction.'

'You are beyond wise, my friend. And I thank you.'

'I don't suppose you have room for this?' Diggleby said.

He opened a drawer in his tummy and took something out. It was wrapped in foil. 'It's chocolate, blueberry and goat's cheese,' he said. 'I made it yesterday.'

'I shall enjoy it with a large glass of Tansel juice on the other side. I believe it is a speciality. Thank you, my dear friend.'

Erasmus wrapped his handkerchief around the cake and stuffed it into his pocket.

'I would advise you that the young lady should return her to her own environment as quickly as possible.'

He stopped talking and there was a clicking sound. Everything went quiet.

'He has turned himself off,' said Erasmus. 'He hates goodbyes.'

He looked over towards me.

'Wait!' said Megan.

She picked up her rucksack and started to open it.

'Keep my things,' I said. 'I don't want them back.'

She ignored me and reached into the bag. She pulled out the 'Grow Your Own Alien' kit.

'I want … I want you to have this,' she said, handing it to Will.

'Thanks,' he said. 'These are cool.'

'We had better be on our way,' said Erasmus. 'Before anyone sees us.'

He looked at Megan. 'If you could just …'

'Of course,' she said.

She closed her eyes. Erasmus put his arm around her shoulder and did the same. The next moment there was a tremendous rush of air, more sand whirled around us in a thick cloud. When it had cleared, they were gone.

Chapter 44

'What are you going to have?' asked Will. 'I'm starving.'

We were sitting outside, at one of the plastic tables at Will's favourite coffee shop in Bridlington. The sun was shining and it was really warm. I turned my face towards the sun and tried to relax.

'Shall we have some ice cream? Or chips?' I asked.

Will looked up from the menu. 'You seem pretty cool about everything,' he said. 'I haven't stopped shaking for days.'

'I'm fine if I'm focusing on ordinary things. It's like the other stuff never happened.'

'It did though.'

'I know.'

'And your mum's OK?'

'Fine. She obviously doesn't remember anything. I mentioned Mr Ward the other day but she didn't seem to know who he was.'

'That's a good thing. I wish I'd never met him.'

'Me neither. No, she seems to be just like she was before. She loves having Mirabel to fuss over and it stops her moaning about Dad being away all the time.'

'He's not coming back all summer?'

'No. He might be staying in London until September now.'

I hadn't had the chance to talk to Dad since all this had happened. I'd wanted to ask him about the Institute but Mum said he was too busy to contact us. It made me wonder about what he was actually doing, especially after what Erasmus had said.

'Did you say you talked to Diggleby again?' I asked.

'Yeah, this morning. There's no news about Erasmus yet.'

'Nothing?'

'No. He's really grumpy.' He paused. 'It all seems a bit far away though now, doesn't it?'

'Almost as though it didn't happen.'

'Except we still have Mirabel.'

'Yeah. That's true.'

'And the whole thing … incredible … I mean to meet another you …'

'Yeah. Even if she was rude and bossy.'

'Like I said. Another you.'

I laughed and kicked him under the table.

'Anyway, I think that changing that streak in your hair to blue is way cooler. Do you think Megan will copy you now that she's seen it?'

I ran my fingers through my fringe and some strands of bright blue hair came away in my hand. 'I think she'd be better not bothering. I may be going bald. Besides, they're not allowed to do stuff like that over at the Institute. She's probably just finding herself another mission.'

'Maybe. I hope so.'

I didn't respond. I knew we were both wondering the

same thing. Had they made it across the Bridge? There was no way of knowing the answer to that question.

'Do you think Megan will look for me over there?' asked Will. 'She said she had never met anyone like me.'

'No one has met anyone like you Will.'

He laughed.

'I think she liked you,' I said, remembering how she had given him the hideous alien thing as a gift. 'But I have to warn you that she was pretty clear she didn't want to marry you.'

'Cheek. I'm a catch.' It was Will's turn to look embarrassed. 'I think I'll go for a mocha latte.'

'It's too hot for one of your stupid coffees. Get a lemonade or something.'

'I'm not five,' he said.

'No comment,' I answered.

I reached into my bag and brought out a new phone.

'Wow,' said Will. 'When did you get that?'

'Yesterday. Mum took a day off from her DIY and took me to Scarborough. She said it was an early birthday present.'

'That is so cool. Are you sure she's alright though?'

'I told you, she's fine. Although I just sort of hinted at the phone and she said I could have it. Maybe she's not quite back to normal yet. That and she felt guilty about not telling me about the fire.'

'Was it true, then?'

I nodded. 'She wanted to know how I found out so I told her that Dad had let something slip ages ago and the photograph made me remember. She said she didn't tell me about it because she still feels terrible although everyone said it wasn't her fault. They have no idea how the fire started and … well, they never understood how I managed to get out of the kitchen.'

'You don't think you did the same as Megan? I mean you travelled …'

'I think Mum's memory is just a bit mixed up,' I said smiling, although I knew I wasn't entirely convincing Will or myself.

'And you had a dog.' He laughed.

'Yeah. After all those times I begged her for a pet.'

'Maybe I should talk to her.'

'Actually, she said I should spend less time with you.'

'What? You're kidding. I thought she liked me?'

'She says you distract me. She thinks I've got too much work on to have a boyfriend.'

'What? We're not …'

'Don't worry. I told her that. And Mirabel spoke up for you. She said you were one of the nicest people she'd ever met. That's what comes of not going to school and meeting lots of people. She's got no one to compare you with.'

Will laughed. He tried to hit me over the head with the menu but he missed. 'She's settled in alright, though?' he asked.

'Yeah. Mum loves her. She's painted Mirabel's room bright pink instead of yellow. Mirabel's really at home now.'

'What about her staying at yours though? I mean what if they try to trace her relatives or …?'

'Don't worry. Diggleby has … well he has made sure that there won't be any problems,' I said. 'All her paperwork is OK anyway. I don't think Erasmus would be too impressed if he knew how he'd done it.'

'I bet.'

'Mirabel asked about her double the other day,' I said. 'If I could find her. I don't think it had occurred to her before.'

'What did you say?'

'Nothing much. I changed the subject. But I went back online later to try to find those articles about the freak storm in Filey. Nothing. I tried putting in Rhiannon Kendrick again but there were no links to the Uni or any mention of a scientist.'

'We should get Diggleby to have another look. See if he can find anything out.'

There was silence between us for a moment.

'You don't think … I mean what you found out about Rhiannon over the Bridge. She will be alright, won't she?' asked Will.

'I don't know,' I said. 'We just have to hope that Erasmus arrived in time to save her.'

'Mirabel doesn't have any idea what's gone on, does she?'

I shook my head. 'No, I haven't said a word. But …' I hesitated.

'But what?' asked Will.

'I suppose it all depends on whether Erasmus is right about who the President is.'

'Yeah. Bloody hell. What if he isn't?'

'Then they're all in trouble.'

We fell quiet again and I pretended to be fascinated by the menu. It was unbearable to think that maybe things had not worked out as well as Erasmus had predicted.

'Maybe we just made all of this up,' said Will at last.

'Both of us? At the same time?'

'It happens. Those mass hallucinations … They say …'

'Will?'

'What?'

'Go and order us some food.'

Will was ages but when he came back he was carrying a giant ice cream bowl in the shape of a heart. It was packed with loads of different flavours of ice cream, a pile of fruit topped off by a mountain of squirty cream and a river of sticky red syrup.

'I thought we were getting chips and coffee?'

'Don't worry. I ordered but they said hot food would be about twenty minutes. I can't wait that long. Anyway, this is on offer today. You get all this and two spoons.'

'It's got "Lover's Cup" written on the side.'

'Try it. It's amazing,' he said, loading his spoon with ice cream. 'Dig in.'

I tried to look cross but I burst out laughing. Will was impossible.

'Do you think Diggleby will be back to baking soon?' he said. 'I miss his cakes.'

'He's too busy with the bingo on the caravan site. Mr Howard's gone.'

'Who's in charge now?' asked Will.

'Some new guy.'

'An alien?'

'I don't think he would like you calling him that. He's from the Rusperian galaxy. Diggleby says they have terrible tempers there.'

'Great. I'll keep out of his way.' He paused. 'Diggleby wants you to go and have another look at the Bridge when he's sorted the camera out. He thinks there's maybe a way to pass messages across.'

'Oooh, ice cream! How fab,' said a familiar voice. There was the sound of yelping and a small brown dog ran up to us. 'Jason! Come back you naughty dog.'

Abbie.

Kathryn was walking at her side, wearing a t-shirt which said, 'Too old to live, too young to die' on the front. There was a picture of a dagger covered in blood.

'Brilliant,' I whispered under my breath. I tried to put my arm casually around the ice cream bowl to stop her from seeing it.

'Is that a Lover's Cup?' she shrieked. 'I knew you two were … we won't disturb.'

'Did you want something?' I asked.

'Yeah, sure. I wondered if Mirabel wanted to come round sometime, now she's here permanently. There's a new nail bar in Scarborough which is like soooo coolio.'

Kathryn had reached over and picked up my spoon. She was digging into the sundae.

'Do you mind?' I said.

'Nope,' she answered, glaring at me. 'Do you?'

I wished we had had her with us when we were facing Mr Ward. She might have been able to solve all of our problems. I was sure even a Kelve would hesitate to pick a fight with Kathryn.

'I think Mirabel has the hots for my big bro. No idea why. Perhaps you could go on a double date.'

'We're good, thanks,' I said.

'Anyway. Later,' said Abbie. 'Oh, Will, I've found some-one else who wants to manage your band. I've got this cousin …'

'I think we're fine,' said Will. 'Thanks all the same.'

'Right,' said Abbie. 'OK.' For the first time she actually looked a bit deflated. 'We'd better go. Come on, Jason.'

The little dog was refusing to move. She picked him up and shoved him under her arm before she walked off. I could tell even from the back of her head that she was annoyed. Kathryn shoved another big scoop of ice cream into her mouth and followed her friend.

There was a scuffling noise from under the table.

'What the hell's that?' I asked.

Will bent down and pulled a large brown rucksack on to his knee. 'Actually, I wanted to show you something else. You're not the only one involved in this fostering lark.'

'What do you mean?'

He reached into his bag and lifted out the scraggy bald cat of Mr Ward's.

'Where the hell did you find that?'

'I didn't. It found me. He said she was called Bess, didn't he? When I went to my caravan she was sitting on the steps. She follows me everywhere.'

'I don't think you should be carrying her around in a bag!'

'I wish I didn't have to. I have to take this stupid thing everywhere with me now because she just keeps appearing wherever I go. I can't let people see her. Poor thing attracts too much unwanted attention. People point and laugh.'

'At you?'

'No, funny. The cat.'

I put out my hand tentatively to stroke her but she hissed and spat at me. 'It's horrible,' I said. 'All cats should have fur. Fact.'

Will covered its ears. 'You'll hurt her feelings,' he said. 'I think she's quite cool.'

'It hasn't … she hasn't turned into anyone, has she?'

'I don't think so. Although there was a woman on the site the other day with these weird yellow eyes. I thought she had those whacky contact lenses in but … you never know.'

The cat looked over at me and then jumped back into the bag. Will put it on the floor.

'Don't zip it right up. It'll suffocate.'

'She's not in there now,' he said. 'She's gone again. But I bet she's on the caravan steps when I get back.'

'Bloody hell,' I said, picking up my spoon and digging into the ice cream. 'Do you think things will ever go back to normal?'

He laughed. 'That would be pretty boring. We have seen some outstanding things.'

'I know.'

'And you, Meg, I can't believe what you did.'

Or what the Esks did, I thought. I wondered where they were now and whether I would ever see them again.

'You were amazing,' Will went on. 'Erasmus said you must be really gifted.'

'Not really I …'

He leaned over. His eyes were bright and excited. 'Bloody hell. You can, can't you?'

I smiled at him. 'Maybe,' I said. 'I did wonder …' I stopped and stared at him.

'What?' he asked.

'Have you got any money?'

'Why?'

'I just need fifty pence.' I held out my hand.

He smiled and reached in his pocket. 'Here you are. But it's all I've got left.'

'You can have it back,' I said, taking it from him. 'Now, do you remember Mr Ward's bungalow? When he told us about the magician?'

'The Great Mancello.'

'Exactly. As you said once, nothing's impossible any more. Watch.'

I opened my mouth and placed the coin on my tongue. I counted to ten and then blew. A small yellow butterfly, its wings as fine as lace, fluttered out and disappeared into the blue Bridlington sky.

The End

About the Author

Janet Blackwell was an English teacher for many years until deciding it was time to have a go at writing her own stories. She studied for an M.A. in Creative Writing at Sheffield Hallam University and it was there that she wrote her first children's novel. The East Coast around Bridlington and Filey provides both the inspiration for her work and the 'What if …?' that underlies it.

If you have enjoyed this story, please consider leaving a review for Janet to let her know what you thought of her work.

You can find out more about Janet on her author page on the Fantastic Books Store. While you're there, why not browse our delightful tales and wonderfully woven prose?

www.fantasticbooksstore.com

Printed in Great Britain
by Amazon